TAMED BY THE BARBARIAN

June Francis

MILLS & BOON®
Pure reading pleasure

All the characters in this book have no existence outside the imagination of the author, and have no relation whatsoever to anyone bearing the same name or names. They are not even distantly inspired by any individual known or unknown to the author, and all the incidents are pure invention.

First published in Great Britain 2007
Large Print edition 2008
Harlequin Mills & Boon Limited,
Eton House, 18-24 Paradise Road, Richmond, Surrey TW9 1SR

ISBN: 978 0 263 20117 8

Set in Times Roman 15½ on 17 pt.
42-0108-83723

Printed and bound in Great Britain
by Antony Rowe Ltd, Chippenham, Wiltshire

TAMED BY THE BARBARIAN

To my dearest John, who is always there for me. He never refuses to help me with my research, be it travelling down an ancient byway or to an abbey in the depths of Yorkshire or abroad or closer to home. A true romantic, he relishes my historical romances with their swashbuckling heroes and feisty heroines, considering them the perfect escapist read.

Chapter One

January 1461

Cicely Milburn's brow furrowed as she stared at the bloodied abrasions on the horse's flank. Whose mount was it? She placed gentle fingers on its neck and the gelding quivered beneath her touch. Yet when she held out a wrinkled apple on the palm of her hand, it lipped the fruit and took it into its mouth. She smiled and moved away to her own palfrey in the neighbouring stall.

Noticing two dried-up burrs picked up on the return journey from her father's steward's house, she removed them. She was worried about her fifteen-year-old brothers and wished Matt had not had to make the journey to Kingston-on-Hull, to enquire of his twin, Jack, and their widower father. He had taken most of the male servants with them, concerned about the rumours of a great host of

Lancastrians in the vicinity of the Duke of York's castle of Sandal a week or so ago. If there had been a battle, then, in the aftermath, one could expect to encounter wandering soldiers on the rampage. She wished her stepbrother, Diccon, was here to share the burden of worry with her, but she had not seen him for the last six months and she feared for his safety. She fingered the dagger that hung from her girdle, then glanced round apprehensively as she heard the sound of approaching footsteps.

Anger surged in her veins at the sight of the man standing there. 'Master Husthwaite! What are you doing here? How could you use this poor horse so cruelly?' she demanded.

'So there you are, Mistress Cicely. I've been looking for you.'

The mousy, lank-haired man ran chilling silver-grey eyes over her in a manner that caused her gloved hands to clench.

'For what purpose?' she asked coldly.

Master Husthwaite sucked in his cheeks and then released them noisily, not answering her question immediately. 'The beast is a slug. My uncle should have insisted on his clients paying their bills more readily and then I could afford a finer horse.'

'What do you mean—should have insisted?'

'My uncle died recently and I am taking over his business.' He approached her, sliding one hand against the other, his eyes fixed on her well-formed bosom. 'So I came here in haste, after speaking to Master Matthew in Knaresborough. I thought you might need my help.'

She stiffened. 'Why should I need *your* help here on my father's manor? I am quite capable of managing the household myself. If in need of further assistance, I can call on Father's steward's wife.'

Master Husthwaite stroked his lantern jaw, his eyes narrowing. 'It is a different kind of help I would offer you. When Master Matthew told me he was travelling to Kingston-on-Hull to seek news of your father from his agent, I was deeply concerned.' He took a step closer to Cicely. 'I fear you must brace yourself for bad tidings.'

'I don't know why you should deem that so,' she retorted. And, feeling a need to put some distance between them, she moved to her horse's head. 'It is not the first time Father has failed to arrive home when expected—especially during the winter months. Stormy weather can delay a ship's departure.'

'No doubt that would be true if your father and brother's arrival was only a few days or a week overdue,' said Master Husthwaite, 'but it is now the feast of St Hilary and, according to your brother, six weeks since he last heard from them. I really do think you have to accept that your father might well be dead.'

'No!' she cried, forcing back the dreadful apprehension roused first by Matt's conviction in the last ten days that his twin brother was in pain. 'I will not believe it is so.'

'Naturally, you don't want to accept his death as a reality, but you must do so because we'll need to consider your future.'

'We? What do you mean? I hope you do not have it in mind to interfere in my affairs,' said Cicely, her fine eyes flashing blue fire. 'It is no concern of yours. I—I am betrothed and will be wed at Easter.'

His deep-set eyes flickered. 'I have found nothing amongst your father's papers about such an arrangement.'

'Nevertheless my wedding will take place.' Cicely was furious that he should have access to her father's private papers. She was certain that if Nat Milburn had known this clerk would dare to step into his dead uncle's shoes, he would have left orders for another man of business to be found instantly.

'So you say. Tell me—who is this so-called betrothed?' demanded Master Husthwaite.

'His name is none of your business. Now will you kindly leave, as I have to prepare for the return of my brothers and father.'

He glared at her, but instead of quitting the stable, he reached for the whip thrust through a strap on his saddle and lashed out at her horse. Cicely let out a scream of rage and, throwing caution to the wind, caught hold of the whip's lash when he would have used it again. Her attempt to disarm the man resulted in her being catapulted against him. The breath was knocked out of her and he swiftly took advantage of her position. His arms went round her and he squeezed her so hard that she could scarcely breathe.

'Unhand me at once! You forget yourself,' she gasped.

He laughed and sank his head into the smooth flesh of her neck. She screamed and resisted as, inch by inch, he forced her down on to the damp straw. In the struggle, her headdress was dislodged and her hair swirled free. He grabbed a handful of it and brought her face close, seeking her mouth with his own. She baulked at the glimpse of his rotting teeth and the smell of his stinking breath, but she managed to get a couple of fingers to his chin and pinched it. He knocked her hand away. 'You'll pay for that,' he snarled.

Cicely feared that she would, but what happened next proved her wrong. Her rescue took place so swiftly that she could barely believe that in moments she was free and Master Husthwaite lay still on the ground. She was lifted to her feet as if she weighed no more than thistledown.

The pressure of her rescuer's hand seemed to sear through her gown and set her skin tingling, a sensation that she found intensely disturbing in a completely different way from the shock of Master Husthwaite's attack on her person.

Her eyes were now on a level with an intricately patterned brooch that gleamed dully like pewter. This fastened a roughly textured woollen cloak at a weatherbeaten neck. Her gaze moved higher and the breath caught in her throat at the sight of the unshaven chin and the strong cheekbones of a man's rugged face, framed in a tangle of chestnut hair that fell to his shoulders. He spoke in a dialect that caused her initial feelings of relief to turn to stunned dismay. Thoughts whirled in her head as she remembered going on a pilgrimage with her dying mother to a priory at Alnmouth not far from the border of England with Scotland. Her mother was from that area and an admirer of the Celtic saints, who had brought the gospel from Ireland.

The man spoke again, but more slowly this time. 'I hope he did not harm you badly, lass?'

She shook her head and her golden hair swirled about her shoulders. His eyes widened as he reached out a gauntleted hand and touched a strand, tucking it behind her ear. She froze, remembering the tales told to her twin brothers by their great-uncle and grandfather. "Enough to chill the blood," her mother had often said. There was no doubt in Cicely's mind that the border Scots were an uncouth race and she feared this man had saved her from Master Husthwaite's foul intent for his own pleasure. If she had been the kind of female given to swooning, she would have chosen that moment to do so. Instead, her fingers crept to the dagger hanging alongside the keys at her girdle and fastened on its string-bound hilt.

Mackillin's gaze skated over her blanched face, noticing that her eyes were the colour of bluebells, which grew beneath the rowan trees near Loch Trool. His mind was not the kind normally given to poetic thoughts, but he reckoned, if asked, that he could write a sonnet to such eyes. She had a heart-shaped face, a perfectly shaped nose and lips that were just asking to be kissed.

There was that in his gaze that caused Cicely to dart out a nervous tongue and wet her lips. She knew that it was now or never to draw her dagger. 'Keep away from me, you—you barbarian!' she said, brandishing the weapon in front of her.

Except for the flare of his nostrils, he appeared unmoved. 'And if I don't, what will you do with that…toy, lass?' he spoke deliberately slowly.

'I would stick it in you. Its edge is sharp!' she warned.

His eyes glinted. 'Such gratitude for rescuing you deserves to be rewarded in kind.' With a carelessness for his own safety that alarmed her, he seized her wrist and twisted, causing her to gasp in pain as the weapon fell to the ground. Then in one smooth movement, his left arm encircled her waist and his right hand cupped the back of her head. 'A kiss for my pains,' he murmured, laying claim to her mouth.

She attempted to ward him off, but found it impossible to make an impression against his hard, muscular strength. The pressure from his mouth eased and now his lips moved gently over hers in a pleasant, tingly fashion. She was alarmed that she found even the abrasive roughness of his stubbly chin peculiarly sensual. Only thrice had she been kissed before and it had not caused sparks to charge through her veins, igniting her nerve ends in a truly thrilling fashion like this one did.

But she had sworn to love Diccon as long as she lived. He was the only man with the right to kiss her in such a beguilingly intimate fashion, despite her father having refused his consent to their betrothal. Still, Cicely believed she could change his mind when he returned. Yet now she was allowing this—this savage to kiss her without putting up a fight. She tore her mouth away and raised a hand to hit him, but the blow never landed because, unexpectedly, he freed her.

She glared at him and gasped, 'My father will make you pay for daring to assault me.'

Mackillin's eyes narrowed. He knew that it had been a mistake kissing her, but the sight of her lips alone were enough to drive a man to forget any code of chivalry he might live by. As for the golden hair that smelt so sweetly of camomile, he had never seen such hair. His breathing deepened as he remembered that same scent on her skin and his body recalled the feel of her breasts against his chest and the jutting bones of her hips against his nether regions. The stirring in his loins did not abate and he said harshly, 'Your father? Is he one of the servants here?'

'God's blood, no! He's…' She paused, uncertain what his reaction would be if he knew she was the daughter of the house. She backed away from him and turned and ran, wondering what he was doing on her father's manor. The Scots had not raided this far south of the border for decades.

No sooner was she outside the stables than she collided with someone. She gasped as her arm was seized and a familiar voice said, 'Cissie, what's wrong? Why did you scream?'

At the welcome sound of her brother's voice, she collapsed against him. Only to realise that his right arm was in a sling. 'It's you, Jack,' she cried gladly. 'But what have you done to yourself?' She touched his shoulder and gazed into his beloved face. 'Matt knew you'd been hurt. Thanks be to our Saviour that you're home. Was it that barbarian in there who damaged your arm?' She gesticulated in the direction of the stable. Mackillin had followed in her wake and stood in the entrance, gazing at them. Cicely eyed him warily. 'Have you a sword, Jack?' she whispered out of the corner of her mouth.

He glanced at her as if she had run mad. 'What use would it be against Mackillin? His skill with a blade is greater than any I have ever seen.'

'So you fought him and lost?'

Jack gazed heavenwards as if for divine intervention. 'No, Cissie. He saved my life!'

She was aghast. 'No! He couldn't have—not his kind. There must be some mistake.'

'You're wrong, Cissie. He's a friend of Father's.'

'He can't be. Father's a cultured man. Well travelled, well read. What could he have in common with that—that Scottish wild man?' She glared at Mackillin, who looked at her with an expression on his face that confused her. 'I must speak to him. Tell him that *he* dared to kiss me!' She turned towards the house.

'Cissie, wait!' called Jack.

'What for? If you think to change my mind, then you're...' She glanced over her shoulder at him and stopped in mid-flight at the sight of the misery in his face. Suddenly she was scared. 'What is it? Why do you look like that?'

The muscles of Jack's throat moved jerkily. 'You won't find Father in the house.'

She retreated her steps. 'Why? Where is he? Has he had an accident?' He hesitated. 'You're scaring me, Jack. Tell me—what's happened to him?' she cried.

'He-he's dead!' croaked her brother. 'Murdered by thieving rogues.' The colour drained from Cicely's face and she shook her head, clutching his undamaged arm. 'I'm so sorry, Cissie,' he added.

'I don't believe it. I *won't* believe it!' Cicely picked up the hem of her brown skirts, revealing the lamb's-wool 'bags' that had encased her legs whilst riding, and raced across the yard. The hens scattered before her as she approached the grey stone house. She ignored the three packhorses waiting patiently to have their loads removed and the man still mounted. She desperately needed to find her father indoors, shouting in his deep voice for his Cissie. She climbed the steps that ran at an angle along the wall to the entrance to the hall and struggled to open the door in the icy wind. At last it gave way beneath her fingers and she went inside.

As Mackillin watched her disappear from sight, that mixture of pity and dismay he felt deepened, overlaid with another emotion that he did not want to acknowledge. He had forgotten Jack had mentioned his sister was comely. If he had remembered, then he might have guessed her identity immediately. Even so, his not knowing she was the daughter of the house did not excuse his handling of her. Yet his body still thrilled with the memory of her in his arms. It was just as well that his sojourn here was of necessity to be short, otherwise he might be tempted to claim the reward the dead Nat Milburn had offered him.

'I'll go after her,' said Jack, looking mortified.

Mackillin stayed him with a hand. 'Allow her time to gain control of herself.'

Jack hesitated before nodding. 'So you kissed her. Is that why she screamed?'

'How could it be? She screamed before I touched her.' There was a noise behind them. 'Here is your explanation,' said Mackillin, facing Master Husthwaite as he appeared, leading his horse.

The man's jaw was swollen and showed signs of bruising. 'So you're returned, Master Jack.'

'Who are you?' asked the scowling youth.

'Gabriel Husthwaite, nephew of your father's man of business. He died recently and I have taken charge of his affairs. This family will have need of my services if my surmise is right and your father is dead.'

'Aye. Set upon and murdered.' Jack looked towards Mackillin with an uncertain expression.

'This is the man Father's agent spoke of in Kingston-on-Hull.'

Mackillin's mouth tightened as Master Husthwaite smiled thinly. 'Mistress Cicely wouldn't have it that he was dead, but I told her it was the most likely explanation for his absence.'

'So that is why she screamed,' said Jack, running his free hand through his fair hair. 'Yet she—'

'Nay, it is not,' growled Mackillin. 'He was making a nuisance of himself, behaving in a manner that was unacceptable to your lovely sister.'

Master Husthwaite cast him a sly look. 'Was my behaviour so different from yours? You demanded a kiss for your pains when you believed her to be a serving girl.'

Mackillin turned to Jack and said in a low voice, 'Forgive me. She called me a barbarian and wanted to stick a knife in me.'

'It's because you're a Borderer, Mackillin. I'm sorry,' said Jack. 'My great-uncle and grandfather used to tell us such hair-raising tales of the Scots reivers that we couldn't sleep nights.'

Master Husthwaite stepped forward, 'Mistress Cicely needs a curbing hand on her bridle. She threatened to do the same to me. I was only defending myself when this Mackillin came in on us.'

'You lie. There was no sign of a blade and you were rolling her in the straw, man,' said Mackillin, his expression disdainful. 'She wanted none of you.'

The man sneered. 'Nor of you. Get back to your own land. This family's affairs are in my hands and have naught to do with you, *barbarian.*'

Mackillin's anger boiled over and he seized Master Husthwaite by the throat of his surcoat and hoisted him into the air. Thrusting him on to his horse, he said, 'Be gone from here before I put my fist down your throat and rip out your tongue.' He hit the horse's flank with the flat of his hand.

Master Husthwaite scrabbled to get hold of the reins and slid sideways but Mackillin forced him upright as the horse set off at a trot towards the beaten-earth track that led to the village and then the highway that would take him to Knaresborough, more than a league away.

Jack frowned. 'I don't like this. Father would never have agreed to such a man taking charge of our business affairs.'

'That man's a rogue. Is there someone else you can turn to help you deal with him?'

Jack nodded. 'There's Diccon, but I don't know where he is…and there's our stepsister's husband Owain, who was a close friend of Father's. I imagine Matt or Cissie will contact them. I wonder where Matt is?' He glanced around. 'He must be out somewhere. Otherwise he would have heard the commotion and come running to see what was going on. I hope he won't be long. You will stay the night and speak to him?'

Mackillin looked up at the louring sky and nodded. 'Aye. We would not get far before darkness fell. Now inside and see to your sister while Robbie and I deal with the horses. And, Jack, do not mention aught about your father's offer to reward me with her hand in marriage. I cannot accept it.' He urged Jack in the direction of the house. 'I will see the baggage is taken indoors for you to unpack at your leisure.'

Jack thanked him and hurried after Cicely.

He found her kneeling in front of the fire, stroking one of the dogs. The face she turned towards him was tear-stained and when she spoke her voice shook. 'I must believe what you say is true. I know you would not jest about such a matter as our dear father's death.'

'I'm sorry, Cissie.' Awkwardly, he put an arm about her shoulders. 'I've dreaded breaking the news to you. Where's Matt?'

'He's gone to Kingston-on-Hull for news of you from Father's shipping agent. It was in his heart that he might find you both there.'

His blue eyes darkened. 'The agent did not mention him. When did he leave?'

'Only this morning and he took most of our men.'

She sighed and got to her feet. 'So you spoke with the agent. What did he have to say?'

'He did not seem surprised to hear that Father was dead and spoke of Master Husthwaite. I had no idea his uncle was dead. A courier should have been sent to one of our agents in Europe, then word would have reached us and Father would have come home.'

'I did not know of the elder Master Husthwaite's demise until now and as far as I know his nephew has had no proper legal training, but only acted as his clerk.' Her voice was strained. 'Anyway, it is pointless discussing this at the moment. We need to get word to Diccon.'

Jack nodded. 'You know where he is?'

Her expression was sombre. 'No. But most likely Kate or Owain will know how to get news to him. They all must be informed of Father's death.' She paused as tears clogged her throat and had to swallow before continuing. 'If Diccon cannot be found, no doubt Owain will help us deal with Master Husthwaite if he should prove really troublesome.'

'Let's hope so.'

Cicely wiped her damp face with the back of her hand. 'Tell me, did Father suffer? Were the devils responsible caught and punished?'

Jack kicked a smouldering brand that had fallen

onto the hearth. 'Death came swiftly for him, but not before he had wrung a promise from Mackillin to see me home safely. He killed one of them and so did Robbie, but another escaped.'

Her fingers curled into the palms of her hands. 'I can't understand how Father believed he could trust a Border reiver to do his bidding,' she cried.

Jack looked uncomfortable. 'He is not what you think. I saw how they recognised each other.'

She was amazed. 'How could Father know such a man?'

Jack sought to scratch his itching arm beneath the splints. 'They've both travelled. Mackillin owns his own ship. They must have met for the first time before Father promised our stepmother to stop his wanderings—after he inherited this manor from our great-uncle and chose to live here, rather than in Grandfather's house, which was ramshackle.'

'I remember. I was twelve summers when Great-uncle Hugo died and left no issue. Father decided to run the two manors as one,' she murmured through lips that quivered.

Jack's expression was sombre. 'Five years ago. Matt and I were ten. Most likely Father and Mackillin met in Calais.'

Cicely sighed and picked up the pillowcase she had been embroidering before she had left the house earlier that day. 'That's where Diccon met Edward of York. Father was angry because he was so taken with him and spoke of allying himself to his cause.' She put the linen down again, too upset to sit and sew.

Jack grimaced. 'You couldn't expect Father not to be. He's supported Henry of Lancaster all his life, despite his being half-mad and a hopeless king. More priest than soldier, so Father said.'

Cicely nodded. 'This is true and why I suppose Diccon *has* gone over to the side of York, despite his having been born and raised in Lancashire.' Yet that was not her father's only reason for withholding his permission for her and Diccon to wed…the fact that he was landless and had little in the way of money most probably had a lot to do with it, too.

Jack sighed. 'I'm tired and in no mood to worry myself about the affairs of York and Lancaster right now. We have enough troubles of our own. Father would expect you to show all courtesy to Mackillin. Food and shelter is the least we can provide him with as he refuses to claim the reward Father offered him.'

Cicely's eyes sharpened. 'So that's what brings him here—the promise of a reward.'

Jack frowned. 'I should not have mentioned it. I told you he has no intention of claiming it.'

'So he says,' she said scornfully. 'He deceives you. He must know Father is a wealthy man. Perhaps he intends to take more than he was offered.'

Jack flushed with anger. 'You insult him. Mackillin could have cut my throat and stolen our extremely valuable property any time these last ten days. I know he kissed you, Cissie, but you mustn't hold that against him. It was a mistake.'

Pink tinged her cheeks and she bent over one of the dogs, noticing it had bits of bramble in its rough coat. She gently removed the thorns and said in a low voice, 'He thought I was a servant girl. That's his excuse for behaving like a savage.'

'He's no savage. You must curb your tongue, Cissie, and be thankful that he sent Master Husthwaite packing.' Jack sighed. 'It seems so strange being home without Matt and Father here. It'll never be the same ever.' His expression was bleak.

She agreed, thinking that the long winter evenings were even more depressing since her stepmother had died two years ago. She could only hope spring would come quickly, so they could at least spend more time outdoors. It was difficult filling the hours at this time of year because most of the tasks suited to the long dark evenings had been completed—the bottling, the pickling, the salting of meat and the making of candles—although there was always embroidery, darning, as well as salves and soap to make to keep her busy, but that left her mind free to wander and worry about Diccon. She sighed heavily, wishing desperately for her father to still be alive, but that was a wish that couldn't come true. Instead she was going to have to be polite to Jack's rescuer and that would not be easy.

As if he had read her thoughts, her brother said, 'A hot meal and a warm bed is little recompense for all Mackillin has done for us. Right now some mulled ale would not go amiss.'

'I suppose you'll want me to give him the best guest bedchamber and prepare a tub for him as well,' she muttered.

'That will not be necessary,' said a voice that caused her heart to leap into her throat and she wondered why the dogs had not barked a warning.

She took a deep breath, pausing to gain her composure before facing Mackillin. He was standing only a few feet away and not only looked unkempt, but stank of horse and dried sweat as well as something indefinably male. She was amazed that her body should have reacted to his the way it had done. He was so large and strong, but she would not be scared of him.

'Of course, you must have the best bedchamber. You saved my brother's life and brought him home to us.' She tried to infuse warmth into her voice, but it sounded stiff.

He inclined his shaggy head. 'I gave your father my word.'

'And you honoured it.'

'Even barbarians keep their word, *occasionally.*' His eyes sent out a challenge to her, daring her to deny that she believed him incapable of behaving like a gentleman.

She held his gaze. 'They have their price, though.'

Mackillin glanced at Jack. 'I did not tell her,' he said hastily.

'Good.' A muscle twitched in Mackillin's jaw. 'I assure you, mistress, you would not wish to pay my price if I were to demand it. Now I would ask only for pallets and blankets for my man, Robbie, and myself. Here in front of the fire will do us both fine.'

But before she could comment, Robbie spoke up. 'Nay, Mackillin, you're a Scottish lord now and should have the best bedchamber.'

Cicely stared at Mackillin in amazement. 'Is this true? You're a Scottish lord?'

He shrugged. 'My title is new to me.'

'That'll explain it,' she said drily.

He raised an eyebrow. 'Explain what?'

She shook her head, knowing she could only say that no sane person would look at him and believe him to be a lord. He could not be blamed for his garments being travel-stained, but they were definitely not made of the finest materials. Beneath his cloak he wore a common leather jerkin instead of the embroidered surcoat and velvet doublet befitting his rank. Her gaze moved downwards and she noted that, instead of silk or costly woollen hose, his legs were shockingly bare. Still, if he was a lord, her father would have expected her to treat him as one.

'I'll prepare the best bedchamber, Lord Mackillin.'

'Despite my appearance?' he said softly. 'Forget it, lass. I will not put you to the bother of preparing a bedchamber for one night. You have enough to trouble you this day.'

She did not deny it and inclined her head. 'If you will excuse me, then. I have yet to tell the servants of my—my father's death.'

He nodded in response and turned to speak to Robbie and Jack.

She had to force herself not to run to the rear of the hall. One of the dogs trotted at her heels. Beneath the stairway that led to the first floor was a door that opened to a passageway. If she turned left, she would come to the staircase that led to the turret where her bedchamber was situated but, instead, went right and soon found herself passing the buttery, the stillroom, the storeroom and the laundry on her way to the kitchen.

She paused in the doorway, watching the cook taking his ease in front of the fire. The serving maid, Tabitha, was chopping herbs. Tom, a male servant, was conversing with her as he stirred a huge blackened pot that dangled on chains over the fire. Martha, a woman in her early middle years, was singing as she rolled out pastry. They had not heard her coming and started at the sound of her voice. 'I have sad tidings.'

Cook slowly got to his feet. Tabitha dropped her knife and Tom and Martha paused and gazed at Cicely. 'What is it, mistress?' asked the cook.

'The master is dead.' Cicely's voice trembled as she fought to not give way to her emotions.

Martha gasped.

'We feared as much,' said the cook with a doleful shake of the head. 'He was a good master. He'll be sadly missed.'

'How did it happen?' asked Martha, wiping her hands on her apron.

Cicely repeated what Jack had said, adding that they had guests for the night in the shape of a Scots lord and his man. 'Perhaps you can use the remains of the mutton to add strength to the barley soup I was going to have for supper,' she said, feeling distraught.

Cook nodded. 'We could kill a couple of chickens, as well…and I'll need to bake more bread.'

She agreed. 'I will leave it to you to do what is

needful.' Running a hand over her hair, she added, 'You'll be using the fire in here, so I will use the hall fire to mull some ale. Tom, will you fetch a couple of pallets and blankets from the chest in the passage by the best bedchamber?'

'Aye, Mistress Cicely.' He hurried out.

Cicely fetched a jug of ale and a jar of honey from a shelf in the storeroom and, from a locked cupboard, removed cinnamon and ginger. Her grief was like a weight in her chest as she carried the items into the hall. There she saw her brother and Mackillin in conversation, standing where the baggage had been stowed in a corner.

At her approach, they moved away and sat on a bench, watching as she placed a griddle on the glowing logs, and on that an iron pot. Aware of Mackillin's eyes on her, she prayed that Diccon would sense her need of him and come home. The disturbing presence of the Scots lord and Master Husthwaite's arrogance made it imperative that she see him as soon as possible. Her concern was that he might have been caught up in fighting between the forces of Lancaster and York. Oh, why did he have to go and give his loyalty to the Duke of York's heir? The trouble was that her stepbrother could be stubborn and, having little in material goods, was determined to make his own way in the world.

Tom appeared with the bedding and placed it

near the fire to air. She whispered to him to see that their guests' horses had enough hay and water before supper was served. After a wary glance at the two strangers, he hurried to the stables, taking a lantern with him.

Cicely did not leave the spices to infuse for long, certain that her brother and the men were so in need of a hot drink that they would not mind it not being too spicy. She fetched cups and ladled the steaming brew into them, whilst all the time she was worrying about how Matt, now heir to the estate, would cope with the terrible news of their father's death.

'I wouldn't be surprised if it snowed in the next few days,' said Jack, watching her approach with their drinks. 'There's an eerie glow in the sky above the fells in the west.'

'That'll be the sunset,' said Cicely, dismayed at the thought that if a blizzard set in they might be cut off and she would have to cater for two guests that she would rather be gone. Now was not a time for having to see to the needs of a guest, and a Scots lord at that! She needed to grieve and devote her hours to prayer for her father's soul and Diccon's safe return.

'Is that cup for me?' asked Mackillin, gazing down at her.

She nodded, steeling herself to meet his eyes with

a coolness she was far from feeling. 'Aye, Lord Mackillin. Is there aught else you need? I could show you to a small bedchamber. Perhaps you'd like to change the garments you've travelled in…and have water to wash your hands, face and feet.'

A devilish glint showed in his eyes, lighting facets of gold and green in the iris. 'Just Mackillin. I appreciate the offer, but I'm warm in my dirt, lass. As for changing my clothes, what's the use of that when I'll be travelling in them on the morrow?' He removed his gauntlets and reached for the pewter cup.

She made certain his fingers did not touch hers. 'As you wish,' she said abruptly. 'If you'll excuse me.'

He inclined his head and she almost fled into the kitchen. He was a savage. She found the women servants plucking chickens and saw that dough was rising on a stone slab close to the fire. Realising that it would be some time before supper was ready, she left them to their tasks. Taking a lantern from a cupboard, she lit the candle inside and made for the door that opened on to a spiral staircase that led up to her turret room.

Built a hundred years ago during the times when the Scots *had* raided this far south of the border, the house had been fortified. Since then, improvements had been made to the property, but her dead stepmother had constantly said it should be pulled down and a cosier, more convenient one built in its place. Her father had laughingly suggested that his wife might prefer his father's house and she had not complained again.

Cicely had been hurt at such criticism of the house she had always liked and had hoped that when she and Diccon wed, he would be willing to live here, so they could all be one big happy family. Now her dreams were all up in the air due to his prolonged absence, and with the changes her father's death would necessarily bring. Her eyes filled with tears again and she brushed them away with her sleeve.

She came to her bedchamber and was grateful for the warmth and light from the charcoal brazier that had been placed there earlier in the day. Darkness had fallen and she could hear a rising wind so, hastily, she crossed the room and closed the shutters.

She yawned and sank on to the bed. Her shoulders drooped as her heart ached with sorrow. She longed to lie down and escape into sleep. Mackillin! Was he being truthful when he'd said he wished for no reward? And what had he meant when he said that *she* would not wish to pay his price if he were to seek it? She remembered the feel of his lips on hers and the hardness of his chest against her breasts. Could he possibly have hinted that bedding her was the reward he would have demanded? The blood rushed to her cheeks and she got up hastily and went over to the chest at the foot of her bed.

She lifted the heavy lid and pushed it back, holding the lantern so she could peer inside. When her stepmother had died, Cicely, aided by her maid, had made mourning clothes to attend her funeral and had worn them almost constantly for months afterwards. Even though there would be no such service for her father here in Yorkshire, Cicely wanted to do everything possible to honour his memory and that meant dressing in a way that was fitting.

She put down the lantern and pulled out a black surcoat and unadorned black gown, knowing that a requiem mass must also be arranged. There was water in the pitcher on the washstand and she poured some into a bowl and washed her hands and face, drying them on a heavy cotton cloth that her father had brought from one of the great fairs in Europe. She removed her muddy shoes and the lamb's-wool bags, as well as her outer garments. Then, over a cream woollen kirtle, she put on the black gown made from the finest wool that her father's tenants' flocks produced. On top of these, she fastened a silk-lined, padded surcoat, trimmed with sable, the fur having been shipped from the Baltic and bought in Bruges.

Again, she rummaged to the bottom of the chest and this time took out a sweet-smelling cedarwood box from its depths. She removed a girdle that was made of links formed in a pattern of silver leaves and fastened it about her hips before lifting a fine silver chain and crucifix from the box and fastening the chain about her neck. She found black ribands in a cloth bag, wove them through strands of her hair and braided them into two plaits. Lastly she slipped on heelless leather slippers before sitting on her bed and wondering what to do next.

Her emotions were in confusion and she felt too close to weeping to face the men downstairs just yet; especially the Scottish lord, whose eyes expressed much that his lips did not say. Lord or not, she still believed him a barbarian at heart. The manner in which he had swept her into his arms and kissed her had been truly shocking. She lay down on the bed, thinking of those moments. Her eyelids drooped and she told herself it was unseemly and sinful to still dwell on his kiss. Instead she should be praying for her father's soul and considering what they should do when Matt returned. Her thoughts began to drift and, within minutes, she was asleep.

Chapter Two

'Where's my sister?' Jack, who had been dozing in front of the fire, blinked up at Martha who was setting the table.

'I don't know, Master Jack, but it's a good four hours since Mistress Cicely came to the kitchen. Supper is ready to be served and we've had no word from her.'

'Perhaps she's in her bedchamber,' suggested Mackillin.

Martha stared curiously at the Scottish lord and her plump face told him exactly what she made of him. 'I'll send Tabitha to look,' she said.

So the maid went upstairs to her mistress's bedchamber and found her slumbering. Uncertain what to do, and knowing Cicely had passed many a sleepless night, worrying about her father and brother, Tabitha was reluctant to disturb her mistress and went downstairs to tell of her discovery.

'Dressed for mourning she is, and lying on top of her bed fast asleep. No doubt she's exhausted, Master Jack. She's been fretting for weeks, worrying herself about you and the master, as well as your stepbrother.'

The youth glanced at Mackillin. 'Should I wake her?'

Mackillin wondered if she was truly asleep or whether she was pretending in order to escape his presence. Either way, it might be best if he were not to see her again before leaving in the morning. 'Let your mistress rest, lass. Sleep is good for her at such a sad time. Make sure she is warm—I think we're in for a cold night.'

'And after you have done that, Tabby, fetch in the supper,' ordered Jack.

'And a bowl of water and a drying cloth,' added Mackillin with a smile. 'I'd like to wash my hands before I eat.'

Cicely started awake and for several moments lay in the darkness, wondering what had disturbed her sleep. She had been dreaming that she was being chased along a castle's battlements, pursued by a large hound and a black-cloaked dark figure. Her heart pounded. Then she heard a shutter banging and the howling of the wind and, although reluctant to get out of bed because she was so snug, knew she had to silence that shutter.

As she sat up, the crucifix slid along its chain and she clasped it. It had been her mother's and she only wore it on special occasions, never in bed. Memories of yesterday came flooding in and a sob broke from her. She would never again see her father's smiling face or hear his deep voice speaking her name. For a moment her grief was such that she could not move, but the shutter banged again and a freezing draught blew across the room. She felt a dampness on her cheek. Pushing down the covers, she climbed out of bed.

No glow came from the charcoal brazier and the candle in her lantern had burnt down. How long had she been asleep? Was it late evening or the middle of the night? Her stomach rumbled. She had missed supper. Why hadn't someone roused her? She remembered Mackillin and groaned. He would surely be thinking the worst of her. Then she asked herself why she should care about what he thought of her. In the morning he would be gone.

The shutter crashed against the stone wall outside once more and icy air gushed into the room. She shivered, remembering her father's promise to bring her a sheet of the finest Flemish glass for her window opening. Her eyes were now accustomed to the darkness, but she wished she had a light and fumbled for a fresh candle and her tinder box in the small cupboard next to the bed.

Another gust of wind fluttered the long sleeves and hem of her gown and she pulled a face, realising it was unlikely she'd get a decent spark in such a strong draught. She placed both items on the chest and crossed to the window. She reached through the aperture and was almost blinded by a flurry of snowflakes. She gasped and frantically groped for the shutter. A sigh of relief escaped her as her fingers touched wood, but she had a struggle pulling the shutter towards her. At last she managed to do so and fastened the hook securely before stepping back. The clothing chest caught her behind her knees and she fell on to it.

Wiping her damp face with her sleeve, she looked around and could just about make out the outline of the door to the stairway. Her stomach rumbled again. Why hadn't she been roused? Perhaps Mackillin had got Jack drunk on her father's wine and cut his throat and was even now plundering the household. Fear clutched her heart. Yet surely she was allowing her imagination to run away with her. Jack trusted him. Even so, she would not rest until she saw for herself that all was well.

She groped for the candle and tinder box, but it was just as hopeless trying to get a spark in the dark. Hopefully, she would find her way downstairs without a light. If she failed, then she would return to her bedchamber. She would not think about Jack lying there with his throat cut—or demons and apparitions, which some said were the souls of the dead come back to haunt the living. She thought of her father and prayed that God would accept him into Heaven. Clutching her crucifix, she felt her way along the wall to the door.

Once outside, there was a lessening of the darkness and she noticed a faint light penetrating the lancet aperture on the stairway. She put her eye to it and saw that snow blanketed the landscape and was still falling in large, fat flakes. Her heart sank, realising she was not going to get rid of the barbaric lord after all. Using extreme caution, she continued down the steps, brushing the wall with her hand.

Once through the door at the bottom, she paused to get her bearings as there were no windows in the passageway. She could still hear the roaring of the gale, albeit the sound was fainter here. Her heart beat heavily as she moved forward through a darkness that seemed to press in on her like a living force. She strained her eyes and ears, alert to any danger. Her hand touched wood. A closed door. She passed it and came to another closed door. She walked on with more confidence, convinced that the kitchen door was straight ahead. She heard the squeak of a latch and started back as the door opened and the light from a lantern temporarily blinded her.

An expletive was swiftly smothered as someone reached out and seized her by the wrist. 'God's blood, lass! What are you doing creeping around in the dark? I could have hurt you,' said Mackillin, lowering the lantern.

She caught a glimpse of his wild hair, unshaven rugged profile and words failed her. Light-headed with hunger and emotional strain, she swayed against him. He smothered another expletive and, placing an arm around her, half-carried her into the kitchen. She stirred in his arms and tried to push him away, but it was like trying to make a dint in a shield with a feather. 'Let me go,' she cried.

'I'll free you once I'm certain you aren't going to swoon again.'

'I did not swoon,' she said indignantly.

'You did.' He placed the lantern on a table and sat down in a chair in front of the fire and drew her onto his knee.

'What are you doing?' Panic strengthened her will and she hit out at him.

'Desist, woman! I intend you no harm, you little fool.'

'I don't believe you. Where's Jack?' She looked wildly about her.

'Where any sensible person is at this time of night—in his bed. Now, don't wriggle. I will release you if you promise to sit still and listen to me.'

She considered what he'd just said and calmed down. 'You mean you'll tell me what you were doing creeping out of the kitchen?'

'I heard banging and wondered at first if it was some misguided traveller, who had lost his way and come seeking shelter,' he said smoothly, not wanting to frighten her. 'I had fallen asleep and had no idea what watch of the night it was when I woke. Not wanting to disturb those sleeping in the hall by opening the main door, and uncertain whether the traveller would be a friend or foe, I decided to make for the kitchen door. When I looked outside I realised that any traveller would have to be a madman to be out on such a night.' His expression was grim. 'It appears I will not be going anywhere in the morning.'

'The snow might not be as deep as we fear,' she said quickly.

'Perhaps. I pray so. My enemies will take my land if I am delayed here too long.' She wondered who his enemies were, but did not ask because he was speaking again. 'What set you to wandering about the house?' he asked.

'The wind had blown my shutter loose and woke me up. I managed to fix it. I realised how hungry I was and came in search of food.'

'Of course, you missed your supper. There is still food aplenty.' She caught the gleam of his strong teeth in the firelight and the arms constraining her slackened.

She shot off his knee as if stung. 'Don't let me keep you from your bed, Lord Mackillin.'

She put some distance between them by going over to the table and leaning against it. She waited for him to leave the kitchen, but he made no move to do so. Tension stiffened her shoulders and she forced herself to relax and walk over to the fire, where an enormous log slumbered, its underbelly glowing red. She estimated it would last out the night, ensuring a fire would not have to be relit in the morning, a difficult task at times. A few feet away, her favourite mouser twitched in its sleep.

'You remind me of night, all black and silver,' said Mackillin abruptly.

His words startled her into staring at him. 'What did you say?'

'If you did not hear, I will not repeat it.' He rose to his feet. 'Sit down by the fire, mistress. I will fetch some bread and fowl. I have slept enough and who is to say that you might not hesitate to knife me if I were to slumber.' His expressive eyes mocked her.

Several times he had shocked her by his words, but that he should believe she would stab him as he slept and the idea that he should wait on her were two things not to be tolerated. 'I would not harm you. Indeed, if you are to extend your stay, you cannot continue to sleep in the hall. You need privacy. As for you fetching and carrying for me… nay, my lord, it is not right.'

'I do not care whether it is right or wrong.' His tone was adamant. 'I am not so high and mighty that I cannot serve another. Did Christ not wait on his disciples during the last supper? No doubt the following days and weeks will prove difficult enough for you in the light of your father's death, so take your ease and do not argue with me. And if you are worried about my hands being dirty, I've washed them.'

He left her to think on that while he fetched food and drink, trying not to dwell on how erotic he found her appearance in her mourning garb. He had to remind himself that she was the daughter of the house and that he could find a far more suitable bride in Scotland. He had almost made up his mind to marry Mary Armstrong. She was the daughter of one of his neighbours, an arrogant man who ruled his household with an iron rod. His wife had died in suspicious circumstances and Mackillin would like to rescue Mary from her father's house.

Besides, his mother, the Lady Joan, had been a great friend of Mary's mother, and she had spoken in favour of such an alliance years ago, although his father had been against it. There had been no love lost between the two men. The disagreement had resulted in one of their quarrels which always ended up with his mother preserving an icy silence towards her husband for days on end. As a young girl she had been carried across Mackillin's father's saddlebow on a border raid like a common wench and she had never forgiven him for treating her in such a fashion.

His mother had found no welcome in her future in-laws' house, one reason being that she could never forget that she belonged to the highborn English family, the Percys. It was to them Mackillin had been sent after his half-brother, Fergus, had tried to kill him seventeen years ago, when he was eight years old. His Scottish half-brothers had resented him, almost as much as they hated his mother. His upbringing would have been less violent if they had been girls instead of boys, but then he might have stayed home instead of leaving to be educated in Northumberland and indulging his love of boats and travel.

Cicely decided that perhaps it was best to do what Mackillin said and sat in the chair he vacated. She stretched her cold feet towards the fire, not knowing what to make of the man. What kind of lord was it that waited on a woman? An unusual one who excused his lowly behaviour by speaking of Christ's humility. She wondered in what other way he would surprise her during his sojourn in her home. What if he ended up staying a sennight or more? She was thankful there was still food in the storeroom: flour, raisins, a side of bacon, salted fish, smoked eel, a little butter, cheese, fresh and bottled fruit, honey, oats and barley. Also, enough logs remained piled high in one of the outhouses. The animals were not forgotten either and there was some straw and hay, as well as corn in the barn.

She heard a noise and, glancing over her shoulder, saw Mackillin carrying a platter. She rose hastily to her feet. 'You should not be doing this, Lor—Mackillin,' she said, taking the platter from him and placing it on the table.

He ignored her comment and put a napkin and knife beside the platter before leaving the kitchen. She sat down, wondering if he would return. No matter. She was famished and the chicken leg and slices of breast meat looked appetising. She picked up the meat and sank her teeth into it. It tasted so good that she closed her eyes in ecstasy.

'This will wash it down,' said a voice.

She opened her eyes and saw that Mackillin was holding a silver-and-glass pitcher of what appeared to be her father's malmsey, a wine he had called the best in the world. 'You've drunk some of that?' she asked.

He nodded. 'Jack said it would go well with the pears and green cheese.'

'But not chicken,' she said firmly. 'We always drink a white wine from a kinsman's vineyard in Kent with fowl.'

'We had some of that, too.'

She stared at him suspiciously. 'My brother was not drunk when he went up to bed, was he?'

Mackillin raised his eyebrows. 'Nay, lass, he wasn't. I drank most of the white wine. Although I have to tell you that I have tasted better. Not your fault, but if I'd known I might be snowed in here, I would have thought of bringing some of my kinsman's vintage from the Loire, instead of shipping it with a courier to my mother. Still, you have the malmsey and that will do you good.' He added conversationally, 'The grape used in making malmsey is from the Monemvasia vine, now grown in Madeira, but native to Greece. Sugar is also cultivated on the island and together they produce this sweet dessert wine.'

'I wanted Father to take me with him on his travels,' she murmured, watching Mackillin pour the tawny-coloured wine into a beautiful Venetian drinking vessel, which seemed out of place in the kitchen.

'Perhaps one day someone else might take you there,' he said, handing the glass to her. '*Bon appetit,* Mistress Cicely. I will leave you to enjoy your wine and see you in the morning.'

She murmured her gratitude, watching him leave the kitchen. He had left the lantern behind, its flame winking on the sparkling glass. Sipping the malmsey, she pondered the unusual behaviour of a certain Scottish lord and sensed it was even more imperative for her peace of mind that he left as soon as possible.

But it was not to be the following morning because although the snow had ceased to fall, it lay thickly over the fields and hills as far as the eye could see. The sky looked heavy with the threat of more to come.

'I hope Matt reached York before the snow came,' said Jack, his youthful face grim as he addressed his sister. 'Perhaps he won't ride on to Kingston-on-Hull when it clears, but come home.'

She nodded, gazing at the path that had been cleared through the snow to the outbuildings. Mackillin, Robbie and Tom had seen to the horses and Jack had fed the hens housed in the barn.

'Even Father's steward won't be able to reach us while it is like this,' said Cicely, chewing her lower lip. 'His concern will be for the tenants' flocks.'

'And who can blame him? Even the best of shepherds will have difficulty keeping all their sheep alive in this weather. We can manage here without him.'

Jack stamped snow from his boots and glanced at their guest as they went indoors. 'I pray you'll forgive me, Mackillin. It's my fault you're stranded here.'

Mackillin shook his head. 'Nay, lad. It is the fault of those murdering curs in Bruges. Besides, you have no control over the weather. We could have been on the road when the blizzard came and we'd have been caught out in the open. If I'm to be delayed, then best it be here.'

'Come and warm yourselves by the fire,' said Cicely. 'I'm mulling ale and have asked Cook to fry some bacon collops. I thought you might be in need of a second breakfast.'

'That's a grand notion,' said Mackillin, rolling the 'r' and smiling down at her. 'Yet you must be cursing me at a time when you need peace and quiet to mourn your father.'

'I deem the house is big enough for all of us to find peace in solitude if need be,' said Cicely, her calm expression concealing the turmoil his nearness caused her. 'As soon as possible we'll have to get a message to Diccon, informing him of Father's death, albeit we'll most likely have to get in touch with Owain ap Rowan first.'

Mackillin's brow furrowed. 'I have heard the name of ap Rowan before.'

'Owain ap Rowan is a horse breeder and has

stud farms in the palatines of Chester and Lancaster,' said Jack.

'He's a good man,' said Cicely, fetching cups from a cupboard and placing them on a table. 'He has travelled Europe, too. Diccon told me that the ap Rowans supplied horses to the present King Henry's armies during the wars with France. He and Father were great friends.'

'I deem that Master ap Rowan has several excellent qualities—but who is Diccon?' asked Mackillin, watching her graceful figure return to the fireplace.

'Our stepbrother,' replied Jack.

'We had hoped he would be home for the Christmas festivities,' said Cicely, ladling the brew into cups, 'but he never arrived.'

'Cissie fears he might have got himself involved with the Yorkists' cause,' said Jack, grimacing.

Cicely tried to frown her brother down, not wanting Mackillin to know too much about Diccon's affairs, but it was too late.

'I met the Duke of York's heir in Calais the other year. I can understand your stepbrother's involvement with him,' said Mackillin, catching that frown of hers and wondering what was behind it. 'He spent a great deal of time talking to merchants and mariners. I saw your father there, too.'

'Then it's likely you met Diccon,' said Jack.

'Diccon Fletcher? He would have been with Father.'

'In that case it's highly likely that I did. I just need to think back to that time and I will remember him.' Mackillin accepted the cup of steaming ale from Cicely. His hazel eyes washed slowly over her lovely pale face and he remembered the feel of her mouth beneath his and would have liked to have repeated the experience, but knew he had to resist such urges. Mary was to be his chosen bride. He did not love her, but then what had marriage to do with love? His father had supposedly fallen in love at first sight with his mother and what good had that done him? Mary would be grateful to him and get on with his mother and together they would organise his household. He would never beat Mary like her father did and he would do his best to make her happy. Although he did not care for Sir Malcolm Armstrong, it would be better to have him as an ally than an enemy.

'Well, have you remembered Diccon?' asked Jack.

Mackillin smiled. 'Not yet. So what is it you fear? That in the power struggle between Lancaster and York, he will be caught in the middle and be lost to you?'

'Aye. That is exactly what I fear,' murmured Cicely, lifting her eyes to his rugged face. 'We are betrothed and I have no wish to have him taken from me before we are even wed.'

Before Mackillin could assimilate her words, Jack burst out, 'Father made no mention of such a betrothal.'

Cicely turned on him. 'You know naught about it. I tell you I could have persuaded Father to change his mind about refusing to give Diccon my hand if he had not been killed.' Her voice broke and, dropping the ladle, she would have fled the hall if Tabitha and Martha had not entered, carrying trays, at that moment.

'The bacon collops, Mistress Cicely,' said Martha, looking askance at her.

Cicely pulled herself together and returned to the table. To her relief, neither man mentioned her outburst, but instead spoke of the baggage that had been unloaded from the packhorses. Mackillin asked whether Jack wanted the packages moved or unpacked first and sorted out.

Jack hesitated. 'Some goods are for customers and others gifts for family and the church. I had thought it was probably best to leave all until Matt returns—but with the weather the way it is it'll give us something to do, unpacking and listing everything.' He turned to his sister. 'You can help me with that, Cissie.'

She had calmed down somewhat and agreed,

stretching out a hand for her bacon collop on the platter in the middle of the table and placing it on a slice of bread. 'Father promised me a sheet of Flemish glass for my bedchamber window. At this time of year so many draughts manage to get through the gaps between the shutters and frame.'

Jack turned to her and his eyes were bright. 'He kept his promise as he always did. He purchased a new kind of glass, not so thick as that in my bed-chamber and much clearer. The trouble was that it was too large to load on to the packhorses—as were some of his other purchases, such as the glass he bought for the village church in memory of our stepmother. The shipping agent is sending them by cart. They were packed carefully and I pray that neither gets broken on the way.'

'Me, too,' she murmured, thinking the glass would be a gift worth waiting for. She took a bite of her food before getting up and wandering over to the pile of baggage.

Mackillin and Jack followed her over, but no one made a move to unpack any of the goods immediately. Cicely was remembering other such times when her father had produced gifts for his women-folk's delectation.

Noticing the sadness in her face and guessing the reason, Mackillin sought to detract her thoughts. 'There is a fine thirteenth-century stained-glass window in the Cathedral of St Maurice in Angers,' he said.

His mention of the saint roused Cicely's interest. 'St Maurice is the patron saint of cloth-makers. Do they make cloth in Angers?'

He shrugged broad shoulders. 'I only know that the women are skilful in tapestry work.'

He had surprised her. 'How do you know this?'

'My mother visited her French kin in Angers as a young girl and a few years ago she asked me to purchase a tapestry for her.'

'Isn't Angers the main city of Anjou?' she asked.

Mackillin nodded. 'The Queen of England's father, King René, has his court there.'

'You have visited his court?' asked Cicely.

A slight smile lifted the corner of Mackillin's lips. 'If I said aye, admit that would surprise you, lass.' She flushed, but did not comment, and he added, 'I was no lord then, but he knew the Percys and so welcomed me. René is a good man, cultured, but with no airs and graces. He likes to talk to his subjects and visitors alike. We discussed painting, music, the law and mathematics.'

Indeed, he had amazed her, thought Cicely, finding it difficult to imagine this man conversing on such topics.

Jack groaned. 'I wish you hadn't mentioned mathematics. Father was adamant that every merchant should have a knowledge of the subject. There are books he wanted me to read. That's why he wished to speak to Master Caxton. I never thought being a merchant would involve so much study.'

Mackillin winked at Cicely and instinctively she smiled. For a moment their eyes held and it was as if a flame passed between them. Her pulses leapt and she thought, this can't be happening! Determinedly, she looked away. Just because he was proving not as uncouth as she had first believed him to be, that did not mean he was to be trusted. She spotted the rolled pallets and blankets in a corner and faced him again. 'I will have the best bedchamber prepared for you.'

'I would appreciate that…and a basin of hot water would not go amiss,' he said, rasping the stubble on his chin with the back of his hand.

Jack swallowed the last bite of his bacon collop. 'We can do better than that for you, Mackillin. Adjacent to the best bedchamber is a room with a tub.'

'Aye,' said Cicely, her eyes brightening. 'I'm sure your lordship will benefit from a soak in hot water and some clean raiment.'

Mackillin desired only a few things more than sinking his smelly and aching body in a tub of steaming water and to don the clean raiment in his saddlebag, and he realised at the top of the list was an urge to bed the lass in front of him. Knowing that was out of the question, he teased her instead. 'I could catch ma death of cold if I were to wash, lass.'

He had to be jesting, thought Cicely and said firmly, 'Then put on an extra garment.'

Jack grinned. 'I deem he does not wish to give you more work, Cissie. I saw Mackillin immerse himself in a barrel of water aboard ship when we crossed the sea. I wouldn't have done it. The wind was freezing and from the north.'

'Hush, laddie,' said Mackillin, laughter in his eyes. 'Your sister might start changing her mind about me.'

Cicely would not allow herself to be drawn on that subject and only said, 'Then you would like the tub filled?'

'If it's not too much trouble.'

'It will be done, even if I have to wind up the buckets of water myself,' she said, picking up one of the parcels and trying to guess its contents by feeling it.

Instantly the laughter died in his eyes and he looked horrified. 'Nay, mistress, it is not a task for you. Robbie will help me to draw water. We'll also fill the empty water butts. It will help pass the time and prevent my body from getting soft.... And before you remind me that lords don't do such menial work,' he added, 'I tell you that this one has done plenty in the past. We'll make a start now. Who's to say when next I'll be able to bathe if the ground freezes and the water in it, too?'

She put the parcel down. 'Then we would have to break the ice and when the water butts ran out we'd dig snow and melt it in pans over the fire,' she said promptly.

'You're a lass of good sense,' he said gravely.

She flushed with pleasure at the compliment and watched as he and Robbie left the hall. 'Has Mackillin mentioned a wife to you, Jack?' she asked casually.

He hesitated. 'Why don't you ask him if you're interested? I'm certain Father did not wish you to marry Diccon.'

'If he did not speak to you about it, how do you know?' demanded Cicely.

Jack's expression changed. 'Take my word for it, Cissie. He had someone else in mind for you.' Before she could ask whom, he hurried after Mackillin and Robbie.

Frustrated, Cicely went upstairs to prepare the best bedchamber for Mackillin.

It was to be a couple of hours before the tub was ready and Mackillin followed her upstairs. His eyes were drawn to the seductive sway of her hips in the black gown and he wondered what Diccon Fletcher was thinking, to leave her here unprotected when he must have known her father was away in Europe. He remembered Diccon now. A pleasant-looking young man, hot for adventure and keen for advancement. After Nat Milburn had introduced them, they had later met in a tavern in company with the young Edward of York and some of his followers. Diccon had drunk too much and spoken of King Henry failing to keep his word and reward him for services rendered. Mackillin did not doubt for a moment that Diccon was now Edward's man. It concerned him only as far as it would affect Cicely's future. Nat Milburn's dying words made him uneasy in the light of what he now knew about his daughter and her relationship with Diccon. What if he was killed in battle? Who would she marry then?

He told himself that it was not his concern, he was for Scotland and a bride of his choosing. Even so he could not take his eyes from Cicely as, holding the lantern high, she turned right and led him along a passage. Now he was only a pace or so behind her and could smell the perfume of her hair. He was reminded of the camomile daisy that grew in profusion on his French kinsman's estate. He had seen the women gathering the flower heads and drying them to use in their washing water, but their scent had never affected him as it did now.

She stopped in front of a large, carved door that stood slightly ajar and pushed it wide. 'I hope you will be comfortable here, Mackillin.'

'I'm sure I shall. You can have no idea of the state of some of the places I've slept in,' he said, indicating that she precede him into the bedchamber.

She hesitated, but then told herself it was unlikely he would make advances to her now he knew that she was the daughter of the house, only to recall seconds later his pulling her on to his lap in the middle of the night. If only Diccon would return. Surely she would not be so affected by this man's presence if he was near?

She placed the lantern next to a bowl of dried rose petals, lavender and gillyflower heads on an ornate circular table. This stood beneath the polished metal of an oval gilt-framed mirror. On the other walls there were several tapestries. The sky had darkened and snow was falling again, but the chill had been taken from the room by a charcoal brazier. The bedchamber was bright with the light from several costly beeswax candles.

It was obvious to Mackillin that much care and money had been lavished on the room. He glanced at the bed that was of a width in which two people could lie in comfort. Its hangings and coverlet were made from a damasked cloth, woven in reds and yellows, and he imagined tossing Cicely on the bed, drawing the curtains and ridding her of clothing before smothering her body with kisses. He felt himself grow hard and forced himself to look away from the bed.

There were two armoires, as well as a large carved chest, and underfoot a floor covering thick enough for his boots to leave an impression. If he had not known already that Jack and Cicely's father was a rich merchant, then he would have recognised just how wealthy he was now. He remembered his parents having separate bedchambers and neither were half as well appointed as this one. He could have laughed out loud at the thought of his mother being introduced to Cicely and finding her wanting as a suitable wife for him because she was a commoner. She had more grace and spirit and good taste than many a lady he had met in his Percy kinsman's Northumberland castle.

He felt out of place in his mud-splattered and smelly garments and a desire to improve his standing in Cicely's eyes swelled inside him. 'This tub?' he asked, noticing his saddlebags had been unpacked by Robbie and raiment laid out on the bed.

'Through here,' said Cicely, casting a glance at the garments.

She led him over to a small door that stood ajar

in the corner of the chamber. As she did so there came a sound at the outer door and a discreet knock. They both turned their heads to see Tom, carrying a steaming bucket. 'More water for his lordship, Mistress Cicely. Shall I top up the tub?'

'Aye, Tom.'

Mackillin held up a hand. 'Nay, man. Just place the bucket inside the room. I'll need to test the water first. Do you know where Robbie is?'

'He's seeing how the horses are doing.'

Mackillin's brow puckered. 'I'll need you then to help me off with my boots. Have you any skill with barbering?'

'Aye, my lord, I used to shave my grandfather,' said Tom.

Mackillin nodded and flashed a smiling glance at Cicely. 'My thanks, lass. I'll not keep you.'

She hurried from the chamber and forced her mind along different channels from that of him shaved and bathed. She had not seen her brother for a while and wondered if he had placed some of the goods that had been unpacked in his bedchamber. She knocked on the door. When there was no answer, she opened it and peeped inside. It was empty.

She searched for him downstairs and when she did not find him, wondered if he was in the stables with Robbie. She hoped he had not done too much by using his damaged arm to cut cords. She decided to return upstairs, wanting to check with Tom that Mackillin had all he needed. On passing the chest in the passage, she noticed a tablet of soap on its lid and thought she must have forgotten to place it alongside the drying cloths in the tub room. She picked it up and hurried to the bedchamber. The door was ajar and she called Tom's name. When he did not answer, she decided that most likely he was with Mackillin. She could hear splashing from the adjoining room, which surely meant his lordship was already in the tub.

'Tom!' she called. No response. 'Mackillin!'

She hesitated before knocking on the antechamber door and peering inside. She could see the tub and a few wisps of steam, but no sign of either man. A whooshing noise caused her to almost jump out of her skin. A head broke the surface of the water and then shoulders and chest. She gaped, staring at the double-wing shaped mat of dark coppery curls and the long silvery scar beneath the left collar bone. She felt such a heat inside her. As if in a trance, she watched him reach blindly for the sword lying on the drying cloth on the stool.

She scooped up his dirty garments as he flicked back his trimmed hair and stood up, water streaming from his body. Cicely gasped and closed her eyes tightly. She had seen her brothers naked in a tub when they were tiny, but never a fully grown man exhibiting such masculinity. She opened her eyes, threw the soap in his direction and fled.

Chapter Three

'Cissie, where are you going in such a rush?' asked Jack, passing her on the stairs. 'You'll break your neck coming down at that speed.'

Thankfully diverted from the vision of the naked Mackillin, she placed the dirty garments behind her back and slowed to a halt, resting her free hand on a baluster. 'Where've you been? I was concerned about you.'

A crack of laughter escaped him. 'Why? What do you think could happen to me when we're snowed in? I'm not such a dolt as to attempt with a damaged arm to ride ten leagues or more in deep snow and the heavens throwing more of it down.'

Alarm caused her to blurt out, 'You've thought of doing so? You're concerned about Matt?'

A wary expression flickered in his eyes. 'Aren't you?'

'Do you sense he's in danger?'

He hesitated. 'I imagine he's anxious and fearful, but that shouldn't surprise either of us in the circumstances. Why don't you sit by the fire with your embroidery and rest?'

'What about the rest of the unpacking of the goods you brought home?'

'They can wait. You're always hurrying hither and thither. I'm sure the servants know well enough what to do about preparing our next meal without you overseeing them more than necessary.'

Cicely considered his words. Sitting quietly by the fire with her embroidery held a definite attraction. But what if Mackillin should come down and find her alone? She did not know how she was going to look him in the face. Her eyes would travel south. No! She must not harbour such a thought. If only he had not come here, she thought fretfully. If only her stepmother had not died, she felt certain her father would not have set out on his travels again. If he had allowed Jack to go abroad with one of his agents, he would still be alive and Mackillin would not have hotfooted it here for a reward. She must keep telling herself that was his only reason for being here. Although, perhaps it would be best not to think of him. Instead, she would consider how they were to get the news of her father's murder to Diccon.

She went and placed Mackillin's dirty clothing in

the laundry room. Then she fetched her embroidery and thought to cover her hair with a black veil to complete her mourning attire before settling in front of the fire. She soon realised it was a waste of time trying to work out a way to get news to Diccon while they were snowed in. Instead she allowed her thoughts to drift to what it would be like to travel the seas on Mackillin's ship and see those places that her father had visited. She regretted deeply that never would she be able to hear his voice describing Venice, Florence, Bruges and all the other cities she would have liked to have seen in his company; but she sensed that his lordship had her father's gift for painting pictures with words.

Mackillin was thoughtful as he rubbed himself vigorously with the drying cloth. His skin glowed and a wry smile creased his face. At least Mistress Cicely should be satisfied that he no longer stank of honest sweat and horse. Had it been she who had thrown the soap? He had glimpsed a whisk of a black skirt vanishing when he opened his eyes and his soiled garments had disappeared. Hopefully she had not seen enough of him to frighten her away. He smiled wryly, remembering on his travels how pleasant it had been to have a wench wash his back and generally make herself useful. Vividly, a picture came into his mind of Cicely behaving in a similar fashion and he imagined the soft swell of her breasts beneath silk brushing his bare shoulder. Desire rushed through him and he shook his head as if to rid himself of such longings. She was not for him, whatever Nat Milburn had promised.

He must concentrate his thoughts on his intended bride. From what he remembered of her from their last meeting, Mary was as different in appearance to Cicely Milburn as could be, but then she had only been a child and would surely have improved. She had dark hair, not the colour of corn like Mistress Cicely. He had never felt it, but doubted it would be as silky as Jack's sister's was when he had seized a handful of it while he had kissed her. Hell and damnation, he must stop thinking of her! Marrying Mary Armstrong would provide him with all he needed. She was sturdy and strong and no doubt could produce healthy sons and pretty daughters. His elder half-brother had wed and sired children, but no offspring had lived beyond infancy. As for the younger one, Fergus, his wife had died in childbirth last year and the baby with her, poor lass.

His lips tightened as he relived Fergus's teasing and bullying, the challenges and hard-fought tussles on the battlements of their grandfather's castle in the south-west of Scotland and his father's keep in the Border country. The scar beneath his collarbone throbbed as if experiencing afresh the plunge of Fergus's blade. Mackillin would never forget the hatred in his eyes for the son of the English woman who had replaced their mother. Now the three men were dead, killed in an ambush. His mother did not seem to know who was responsible. Due to his half-brothers leaving no heirs, Mackillin had inherited Killin Keep and its lands.

He was reminded again of Cicely, wondering if she would change her mind about his being a barbarian if she knew he was half-English. At least his altered appearance might convince her that he was no savage. He ran a hand over his freshly shaven jaw as he strolled into the bedchamber with the drying cloth slung about his lean hips.

Mackillin reached for his drawers and hose and pulled them on. He then put on a *petticote* beneath a linen shirt and donned a green woollen doublet, embroidered at neck, cuffs and hem. Over this he pulled on a sleeveless brown velvet surcoat that reached to his hose-covered calves before placing a vellum-backed book inside a concealed pocket. He combed his hair, which had been cut to just below his ears. Now he felt fit to be in a woman's company.

Thinking of Cicely again brought a lift to his heart, but a frown to his face as he slipped on a pair of leather shoes that laced up the sides. He took the lantern from the table and left the bedchamber, locking the door behind him. He placed the key in his pocket and strolled down the passage. As he went downstairs, he spotted Cicely sitting by the fire and scowled. She had covered her hair with a black veil; with her black gown and surcoat, this gave her a nun-like appearance. Was it deliberate? Was she saying, *Do not touch?*

As he approached, the dogs lifted their heads and she glanced up from her sewing. He saw her eyes widen and knew he had achieved the effect he had aimed for. His mood lightened. She half rose in her chair, but he told her not to disturb herself, so she resumed her seat and bent her head over her embroidery.

Mackillin settled himself in a chair close to the fire and took out his book. It was one that an elderly Percy relative had left him in his will and was over fifty years old. Fortunately the handwriting was still legible. As he carefully turned the pages, he was aware that Cicely was watching him.

'Whenever I take up this book, I think of the copyist working for months on end, writing out thousands of words,' he said.

'What book is it?' asked Cicely, impressed not only by his appearance but that he should produce a book and to all purposes seem intent on reading it. She was relieved that he appeared to have no idea that she had seen him in his skin and yet felt vexed with herself for wanting to touch his shaven cheek and run her fingers through the chestnut hair that curled about his ears. What would her father have thought of her for having such desires? How could she be grieving for him, be in love with Diccon and yet still be attracted to this man?

'*The Canterbury Tales*—have you heard of it?' asked Mackillin.

'Aye. But I've never seen a copy before.' She was surprised that her voice sounded normal.

'Perhaps you'd like me to read some to you?' He had found the place where he had left off and, without waiting for her answer, added, 'This is part of "The Monk's Tale", a piece written about Count Ugolino of Pisa.'

'Who was this Count, my lord?'

'Mackillin,' he said automatically, reading in silence for a few moments before lifting his head and grimacing. 'Perhaps not.'

'Why—why not?' She stared at him and their eyes met and held for several quickened heartbeats.

'Because it is a tragedy and you have enough sadness to deal with at the moment,' he said brusquely, lowering his gaze and turning pages. '"The Miller's Tale" is amusing and brings tears to the eyes, but it is not suitable for a maid's ears. Perhaps "The Second Nun's Tale" would be best. There's an "Invocation to Mary", daughter and mother of our Saviour in its pages.'

'Daughter and mother?'

'Aye, such is what the writer has written here… *maid and mother, daughter of thy son.*'

'I have never thought of our Lady being both daughter and mother to our Saviour before….' She stumbled over the words, but added, 'Of course, if He is part of the Trinity—Father, Son and Holy Ghost, three in one—then it must be so. And yet…'

'It is a mystery, I agree. Do you wish me to read on? Or would you rather I read…what have we here?' He smiled. 'An "Interpretatio Nominis Ceciliae". Did you know that the name *Cecilia* in the English tongue means *Lily of Heaven?*'

'Aye! My father told me so. Cecilia was a highborn Roman woman and my name derives from hers.' Cicely was amazed that they were having such a conversation and not only because she was reneging on her decision to distance herself from him.

'You know her story?'

She nodded, filling in a flower petal with blue thread and thinking of the Cecilia who had converted her pagan husband to Christianity. 'If you have not read it before, then I do not mind hearing it again,' she murmured.

'It is of no matter. I know the story.'

He closed the book and, excusing himself, rose and went over to where some of the baggage was still piled in a heap. Silence reigned but for the crackling of the fire. He wondered if she was tired after their disturbed night and that was why no more inroads had been made on exploring the contents of the goods here. Perhaps it would be wiser to leave her alone to her embroidery and her grief. Yet he found himself wondering if this was the only leisure pastime she occupied herself with to help pass the winter days when the weather kept her indoors. Even when Nat was alive it must have been a lonely life for her after her stepmother died and with the males of the family busy elsewhere.

He recalled the moment when a courier had arrived at his kinsman's manor in France. His mother had pleaded with him to return to the keep in the Border country, which had never felt like a home; rather he had considered his own house in the port of Kirkcudbright with its busy harbour as home. As his eyes roamed the tapestry-covered walls, he realised why he felt relaxed here. 'This hall reminds me of my house in Kir'coo-bri.' He pronounced the name in the dialect of that area of Scotland. 'It was to that port I used to escape when life became unbearable when we stayed at my grandfather's castle—and there I discovered a love of ships and a longing to travel.'

'In what way does this hall remind you of your house?' asked Cicely, wondering why he had found his grandfather's castle unbearable.

'Its size and...' He went over to a wall and fingered a tapestry of *The Chase*. 'This tapestry. I wager your father bought this in Angers.'

'I cannot say for sure. France certainly.' She gazed openly at his back, her eyes lingering on the hair at the nape of his strong neck, his broad shoulders and the firm muscles of his calves.

He turned suddenly and she lowered her eyes swiftly, feeling her cheeks burn with embarrassment because he had caught her looking at him...and looking in a way that was unseemly. She cleared her throat and rushed into speech. 'Father had one of his agents purchase several for my stepmother soon after we moved here. The walls were unadorned and filthy after the smoke from the winter's fires...as they are now. But you being a lord, surely you will live in a castle with a great hall when you return home to Scotland?'

Frowning, he glanced over his shoulder. 'No. My father's elder brother inherited the castle. Have you ever visited the Scottish Borders, Mistress Cicely? The place I return to is not like the great edifices of England, such as my kinsman Northumberland's at Alnwick. The building that I have inherited is a keep in a wild lonely place. At the moment my mother is Killin's chatelaine, which is within a day's journey of Berwick-on-Tweed.'

She dug her needle into the linen and murmured,

'My father used to speak of Berwick-on-Tweed. Is it not on the Eastern seaboard and has changed hands several times—as did the border during the wars between our countries?' she asked.

'You are well informed,' he said approvingly, returning to the fireplace.

She flushed. 'I am a merchant's daughter and as such am interested in the places my father visited. He has estranged kin up near the border, but we have naught to do with them.'

There was a silence before he said carefully, 'Then they have never visited this manor?'

'Not while I've lived here. Probably they might have visited during my great-uncle's time.' She looked up at him. 'Why do you ask? Are you acquainted with them?'

He hesitated. 'Not at all, but I suspect they could have been behind your father's murder.'

She started and stared at him from dismayed blue eyes. 'Why should you think that?'

He was unsure whether to burden her further but, remembering the way she had threatened him with her dagger, decided she was strong enough to know the truth so as to be forewarned. 'Robbie recognised a man he killed in Bruges as a Milburn he had seen in the Border country.'

She was astounded. 'You have spoken to Jack of this?'

He shook his head. 'Perhaps I should have, but at the time I thought he had enough to worry about, having seen his father die and fretting over how he was going to break the tragic news of Nat's death to you and his twin.'

A furrow appeared between her finely etched brows. 'I deem you've told me to put me on my guard?'

Mackillin nodded. 'The man might have been acting on his own account, but we don't know for sure.'

Her concern deepened. 'How did this kinsman know where to find Father?'

Mackillin shrugged. 'If he wanted to find Nat and knew enough about his business, then it would be easy enough for him to make enquiries.'

'Of course. But why?' she asked of him, realising she trusted him enough to believe that he would give her an honest and sensible answer.

'Money, power? Perhaps your northern kinsman thought he should have inherited this manor instead of your father.'

She bit her lower lip, thinking about what he said. 'That would make sense despite my great-uncle and grandfather having quarrelled with their brother up north. It was my great-uncle's wish that Father inherit this manor and he made it legal by stating so in his will.'

'Even so, speak to your brothers when Matt comes home about this matter. It could be that it is not finished.'

She nodded. 'I will do so.'

His frown deepened and he thought again of his half-brothers and how they would have hated his inheriting in their place. There could be that there would be others on the Borders who would not approve of his doing so. He rose from his chair and began to pace the floor, thinking of the times he had had to ride for his life, not only from his half-brothers but his Scottish cousins, as well. So much hatred in a family, which he had to admit had sometimes been fuelled by his mother's disdain of their simple way of life. Another reason perhaps why he had turned down Nat's offer of his daughter. She was accustomed to the luxuries that money could buy and might prove to be another like his mother. Perhaps that was the reason why he, himself, had been determined to make his fortune.

Cicely wondered what was on Mackillin's mind—the way he could not keep still suggested his control over his emotions was uncertain. He was obviously desperate to be up in his wild country dealing with what needed to be done for his future in that land. Well, the sooner he could leave the better it would be. She would be able to get on with all that needed doing in the wake of her father's death.

The door opened and Martha appeared. Her jaw dropped as she stared at Mackillin. Amused by the serving woman's expression, Cicely said, 'You may well look surprised—Mackillin looks like a nobleman now, doesn't he?'

Martha nodded and bobbed a curtsy in his direction. He raised an eyebrow and a smile tugged at the corner of his mouth. 'I'm glad you approve, Mistress Cicely.'

She blushed and turned to Martha. 'Is supper ready to be served?'

'Aye, mistress.'

'Then I'll fetch my brother.' She folded her sewing and hurried upstairs, needing to escape Mackillin's charismatic presence for a while.

Over the meal, Cicely spoke little but she was intensely aware of Mackillin sitting across from her. Their earlier conversation had been fascinating and frightening in equal measure. She appreciated that he had not talked to her in that condescending manner some men adopted when speaking to a woman. He had given her a problem, though—did she wait until Matt returned home as he had suggested, or tell Jack before then what Mackillin had said about their northern kin?

She pondered the matter on and off for the rest of the evening, as they unpacked some of the items Nat had bought in Europe. Amongst the goods he had purchased on behalf of his regular customers, she discovered a great gift from her father. Tears filled her eyes as she turned the pages of *The Book of Hours,* a layperson's book of devotion that Jack told her was Nat's belated extra birthday present for her. She was tempted to wander over to the fire and delve further into it, but at that moment Mackillin produced a lute from wrappings of thickly woven cloth.

'Who's that for?' she asked, clutching her precious book to her breast.

Jack paused in the act of opening a box containing jars of pepper that had also been purchased in Venice, the city controlling a large part in the market of that commodity. 'Owain asked Father to have one specially made for Anna in Venice. Gareth accidentally dropped hers down the stairs—unfortunately it was smashed beyond repair.'

'Who are Anna and Gareth?' asked Mackillin absently, inspecting the inlaid mother-of-pearl patterning on the musical instrument.

'Anna is Owain's much younger half-sister and Gareth is his son,' answered Cicely.

'It's a wonderful gift,' said Mackillin, carefully plucking a couple of the strings.

'You play?' asked Cicely, her eyes suddenly alight. 'Matt plays the guitar and Jack makes a noise on the drums. Sometimes they create sounds that cause me to cover my ears and yet at others—'

'At others,' interrupted Jack with a grin, 'you were wont to sing and dance. I remember Father—' He stopped abruptly and his lips quivered.

Mackillin placed the lute on a table. 'I am certain Nat would not want the music in this house to end with his death,' he said firmly. 'I remember meeting him in Marseilles a while ago and he would insist on singing after we'd downed enough wine and brandy to float a ship.'

Cicely and Jack groaned in unison. 'Father loved music, but he always sang off key,' said the latter.

'Yet right now I'd give anything to hear him sing,' said Cicely, a catch in her voice.

Jack nodded and Mackillin noticed that his eyes were shiny with tears. The youth left the box he'd been unpacking and walked over to the fireplace. Cicely followed him, putting an arm around him as her brother gazed into the fire. Mackillin cursed himself for telling that tale and racked his brains for something to do to take the youth's mind off his sorrow. Then he remembered the chessboard he had seen set up on a side table and suggested to Jack that they could make a match of it.

'I've never played,' he admitted, looking slightly shame-faced. 'It was Father and Cissie who enjoyed testing the other's wits.'

'I could teach you,' suggested Mackillin.

Jack hesitated and then nodded.

Cicely left them to it and sat down and opened *The Book of Hours.*

Now the only sounds to be heard were the occasional murmur of voices, the turning of pages, the crackling of the fire and the roar of the wind in the chimney. Even so Cicely found it difficult to keep her mind on the pages of her book. Her attention kept wandering to the table where their guest was instructing her brother. He had surprised her again in more ways than one. He was extremely patient with Jack and she wondered where such a man as he had developed such a gift. Several times she caught him glancing her way and she lowered her eyes instantly. Suppressing her attraction to this man was essential if she was to maintain a distance between them until he left.

Two days later when Cicely threw back the shutters, the sun poured in. The air might be bitterly cold, but the brightness of the day lifted her spirits. She wanted to be outside, and after washing and dressing, hurried downstairs. On entering the hall, she found Tabitha shovelling ashes from the fire into a pail.

'We'll be needing those ashes,' said Mackillin, appearing in the main entrance. 'I've been outside, and the steps and yard where the snow has been cleared are slippery.'

Cicely's pulses leapt. 'Have you measured the deepness of the snow?' she asked.

His hazel eyes creased at the corners as his gaze rested on her heart-shaped face. 'I have been no further than the stables. You have it in mind to go somewhere?'

Had she? 'I would like to go to the village. It is but half a mile away. I need to speak to the priest.' She paused and felt a lump in her throat. 'I deem he needs to know what has happened to Father as soon as possible so prayers can be said for his soul in church.'

He looked thoughtful. 'I am willing to attempt a ride that far with you. If the snow proves too deep, then we will return.' He picked up the pail of ashes.

Before Cicely could protest at his doing such a menial task, he had gone. She presumed they would break their fast before attempting to reach the village and went with Tabitha to speak to Cook.

It was just over an hour later that Mackillin and Cicely left the confines of the yard. The surface of the snow was frozen and crunched beneath the horses' hooves as they picked their way gingerly towards the track of beaten earth. It was only recognisable as such by the stark outline of the leafless trees that grew on one side of it; on the other was a ditch. Cicely noticed that Mackillin had a staff and a coiled rope attached to his saddle and wondered what use he would make of them. Her cheeks and the tip of her nose were pink with cold and her breath misted in the icy air; even so she was glad to be out of the house. For extra warmth she had wound a length of thick woollen material over her head and round her neck and her legs were encased in her lamb's-wool bags beneath her skirts.

Even Mackillin had made a concession to the freezing weather by wearing a russet felt hat with a rolled-up brim. Neither of them spoke, although each were extremely aware of the other. Mackillin was questioning his reason for offering to accompany her when Tom could have easily done so. It would have been wiser to spend less time in her company, not more. Yet he was glad to have her at his side. She was a delight to look upon and surprisingly she rode astride her mount. He wondered if she had had cause to ride like the wind to escape an enemy at any time or because she enjoyed a good gallop and was more likely to remain in the saddle that way. He thought of last evening and of her reading the book her father had bought her. He mentioned the fact that she was able to read now.

She glanced at him. 'Sometimes Father would be away for months on end and Mother never learnt to read or write, so he had the priest teach me along with my brothers. They were skills she seemed unable to grasp, so I kept the housekeeping accounts and she dictated messages to me to send to him.' She hesitated. 'I would like to read the gospel in English some day. Father told me once that his grandfather was imprisoned because he had read one of John Wycliffe's translations. He was a follower of the Lollards. Have you heard of these men?'

Mackillin nodded. 'Because they read the gospels in their own tongue, they began to question not only the Church's interpretation of God's word, but also the structure of society itself. They stirred up the common people to revolt and were ruthlessly put down at the instigation of the Church.'

She nodded, thinking he had surprised her again by being so well informed. 'Some believe the movement has died out, but others have spoken of it having gone underground.'

His gaze washed over her face. 'That wouldn't surprise me. Dissatisfaction with the Church's teaching is growing in some quarters in Europe too. There are men in the Low Countries determined to print copies of the gospels in their own tongue on the new printing presses. I do not doubt they will find a market and sell in their hundreds.'

Cicely's eyes widened. 'Is this possible?'

'Aye. Although, no doubt, the Church will try to prevent it.'

'Then there must be some truth in what the Lollards taught,' she said firmly, 'if the Church is so determined to prevent men reading God's word for themselves.'

'Men doing so could turn the world upside down.'

She did not say so, but she agreed with him. The Church had such power that it would surely fight any challenge to its authority.

Mackillin said, 'Does Master Fletcher share your interest in reading the gospels in English?'

'It is a matter we've not touched upon,' she said in a stilted voice.

Mackillin frowned. 'Yet you want to marry him. Do you have a day in mind?'

She flushed, sensing a criticism of either herself or Diccon in his comment. 'Eastertide,' she muttered. 'If the quarrels between the houses of York and Lancaster do not spoil my plans and Master Husthwaite keeps his nose out of my affairs.'

He raised his eyebrows. 'Master Husthwaite! You speak of that lantern-jawed cur who claimed to be your father's new man of business?'

'The very same! I do not trust him.'

'You show sense. In my experience, it is not unknown for such men to act inappropriately with their clients' funds. You would do well—' He broke off as his mount lurched to the right and, steadying it with a firm hand, he looked down to where the wind had blown the snow into a drift that blocked the path. Their conversation was forgotten as he dismounted.

Cicely watched as he unfastened the straps that held the staff to his saddle. She hazarded a guess that he intended to test the depth of the drift. His booted foot sank into the snow past his knee as he plunged the staff into the snow a few inches in front of him. The staff disappeared from sight and he lost his balance, toppling face down in the snow. She bit back a laugh.

He lifted his head. 'Don't you dare!'

She giggled.

He glanced at her over his shoulder. 'Stop your cackling, woman. It's not helpful.'

'I'm not cackling,' she said indignantly. 'I was about to dismount and offer you my hand. Now I've a good mind to leave you to your fate and ride back. Perhaps someone will find you after the thaw.'

He groaned. 'You have to be jesting. I've a plan.'

'So have I. I'll fetch Robbie.'

'And have him laugh his boots off? That's not kind, Cissie.'

He had called her *Cissie!* 'I don't see why it isn't,' she teased. 'Laughter is good for the soul.'

'Cissie, if you dare fetch him, I'll…'

He had called her Cissie again and his doing so gave her an odd feeling, as if a barrier had been removed. 'You'll what?' she said sweetly. 'You're in no position to threaten me, Mackillin.'

He twisted his head and sighed. 'That is no way to speak to a lord. You'll have to help me, but don't make a move until I say so.'

For a few moments Cicely had forgotten both that he was a lord and her decision to keep him at a distance because she had so enjoyed mocking him. 'I beg your pardon, *Lord* Mackillin. Sing loud when you want my help.'

She dismounted, waiting for his command. It was obvious that he could not get up unaided. The snow might be hard on the surface, but it was soft underneath. If he tried to push himself up, then his arms would plunge beneath the snow and he would sink deeper into it.

'Take the rope from my saddle and tie one end to the pommel and throw the other end to me where I can reach it.'

Instantly she realised what his plan was and wasted no time obeying him, reminded of a day on the fells when she had come upon a sheep that had wandered into a mire. She had wanted to help the poor creature, but couldn't, and it had vanished beneath the surface. Mackillin's situation was fortunately different because she was able to help him.

Having fastened the rope to the pommel, she watched Mackillin ease the other end of it round his chest and back and knot it beneath an armpit. He signalled to her to urge his horse along the path the way they had come. She did so and Mackillin spun round slowly and slid along the surface of the snow. In no time at all, he was free of the snowdrift and standing upright. She approached him, reaching out a hand, thinking only to help him unfasten the rope and brush the snow from his clothing.

But he seized her wrist and drew her towards him, a glint in his green-coppery hued eyes. 'I should punish you for laughing at me,' he said in a teasing voice.

She was breathlessly indignant. 'I rescued you! I deserve a reward.'

'Then you decide which it is to be.' Smiling, he lowered his head and brushed his lips against hers in a tantalising fashion. It was so pleasant that instinctively his arms went round her and he brought her against him so that her head rested in the crook of his shoulder.

With a heavily beating heart Cicely gazed up at him, knowing she felt his kiss had been no punishment. Perhaps he saw her answer in her eyes and that was why he followed it up with another kiss that was longer, deeper and intensely satisfying. She should have struggled, but she had no desire to resist him. Her lips parted beneath the insistent pressure of his mouth and she felt a further thrill as the tip of his tongue danced along the inside of her lip. It felt so sensual that her own tongue flickered against the side of his. Instantly she was aware of the quiver that passed through him and knew she should pull away, but her insides seemed to be melting like butter on hot bread and she didn't want the moment to end.

Then a horse whinnied and attempted to thrust its head between them. Instantly Mackillin released her and his expression was so thunderous that Cicely was shocked and hastily turned away from him and went to her own horse, fumbling at the beast's accoutrements with shaking hands. She dragged herself up into the saddle. Did he blame her for what had just happened between them? What *was* happening to her? What were these unfamiliar urges she felt towards him? It had been such fun and satisfying when they had worked together to free him from the snowdrift. If only she and Diccon could share such moments of being in harmony. She needed Mackillin to go far away so that she could concentrate her thoughts on praying for Diccon's return. She needed inner peace instead of the tumultuous feelings that gripped her now.

She must hold steadfast to her decision to keep her distance from Mackillin for the remainder of his stay at Milburn Manor.

'We must go back.' The harshness in his voice was enough to make her school her features before looking at him.

'It would be foolish to continue,' she said, sensing the tension in him as he held himself erect in the saddle.

He clenched his jaw and dug his heels into his horse's flanks. There were words he would have liked to say to her, but it would indeed be folly to speak them. He was shocked that a kiss he had intended as part of the fun they had shared had turned into something far deeper. What did he think he was playing at? He had made up his mind to marry Mary Armstrong, knowing it was sensible. He did not expect to reach the heights in his alliance with her, knowing that the love that the poets and minstrels raved about scarcely existed between man and wife. Yet just now he had felt such an explosion of feeling inside him that a certain part of his body still throbbed with arousal. He could not help wondering whether Cicely was attracted to him, as he was to her, against her better judgement. He certainly could not allow it to interfere with his plans. After years of travelling and adventure it was time to settle down and raise a family. For that he needed allies to make his position more secure. For the remainder of his stay he would make sure not to be alone with Cicely.

Having made their decisions, both prayed that God would be kind to them and send a thaw.

Chapter Four

The sound of rushing water swirling round rocks filled Cicely's ears. Standing on a boulder, she watched a vole struggle towards the opposite bank of the river and saw a similarity in its plight to her own. For she, too, felt that she was trying to reach firm ground again because the world that she thought secure had collapsed with the death of her father and the news that their northern kin were a threat to her and the twins' safety.

'What will you do, Mackillin?' Jack's voice drew her attention away from her thoughts and the tiny creature's plight. 'The water level is dangerously high. Will you delay your departure until Matt returns? He'll be able to tell you the state of the rivers and bridges on the road to York and perhaps Kingston-on-Hull, too.'

Cicely gazed towards where her brother and the Scots lord were inspecting the bridge and held her breath as she waited for Mackillin's reply. Since she had first heard the rain two nights ago, differing emotions had warred inside her. Now she told herself, not for the first time, that she must put him out of her mind and concentrate on getting in touch with Diccon.

Mackillin's eyes met hers, so that when he responded to Jack's words it felt as if he was speaking directly to her. 'When I parted from my master mariner, I ordered him to return for me and Robbie within the week. We are already late for our rendezvous. Of course, it's possible the weather has sunk my ship or at the least delayed it putting into Kingston-on-Hull as arranged. In that case I would have to ride north. Whatever has happened, I cannot delay any longer.'

'I so wanted you to meet Matt,' said Jack, sounding disappointed.

Cicely said lightly, 'It's possible Mackillin might meet our brother on his way to Kingston-on-Hull. He will have no trouble recognising him with you and Matt alike as two ripe berries on a bramble bush.'

'I will certainly look out for him,' said Mackillin, strolling towards her. He reached up both arms to help her down from the boulder. Was that regret he could see glistening in her lovely eyes? He wanted to sweep her off her feet and do what his father had done with his mother twenty-six years ago. He imagined placing Cicely on his horse and carrying her off to his keep in the north. Yet he knew it would be foolish to act so recklessly with his parents' example before him.

As soon as he set her on her feet, she stepped back and, forcing a smile, said, 'Fare thee well, Mackillin. God grant you a safe journey.'

He thanked her and rashly took one of her hands and brushed the back of it with his lips before turning and striding away.

She was immensely touched by his action and could feel her skin tingling where his lips had touched it. She chose not to watch him until he was out of sight, but gazed over the river. She hoped the vole had reached the far bank safely and prayed that the emotions striving for prominence inside her would abate and she could feel her customary calm, sensible, accepting and adaptable self. She loved her home and the twins; although she would grieve for her father for some time, once Diccon returned and they married, they would live happily after, helping her brothers to cope with the heavy responsibilities that had fallen on to their shoulders.

Mackillin gazed down at Jack with a smile. 'You will behave sensibly and not use that arm more than necessary?'

Jack swung his arm back and forth and bit back a wince, saying, 'See. It's fine. Will you not come and visit us again, Mackillin?'

'I can make no promises, Jack. You will have a care for your sister?'

'Aye. But it should have been your task,' he said boldly. 'You should not be leaving without your reward. If Father knew you were going empty-handed, he would not be pleased.'

'We've spoken of this already, Jack,' rasped Mackillin, trying to be patient. 'I cannot marry your sister. Besides, aught else, she is intent on marrying Diccon Fletcher.'

'But Cissie would make you a good wife,' insisted Jack. 'You cannot have failed to notice how admirable she is in so many ways. Where she might fail in your notion of the perfect wife, Father would say she is young enough to be moulded into shape.'

Mackillin sighed heavily. 'I am aware of your sister's fine qualities, but it cannot be. I need allies, Jack. I must take a Scottish bride.'

Jack looked deeply disappointed. 'But Father wanted you to marry Cissie. He must have believed you were right for each other. If you don't marry her and Diccon gets killed, then that horrible Husthwaite might return and…'

Mackillin steadied his horse, which was desperate to get the fidgets out of its legs. 'Then you must waste no time getting in touch with Master Fletcher, so he can deal with him.'

Jack frowned and kicked at a pebble. 'I can't do that until Matt comes home, but don't you concern yourself any more about us. We'll manage. Thank you for bringing me home and I pray you have a safe journey,' he said in polite tones before turning and walking towards the house.

Mackillin felt thoroughly bad-tempered. Jack made him feel in the wrong, but then he was only a lad and didn't understand that marriage was a serious matter and involved making useful alliances. He signalled to Robbie, who was standing by the stable entrance, talking to Martha. She looked vexed, but Robbie shrugged and climbed on to his horse. Gathering the reins of the hired packhorses together, he followed Mackillin towards the path that led to the highway.

Fortunately the road was passable and they only had to make one diversion due to flooding. They met few travellers on the way, and none that resembled Jack. By late afternoon they had reached York where they broke their journey. It was there that Mackillin received what was to be his first indication that his plans might be altered by the quarrels between the Lancastrians and Yorkists. They had skirted York on the journey to Milburn Manor, but now they saw the heads displayed on the Micklebar

Gate. Mackillin felt sickened and his mouth set grim. His thoughts flew to Cicely and he wondered whether Diccon had been caught up in the latest battle. If so, was he dead? If she suffered the loss of another that she loved, might it break her heart? He decided he needed information.

Over supper in a tavern, Mackillin got into conversation with an injured mercenary. Apparently the Duke of York had left the safety of his castle walls on the eve of the New Year to do battle with a greater force of Lancastrians. The result of this folly was that he and his sixteen-year-old son had been killed.

'What of York's heir, Edward?' Mackillin asked.

The man lowered his voice. 'Some say he's the rightful king of England. That parliament agreed to the seven-year-old Prince of Wales being set aside and York declared Henry's heir. The King's said to have put his name to it, but the Queen's like a she-wolf fighting for her young and won't accept it.'

'So young Edward's still alive?'

'He weren't at Wakefield. It's believed he spent Christmas at his father's castle at Ludlow.'

Mackillin was relieved. He considered it unlikely Diccon would have fought in the recent battle if Edward was not involved, so he need not worry himself about Cicely being left without a husband.

Yet that night he dreamt of her and woke fevered and aroused. He lay, imagining her in his arms, picturing her sweet, sad face, wanting to wipe away her grief and plant laughter in her eyes. He told himself he must banish such imaginings and concentrate his thoughts on getting safely to Scotland to take up the reins of his new life. It was going to be difficult enough settling down in one place without yearning for a Yorkshire lass who had shared his kisses.

The next day Mackillin and Robbie made good speed despite there being much trafficking on the road between Kingston-on-Hull and York. When they arrived in the port, Mackillin left it to Robbie to return the packhorses to the Milburns' shipping agent and headed through the bustling streets to the quayside near the junction of the rivers Hull and Humber. Gulls screeched overheard and there was a keen wind. The salty tang of the sea brought him a momentary calm and he told himself that he really was looking forward to setting sail again.

He praised God when he found his ship at the quayside and wasted no time hailing the mariner on deck. Soon he was sitting in his cabin, eating oaten bread and grilled herring washed down with a tankard of hot spiced wine. When he had finished, his master mariner handed over two scrolls.

'One is from your lady mother and a messenger delivered the other to Killin Keep. As you will note, the seal has the royal crest stamped on it.'

Mackillin frowned, wondering what the young king of Scotland wanted from him. He untied the ribbon and broke the royal seal and flattened the parchment on the table. The message was addressed simply to the Laird of Killin and summoned him and his men to foregather in support of Queen Margaret, wife of Henry VI of England, to free her husband from the Yorkist rebels. Apparently it was imperative that he did this as it was in Scotland's interest that Henry was restored to his throne. There was no reason given why it was imperative and that annoyed Mackillin somewhat.

He rolled up the scroll and stretched out a hand for that sent by his mother and broke the seal.

To my son, the new Lord of Killin,

I pray to the Holy Trinity and all the Saints that this letter will find you in bodily health and in good spirits. It was with deep foreboding I received your courier under my roof, but he soon assured me of your well being and gave me your missive concerning your promise to this dying merchant. You are a fool, Rory, and I can only hope that you do not regret the promise you made to him. I look forward to seeing you as soon as Almighty God brings you safely home. I do hope you will be pleased

to know that Mary Armstrong is keeping me company. She is now eighteen and is looking forward to being reacquainted with you. She talks of your being her brave lord. I pray you will not disillusion the poor child. Her father is keen on a match between the two of you. Unfortunately he and most of his clan have been called away on the orders of the king and I fear the message that has come for you will contain a similar command. I am making what preparations I can to keep your inheritance safe and I pray for the day when we can toast your health in the excellent vintage you sent home.
Your mother, Lady Joan Mackillin.

Mackillin swore beneath his breath as he reread both messages and felt a rising fury. Why in God's name should he have to embroil himself in a cause he had no reason to support and, in so doing, possibly sacrifice his life? He rolled up the scroll and tapped it against his teeth, aware of his master mariner's eyes upon him. Did he have any idea what was written in the scrolls? If not, all Mackillin had to do was to give the order to set sail for home.

Yet an inbuilt honesty prevented him from doing so. 'Angus, do you know aught of the contents of these missives?'

'Aye, Mackillin. King James and the dowager

Queen have summoned as many fighting men as they can to support the King of England's cause.'

'And what can we expect in return? What good will it do Scotland if we fight?' he rasped. 'What encouragement can I give to Killin's men to risk their lives for the sake of the King and Queen—of England of all places? How am I to pay their wages if I agree to answer this royal summons? What rewards are on offer?'

'No wages are to be paid from what I've heard,' Angus answered, shaking his hoary head. 'I do know you are not the only Borderer to be summoned in like manner.'

'My mother speaks of the Armstrongs answering the King's summons.' He scowled, recognising the quandary he was in.

'Rumour has it that no northern lands or the Midlands of England are to be raided, but further south where the Yorkist strongholds exist can be.'

Mackillin's scowl deepened. He did not like what he was hearing despite the knowledge that it was common practice for armies to pillage for food and fodder. He despised such behaviour and thought it would definitely not endear the Scots to the southern English. At least he could console himself with the thought that Cicely and the twins would be free of attack at Milburn Manor because of it being in the north.

He pictured her safe indoors, working at her embroidery. The image was shattered by the sound of hurrying feet. The door burst open and Robbie entered the cabin. There was such an air of suppressed excitement about him that Mackillin started to his feet. 'What is it? What's wrong?'

Robbie gripped the other side of the table and gazed across at him. 'Several kinsmen of the Milburn I slew in Bruges are in the shipping agent's house. I saw them with my own eyes.'

Mackillin's eyebrows shot up. 'Did they recognise you?'

'One of them knew me all right,' he said grimly. 'I think they're up to no good, so I promised a lad half a groat to keep a watch on them.'

Mackillin's eyes burned in his weatherbeaten face. 'Good man. Eat and drink and then return there. I want to know what mischief they are brewing and whether it has anything to do with Mistress Cicely and the twins. In the meantime I must write a message for my mother.'

Robbie stayed him with a hand. 'I think the Milburns and the agent are in league with each other. I caught a glimpse of a youth in a back room and he appeared none too happy. His face was swollen and bruised, but he reminded me of Jack.'

Mackillin clenched his fist. 'It must be Matt. Possibly he looked downcast because the agent has told him of his father's death.' He frowned. 'Nay, it has to be more than that. He'd waste no time hurrying home to Jack and Cissie…and why the bruised face? His kin must have beaten him up and no doubt they plan worse.'

'I reckon they have murder in their black hearts,' growled Robbie.

Mackillin nodded. 'I wonder if that slimy toad Husthwaite is in this as well. If so, Cissie and Jack could be in danger.'

'What are you going to do?'

Mackillin rubbed his unshaven jaw. 'It looks like I'm going to have to change my plans yet again.' He ordered food to be brought for Robbie, and as his groom ate, Mackillin told both his master mariner and Robbie exactly what he intended doing and what he wanted them to do.

Cicely could no longer keep still and began to pace the floor. Not only had Matt and their men failed to return, but while she had been in the village, Jack had gone off in search of his twin. Fortunately he had taken Tom and the dogs with him; even so, she was frightened for him.

She toyed with the crucifix about her neck, thinking it was five days since Mackillin had left and within hours of his departure Jack had climbed into the saddle. He had not ridden far that first day, but on the second he had travelled into Knaresborough and returned, exhausted and in pain, with the news that Master Husthwaite was not at his house but, according to his servant, had left for Kingston-on-Hull several days ago. Cicely could only be glad that the man was miles away but, even so, she wondered what had taken him to Kingston-on-Hull. What if he was in cahoots with the shipping agent and the Milburns? What if Matt…?

She shook her head, not prepared to believe he could be dead. Jack would have known of it. The twins sensed when the other was in trouble. She continued her pacing, her prayers for her brothers interspersed with thoughts of Mackillin: his smile, the tales of his travels that he had spun in his attractively accented voice. She could see him in her mind's eye raising an eyebrow as if questioning her belief in his ability to stop Jack behaving foolishly. Even so, she would have trusted him to do so if he had still been here.

Would she have trusted Diccon to the same extent? She screwed up her face in anguish, knowing she had to stop thinking about Mackillin and have faith in Diccon. It was unlikely that she would ever see the Borderer again and that had to be for the good. She must look to Diccon for help. Why hadn't he sent word? Where was he? Was he alive or dead? If he cared for her as much as he'd said he did, then he should not have stayed away so long. Hurt and anger rose within her and she could hardly contain it, so began to pace the floor once more.

Suddenly she heard voices outside of the house and instantly hurried towards the entrance, only to still when the door opened to reveal Master Husthwaite and two rough-looking strangers standing there. Her heart bumped uncomfortably against her ribs and she reached for the dagger at her waist, only to remember she had dispensed with it since putting on mourning. She swallowed to ease the tightness in her throat and said, 'What are you doing here, Master Husthwaite? Who are these men?'

The clerk's eyes darted about the hall and he smirked in a manner that sickened her. 'All alone, Mistress Cicely?' he said, strutting across the hall towards her.

She was more alone than he realised because Martha and Tabitha had gone into the village to visit their families and had not returned yet. But this horrible man was not to know that. 'It might appear so, Master Husthwaite, but my brother is within call…and Mackillin, too,' she added for good measure.

His smirk vanished. 'You lie! I returned from

Kingston-on-Hull three days ago and I received news this morning from my companions that the barbarian was seen there. No doubt he'll have discovered by now that Queen Margaret is gathering a great force in Scotland to rescue her husband, King Henry, from captivity, and he'll be bidden to join that host.'

His words so shocked her that she felt dizzy and had to grip a nearby chair. 'It doesn't make sense. Why should the Scots support the queen of England?'

He shrugged. 'It's true, none the less. Also, I regret to inform you that your brother's shipping agent has seen no sign of Master Matthew.' There was an expression of malevolent pleasure in his mud-coloured eyes. 'Perhaps he and his men were caught out in the blizzard on their way to Kingston and wandered off the road into a mere. We shall never know,' he added.

His words intensified her fear and she felt chilled to the bone and hugged herself in an attempt to infuse some warmth into her body. Then a thought presented itself to her. 'What is your purpose in bringing me such news? Unless you have proof, your words are just supposition and worthless. I would ask you to leave.'

His brows hooded his eyes and he sneered, 'Surely his continued absence is proof enough.

Why is it, Mistress Cicely, you never believe me when I tell you the truth? Was I not right about your father?'

'Aye! A matter I find suspicious now.' Her glance darted to his unsavoury-looking companions. 'Will you please go and take your friends with you.'

'I'm not going anywhere,' growled the fairer-haired one, whose beard covered half his chest. 'I'm your cousin, wench, and me and my brother are here to take over as masters of this manor.'

'Never,' she cried, remembering what Mackillin had said about her northern kin. 'Even if Matt were dead, which I don't believe,' she added stoutly, 'Jack would inherit.'

'Soon get rid of him,' said the other man, swaggering over to her. He made to chuck her under the chin, but anger replaced her fear and she smacked his hand away and darted behind a table. 'Get out! Our great-uncle disowned your branch of the family and you do not belong here.'

His eyes darted venom. 'You said she needed a strong hand, Husthwaite. I deem we should show her now who's in charge here.'

Husthwaite spat out, 'Remember what we decided! You'll get naught without my aid. I'll see she gets what she deserves.'

'You have no right to come here and threaten me,' said Cicely, trying to infuse steel into her voice.

'No right, you say!' Husthwaite breathed deeply through his thin nose and from a leather satchel withdrew a sheet of parchment. 'I have more right than you think. I have your father's will here. I find it satisfying that a sum of a thousand pounds has been left to provide you with a dowry and that in my uncle's place I am your guardian.'

She was aghast. 'You my guardian? Never! If I was to need a guardian, then Father would have named my stepbrother or my stepsister's husband, Owain ap Rowan, to fill that role.' She leant across the table and almost managed to snatch the parchment from his hand. As it was she tore a strip off the bottom before he was able to draw back his arm.

'That was foolish,' he said, his eyes cold. 'Give that piece to me!'

Cicely clenched her fingers on the parchment. 'Certainly not. Now get out of here!'

'You are in no position to give me orders. Your kinsmen have agreed to my becoming your husband. I'll have the banns called in the week,' he said with a laugh.

Cicely's distaste showed in her face. 'I would rather die,' she said scornfully, and before they could prevent her, she ran from the hall.

'Follow her, man, and see where she goes,' snapped Master Husthwaite. 'Do not let her leave this house.'

Instantly one of the brothers went after her.

Realising that it was unlikely she would manage to reach the kitchen and escape that way, Cicely slipped through the door at the bottom of her staircase. She locked and bolted the door and fled up the steps. Once inside her bedchamber she bolted that door and sank on to her bed. Her heart was racing and it was a minute or so before it steadied its beat. Only then did she glance at the strip of parchment and knew for certain Husthwaite had lied. She would have recognised her father's signature anywhere and this one was definitely a forgery.

She slipped the parchment beneath her pillow and prayed that what the man had said about Matt was also false. A sob rose in her throat, but she forced it down. Now was not the time for tears. She had to escape, find Jack and tell him what had happened. If only Mackillin or—or Diccon was here, then they would deal with her enemies. As it was, she was going to have to cope with this herself.

She went over to her window and opened a shutter. She could smell damp air and hoped it did not forecast rain. She hoisted herself up on to the sill and gazed down at the ground. There was a chance she could get down if only she had a rope. She thought for a moment, her eyes scanning the path that led to the village and the distant fells.

Moving away from the window, she went over to

the door and opened it. She could hear banging. They must be trying to knock the door down. A smile eased her mouth. The wood was extremely thick. Even with an axe it would take them several hours to break through. She closed her chamber door and locked it and sat on her bed and thought some more as shadows began to fill her room.

She rose and took the sheets from her bed and knotted them together. Then she donned her sheepskin bags and put on her cloak, a hat and gloves. She pocketed her tinder box, a candle, her dagger and took coin from a small tin in the chest. She returned to the window and gazed out over the darkening landscape, but could see no one, so she tied one end of her improvised rope to the bedpost and then fed the other end through the opening. Taking a deep breath, she tested the rope was secure before climbing on to the window ledge. For a moment she sat there, praying that the knot would not come apart. Then she took a deep breath and was about to lower herself off the ledge when she heard a familiar voice enquire, 'Where are you going to, my pretty lass?'

Her heart jerked excitedly within her breast and she almost fell off the sill. 'Mackillin!' she cried.

'Aye! Get back inside your chamber and take your *rope* with you. I'm coming up.'

'B-but how c-can you with-without a-a rope?' she

stammered, trying to make out his face in the twilight.

'I have a rope—remember that time in the snow? I'll toss the end up to you. Attach it to the bed with a good strong knot. You can tie a decent knot, can't you?'

'Of a surety I can,' she retorted in an indignant whisper. 'Father taught me.' She wondered how Mackillin came to be there when he was supposed to be in Kingston-on-Hull, but did not ask. 'What's wrong with my rope?' she demanded. 'I went to a great deal of trouble tying the sheets together.'

He shook his head at her. 'It won't take my weight and I've no intention of crashing to the ground.'

'Why can't I come down to you?'

'Because the front door is bolted and I want to get inside and surprise the curs.'

She clung to her rope, blinking down at him. 'You know who's in the hall?'

'I guess Master Husthwaite and two of your kinsmen who managed to slip away before we could stop them. Now stop blathering and be ready to catch my rope.'

She did as he said, thinking that if her heart had not already reacted positively to the sound of his voice, then it would have done so when she saw him smiling up at her so confidently. He threw up the rope, but it took her several attempts to catch it. Removing her gloves, she set about securing the rope to the leg of her bed. Once she had done that, she informed him of it.

He pulled hard on the rope and she heard the fibres stretch, but the knot held. For added safety she drew part of the rope about her hand, concerned that the rough stone of the sill might saw through the fibres.

When he began to swarm up the rope, his weight was such that her arm was almost pulled from its socket and the bed moved. Determinedly, she hung on until he was through the window and only then did the burning ache in her shoulder ease. She could hear Mackillin's rapid breathing as he loomed over her. Her own breath seemed to match his as he slipped the rope from about her hand. Before she realised what he was about his fingers grazed her skin. She winced as his fingertips explored the weal made by the rope.

'Fool,' he muttered, licking the abrasion and sending shimmers of sensation along her nerve ends.

'Don't do that! It's naught to worry about.' She realised she wanted him to take her in his arms so she could weep on his chest and blurt out her fears, but that would never do.

Chapter Five

'Have you salve? You must anoint it so the broken skin doesn't putrefy.' His voice was deep with concern.

'I will later,' she assured him, tugging her hand free. 'Tell me, how did you know those men were downstairs? Master Husthwaite said that Matt never reached Kingston-on-Hull.'

'He speaks false.' Mackillin moved away to haul up his rope.

She felt weak with relief. 'Thank God!'

'Aye,' he said. 'Now light me a candle.'

She did so, fixing it in a holder and watching him close the shutters before facing her. The flickering flame cast shadows over the planes of his rugged features, darkening the hollows beneath his cheekbones. She felt such a hunger for him that, without realising she was doing it, she licked her lips.

He stared at her and swallowed, wanting to kiss

her so badly that he had to look away. He placed the rope on the chest. 'Sit down.'

She hesitated before sinking on to the bed. 'Why are you not on your way to Scotland?'

Mackillin sat beside her. His instincts were still telling him to draw her into his arms and comfort her with such lovemaking that all fears would be forgotten in bodily delights, but that was out of the question. Not only because of all the reasons he had already voiced to himself, but also because he did not know how long the twins would obey him and stay in the village.

'When Robbie caught sight of your kinsmen and Matt at the house of the shipping agent, I knew I had to change my plans.'

'I'm glad you did,' said Cicely, facing him and placing a hand on his surcoat. 'So where is Matt now—and have you seen Jack?'

'Aye. They're both safe.' He covered her hand with his, intending to remove it and put it on her lap, but instead he stroked the soft swelling at the base of her thumb with his own and drew circles on her palm with a tip of a finger. 'Your father's shipping agent is not to be trusted. He played not only your father false, but Matt, too.'

'But why?' she asked, knowing she should tug her hand free, but was so enjoying his gentle caress.

'Your kinsmen apparently promised him a greater

percentage of income on the goods he handled if he helped them by informing them of your father's movements.'

'But how did Husthwaite and my father's cousins come to know each other?'

'I don't know. But somehow they all became acquainted and plotted to take over the business and this manor.'

Cicely gulped and squeezed Mackillin's hand. 'If it were not for you, then Jack would be dead… and Matt, too. Where are they?'

'In the village. I'll explain the rest later. Suffice for you to know that we rescued Matt and met Jack and Tom in Knaresborough. We'd planned to confront Husthwaite at his house. Instead, his servant told us that he had come here with two of your kinsmen.'

She closed her eyes briefly and when she opened them again there was such warmth in their depths that Mackillin guessed that if he kissed her now then she would respond.

'I don't know how to repay you,' she said.

He could think of a way, but knew that now was not the time for dalliance. He released her hand and stood up. 'I'm sorry to tell you that most of your servants were killed when Matt was captured.'

'Oh, no!' she cried, distressed not only with the thought of their sacrificing their lives for her brother, but she pitied their wives and children.

'Don't ask me why they didn't kill Matt, too. Maybe they wanted a bargaining tool if their plan went wrong. Which reminds me, it's time to deal with our enemies below.' He went over to the door.

She picked up the candle and followed him. 'Are you completely alone, then?' she whispered.

'The twins would have come, but Jack's arm would fail him in a fight and Matt sustained a small wound in the skirmish. I deemed it wiser that they stayed behind. I brought Robbie. He is keeping an eye on the back of the house and the stables if our enemies should try to escape.'

Mackillin eased back the bolt and opened the door.

All was quiet.

Cicely supposed she had to accept that Mackillin knew what he was doing, but she was not going to allow him to face their enemies alone, so was at his heels as he made his way soft-footedly down the winding staircase.

When they reached the bottom, she whispered, 'Let me go first.' He glanced over his shoulder and his expression told her exactly what he thought of that suggestion. 'Consider, Mackillin, that my appearance will be of no surprise to whoever is there,' she added. 'He will be off guard and you'll have the advantage.'

Mackillin's lips curled into a smile. 'Your idea has merit.'

She felt a glow inside her. 'Of course it has. I'm no fool.'

Another bend in the stairway and the door was in front of them. A panel had splintered, but the axe had not broken through yet. She descended to the door and Mackillin concealed himself behind it. She turned the key, eased back the bolt and opened the door. Instantly one of her Milburn kin pushed himself away from the wall and came towards her with a lantern. He seized her wrist and dragged her away from the door. They were only a little way along the passage when Mackillin struck and the man fell as if pole-axed.

'Is he dead?' asked Cicely, bending over him.

Mackillin felt the man's pulse and shook his head. 'He'll no stir for a while, though.' She caught the glint of light reflecting off steel as he straightened and stared at her. For a moment she thought he was going to kiss her, but he only touched her cheek with the back of his hand. 'You stay here,' he said, before heading for the hall.

Cicely wasted no time before following Mackillin. She did not consider Master Husthwaite much of a fighting man, but she remembered his use of a whip on her horse and feared he might pick up something heavy and hurl it at Mackillin whilst he fought her other kinsman. If she could do naught else, she could keep her eye on their so-called new man-of-business and try to thwart any such attempt.

She entered the hall a few moments after Mackillin and was in time to see her kinsman start up from the table. She could not make out what he said, but presumed it was a warning to Master Husthwaite, who had his back to them. The latter staggered to his feet and it was clear to see that he'd been imbibing freely of her father's wine. He blinked rapidly as if he could not believe his eyes when he saw Mackillin and clung to the table.

Her kinsman drew his sword and, with a fearsome yell, charged towards them. Mackillin went forward to meet him. Her heart was in her mouth, but then she remembered what Jack had said about Mackillin being skilled with a blade; even so she thought it would be useful to have a weapon of her own. She rushed over to the fireplace and reached for the poker. As she picked it up something whizzed past her cheek and shattered on the hearth. Realising it was one of the precious Venetian drinking vessels her father had brought from that city eighteen months ago, she was furious. Only Husthwaite could be responsible and she was not going to let him get away with it.

She flew at him with the poker. The breath whistled out of him as she caught him in the stomach with its point and he doubled over. Darting behind him, she hit him across the back and he sank on to the floor. Despite the temptation to place her foot on his neck and perform a victory dance, she made do with standing over him with her weapon at the ready should he attempt to rise. She risked a glance in Mackillin's direction and saw that there was blood on his cheek, but his opponent was in a worse condition. He had been wounded in the arm and blood soaked his sleeve, trickling between his fingers. His grasp on the weapon's hilt must have been slippery with blood, but he still attempted to stab Mackillin through the heart. It was her kinsman's last mistake. Mackillin drove his sword under his guard and finished him off.

As he slumped to the floor, Husthwaite attempted to rise, but Cicely threatened him with the poker. He lunged towards her, but she whacked him on the shoulder. Then Mackillin was beside her and the man sank back. She glanced at his lordship as he wiped the blood from his face with his sleeve. He grinned. 'I'm glad you're on my side, lass.'

She smiled. Reaching up, she touched Mackillin's cut cheek and felt a muscle quiver beneath her fingers. 'I'm sorry my kinsman wounded you,' she said with concern. 'I'll tend it later.'

He grasped her wrist. 'It's but a scratch. Think instead about what we should do with Husthwaite and the man in the passage.'

'Perhaps we could tie them up with your rope and lock them in the laundry room until we can take them to the sheriff,' she suggested.

Husthwaite started up. 'You had no right to attack me,' he snarled. 'I came here on legitimate business.'

'I have every right,' said Cicely, her eyes flashing blue fire. 'The signature on that so-called will of my father's is a forgery. You thought to get your filthy hands on my dowry as well as assist my kinsmen to cheat my brothers of their inheritance. You will be punished for that.'

Husthwaite let out a string of curses, but Mackillin cut him short with a blow to the jaw that knocked him out.

'Well, that finished that conversation,' said Cicely, a twinkle in her eyes.

'He insulted you,' he murmured. 'Now let's see how your kinsman in the passage does.'

They found him stirring and Cicely ran upstairs to her bedchamber for Mackillin's rope. When she returned, the man was sullen and bloody of face and she presumed he had fought Mackillin whilst she was upstairs. He struggled as he was tied up, but was overcome and placed in the laundry room. When they returned to the hall, to their dismay there was no sign of Husthwaite.

'I should not have left him alone,' said Mackillin,

annoyed with himself. 'But if he's made for the stable then hopefully Robbie will have dealt with him. I'll go and see.' He smiled down at her. 'In the meantime, lass, a hot drink wouldn't go amiss.'

She agreed, so hurried to the kitchen where she found Cook slumped in a chair. At first she thought he was dead, but he proved to be only unconscious. She opened the kitchen door and looked outside. It was as dark as pitch and the wind blew rain into her face, but above the sound of the storm she thought she heard the sound of hoof beats.

She called out and a few moments later Mackillin appeared, looking grim-faced. 'What's wrong?' she asked.

'He surprised Robbie and knocked him out. The cur's escaped. Although he's a wily devil and could have set the horse free to deceive us and be hiding. It's turning into a filthy night and he might not be prepared to risk the journey to Knaresborough. I'll check the outhouses.'

'I'll fetch a lantern,' said Cicely, hurrying back into the kitchen.

He took the light from her and told her to lock the door behind her. A sound from the kitchen drew her attention and she realised that Cook was coming round.

She went over to him. 'Are you all right?' she asked, placing a hand on his shoulder.

'Just a sore head, mistress,' he said, gingerly feeling the lump on his head. 'I've no notion why they hit me.'

'Probably so you could not help me. Mackillin has killed one of my kinsmen and another is locked in the laundry room. Unfortunately, Husthwaite managed to escape, but his lordship is checking the outhouses in case he is lurking there.'

Cook's face lit up. 'His lordship is here. That's good.' Then his expression changed. 'But he'll be hungry and those rogues ate yours and Master Jack's supper.'

Cicely wished she had Husthwaite at her mercy so she could have given him another whack with the poker for eating the food she could have shared with Mackillin. They would have to make do with bread, cheese, eggs and apples. At least she would be able to make Mackillin a hot drink.

By the time his lordship returned, half carrying Robbie, she had mulled wine and set the table with the simplest of fare. As she watched him lay Robbie on a cushioned settle, she said, 'I presume you saw no sign of Husthwaite?'

Mackillin shook his head.

He looked wet and weary and she suggested that he sit down and eat supper. 'You should get out of those damp clothes as soon as possible or you'll catch a chill,' she said solicitously.

He emptied the vessel of mulled wine thirstily before saying, 'I've been wetter than this, lass, and survived, but I appreciate what you say.' He reached for bread and cheese, thinking that he was enjoying her fussing over him.

They ate in silence for a few minutes and then he said, 'I am concerned about Robbie. I might have to leave him here when I return to Kingston-on-Hull.'

'He's welcome to stay as long as needful, as are you,' she said, having forgotten her resolve of a few days ago. 'Although I know you must be impatient to go to Scotland,' she added hastily, remembering Diccon.

Mackillin reached for more bread. 'A thought occurred to me whilst I was searching the outhouses.'

'And what is that?' she asked, refilling his cup.

'Husthwaite mightn't have left the house.'

She started and spilt some of the wine. 'You mean he could be hiding here?' Involuntarily she glanced over her shoulder.

Quickly he said, 'There is naught to fear. I will protect you.'

All night! she thought, gazing at his strong frame and remembering what it felt like to be held in his arms and thoroughly kissed. A thrill raced through her and she was unsure whether it was due to excitement or fear. She gulped down half her wine before asking should they search the house.

'I will search the house. You will go into your bedchamber and lock the door and remain there until I tell you that he is either under lock and key or not here.' He finished his bread and held out a hand to her. 'Your keys.'

She gazed at his outstretched hand and then took another sip of wine. 'I will not be locked away like a damsel waiting to be rescued in a tale of romance. It makes more sense for me to accompany you. Left alone, I'll picture him coming up behind you and hitting you over the head—and where will that leave me?'

He pulled a face and rubbed his unshaven jaw. 'Why couldn't you imagine my hitting Husthwaite over the head?'

'I don't care about his getting killed, but I do…' Her voice trailed off as she realised what she'd been about to say and quickly lowered her gaze beneath the sudden blaze in his hazel eyes.

'I'm gratified that you care about me.'

She flushed. 'You are a guest in my home and not only have you saved my brothers' lives, but you've saved mine.' A tiny smile lifted the corners of her mouth. 'You were of great help. And now it makes sense for me to help you search the house. I know it better than you.'

He gave in and suggested that Cook came and sat with Robbie, whilst they combed the likely hiding places for Husthwaite. They wasted no more time in conversation.

As soon as they had finished eating, Cook was fetched. Then Mackillin picked up a lantern and they made their way over to the stairs.

'We'll need to go as silently as we can,' whispered Cicely, light-headed with wine and excitement. 'Your boots…'

He stared down at her with a fixed expression. 'If you're hinting that Husthwaite might hear any noise I make, might I say that whispers carry.'

She was about to tell him what she thought of that remark when she caught the twinkle in his eye. 'Whatever you say, Lord Mackillin,' she mouthed silently.

He was not fooled by her assumed meekness. A lass who could handle a poker the way she did had fire in her belly. He could imagine her standing shoulder to shoulder with him before his enemies. He blinked and shook his head to rid himself of the thought and mounted the stairs with the lightest of treads.

Smiling, she followed him on tiptoe. The light from the lantern sent shadows dancing along the walls as they moved silently along the passage leading to the guest chamber and those of her brothers. Mackillin checked them all, but the rooms were deserted. They turned and went along the passage the other side of the stairway. She hummed nervously beneath her breath. He turned and raised both eyebrows. She put a hand guiltily over her mouth. He carried on walking and she swiftly followed him in the direction of a small guest chamber and the bedchamber that had once belonged to her parents. A lump rose in her throat and she wondered what they would think if they knew she was wandering about upstairs alone with this man. No doubt her mother would be shocked, but perhaps her father would see the sense in their actions. He must have had a lot of faith in this Scots lord to entrust Jack into his hands.

Mackillin stopped in front of a door and held out a hand for her keys. The small guest chamber was devoid of life and he locked it behind them before going on to the next chamber. Suddenly they heard a noise coming towards them out of the darkness. Both froze. Cicely thought if Husthwaite really was up here hiding behind a door or cupboard, he might spring out and hit Mackillin with a blunt weapon or even stab him. A cold draught fluttered her skirts and she drew closer to him.

He did not speak, but reached out a hand and she slipped her small one into his larger one. The sound was coming from the main bedchamber and the door stood ajar. She looked sidelong at Mackillin. He handed her the lantern and drew his sword. He indicated that she back away and pushed the door wide with his booted foot and entered swiftly.

She waited several moments, listening to her heartbeat. Then there came a yelp and what sounded like falling furniture. Something shot out of the room, brushed her skirts and was gone. She turned and gazed along the passageway and saw her favourite mouser. A bubble of laughter rose in her throat and she was giggling as she entered the bedchamber to find Mackillin sitting on the bed, rubbing his shin. A stool had been knocked over. The cold air was coming from the window where the shutters were open. A branch of ivy creaked in the wind and a twig tapped against the wooden shutter. Who could have opened it? Could Husthwaite have been up here and escaped that way whilst they were in the hall? No. It didn't make sense. Probably it was just the wind.

She sat down beside Mackillin on the bed and breathed in the scent of wood smoke, horse and his own particular scent. 'Are you all right?'

He nodded and then laughed. 'A cat! Husthwaite has gone. I was thinking myself into his shoes and what I would do in his situation. But he's run like the coward he is.'

'Will you go after him on the morrow?'

'Aye. Most likely I'll see if he's returned to his house.' He glanced down at Cicely. 'You're not frightened, are you?'

She wasn't with him there, but was tempted to say, 'A little. Husthwaite might have concealed himself in the armoire.' There was a smile in her voice.

He got up and had a look and then came back over to the bed and sat closer to her this time. 'I meant you're not frightened of being alone with me?'

She shook her head. 'To be honest, I feel strangely at peace now all the excitement is over.'

He was far from feeling that all the excitement was over and was struggling with the temptation to kiss her lovely neck and then her mouth. He imagined her breasts squashed against the hard wall of his chest, but maybe this time she would resist and smack his face. Besides, hadn't he made up his mind that a marriage between them would be a mistake?

'Why are we sitting here so long?' she murmured after he made no sign of moving. 'Are you not feeling well after your fight with my kinsmen and then falling over in here?'

'I am fine,' he said stiffly. 'You deem me so weak that I need rest after so little exertion?'

'Of course not,' she replied apologetically. 'I

thought you'd had lots of exertion what with riding from Kingston-on-Hull after rescuing Matt and then coming here and all that you've done since. I was worried that you might have hurt your head on top of everything else.'

'Well, I haven't,' he said, getting to his feet and walking over to the door.

Picking up the lantern, she followed, disappointed that he sounded so cross with her. They walked silently downstairs. After making certain Robbie was all right, she asked Mackillin what he was going to do about her dead kinsman.

'I'll find somewhere to put him, don't worry yourself, lassie,' he grumbled.

She decided that she was not going to worry and bid him goodnight and went up to her bedchamber, leaving it to him to make certain the house was secure for the night. She doubted that the twins or Tabitha and Martha would make the journey from the village home in such wild weather until morning. When she reached her bedchamber, it was to look about her remembering how she had felt when Mackillin had called up to her. Excitement! She had felt relief as well, but excitement had been her uppermost feeling. He was back and life was no longer drab. He had rescued her brother and come to her aid. Instead of going to Scotland, as was his intention, he had set his own affairs aside once he realised they were in trouble. She thanked God that he had not abandoned her brothers and herself. Whether this was due to his friendship with her father or because it was just Mackillin's way, she did not know. What she did know was that he deserved the reward her father had offered him. As she slipped beneath the bedcovers, Cicely remembered saying to him that she didn't know how to thank him. He had looked at her in such a way that her belly had began to quiver—such a strange feeling. She fell asleep and dreamed of his kissing her in such a way that her whole body shimmied in response and she was in danger of surrendering herself to him—and that would never do.

Cicely gazed at Mackillin, watching his strong fingers wield a knife as he peeled an apple. Tabitha and Martha had returned at sunrise not half an hour after Tom, who had ridden on ahead of the twins. Now she and Mackillin were just finishing breakfast and awaiting the return of her brothers. The tumultuous emotions caused by her dreams had calmed somewhat, due, no doubt, to his lordship's manners being impeccable. She thought of Diccon and determined to go in search of him once Mackillin left for Scotland as he surely would. She then thought of Husthwaite and felt loathing towards the clerk. He must have escaped on his horse, but whether he had reached Knaresborough was a different matter altogether.

Cicely was roused from her reverie by Mackillin offering her a slice of apple on the point of his knife. She thanked him. 'What will you do with our prisoner?' she asked, popping the fruit into her mouth.

'I'll leave it to your brothers and Robbie to make that decision. It's possible, if threatened with being taken before the sheriff, that he might be persuaded to give you more information about the border branch of your family. I aim to call at Master Husthwaite's house before returning to Kingston-on-Hull.'

'So you are leaving Robbie here?'

He nodded. 'He needs a few days to recover from that bang on the head. Also, you could do with a man who's a canny fighter, until either Master ap Rowan or Diccon arrives.'

'I appreciate your doing so, but that does mean you will have to travel alone,' she blurted out.

He put down the knife and gazed across at her with a faint smile. 'You mustn't worry about me.'

She said lightly, 'Why should you think I am worried? From what I have seen of you, it's obvious you're capable of looking after yourself.'

He nodded. 'I'll stay here until your brothers arrive.'

They did not have to wait long for the twins' return. Within the hour they came riding into the stable yard. Cicely hurried down the steps as her brothers dismounted. Immediately she rushed over to Matt. 'I've been so concerned for you.' Her voice was muffled against his shoulder as she hugged him.

'I've felt the same about you, Cissie.' He held her at arm's length and his blue eyes gazed into her pale face. 'You really are unhurt? Husthwaite and our kinsmen didn't harm you?'

'They might have if Mackillin hadn't arrived on the scene.' Cicely glanced towards the steps where his lordship stood, watching them. He winked and she felt the blood rush to her cheeks.

Matt's expression was thoughtful. 'I can understand why Father held him in such high esteem. How do you find him, Cissie?'

'He has courage and is thoughtful, also more cultured than I ever thought possible of a Borderer.'

'And his appearance?'

She did not answer immediately, but gazed up at Mackillin as he descended the steps. In a low voice she said, 'Why do you ask me such a question?'

Matt's youthful features were austere. 'I have my reasons.'

'I do think he deserves a reward for all that he has done for us,' she murmured, 'but how do you reward a lord?'

'Strange that you should say that,' said Matt.

Cicely waited for him to say something more, but he just walked away and over to Mackillin.

'Well met, my lord. Thank you for saving my sister.' Matt held out a hand.

Mackillin shook it before placing a hand on the youth's shoulder. 'I am angry with myself that I allowed Husthwaite to escape.'

'It's possible his escape was ill fated,' said Cicely, coming up to them. 'It was a foul night with no moon or stars to light his way. He could have perished.'

'At least Mackillin has rid us of another of our kinsmen,' said Jack, joining them. 'We'll need to bury him. What of the other?'

Mackillin told the twins his plan.

Instantly Matt said, 'I appreciate all you are doing for us, Mackillin. I just wish you did not have to return to Scotland and could stay longer. It should have been our stepbrother who was here to help us.'

'He has other things he deems more important,' said Jack, scowling. 'More important than Cissie, who she tells us he is going to marry.'

'Stop it!' ordered Cicely. 'Leave Diccon out of this. He has no idea Father is dead, so how can he know we have need of him?'

Mackillin said sternly, 'There is truth in what your sister says. Now I must be off. I will ride to Knaresborough and see if I can discover what has befallen Husthwaite before returning to Kingston-on-Hull. I will only return here if I have vital news of him that affects your safety.'

'Fare thee well, Mackillin,' said Cicely, knowing she was going to miss him, which made it even more important that he was out of her life as soon as possible.

His face softened. 'I wish you well and hope that you and Diccon will be happy.' Without a backward glance, he strode across the yard towards the stables.

Matt turned to Cissie. 'He's worth ten of Diccon, who is a fool for getting himself involved in a fight that he could have avoided,' he said. 'His loyalty certainly isn't to this family. No wonder Father didn't want you marrying him and offered you to Mackillin.'

'Hold your tongue, Matt,' warned Jack. 'I told you to keep quiet about that.'

'Father did what?' she asked, thinking she must have misheard him.

Matt did not answer, but pressed his lips tightly together and went after Mackillin.

Cicely turned on Jack. 'Did Father really offer me to Mackillin?'

He hesitated. It was enough to convince her of the truth. She was aghast and said in a choking voice, 'How could he do such a thing without ever mentioning Mackillin to me all the years he had known him? I deem he did it to try to prevent my marrying Diccon.'

Jack rubbed his aching arm. 'I can understand your being upset, but Mackillin did refuse his offer.'

Her brother's words made her feel worse. 'Refused! But he hadn't even set eyes on me. Did he know Father was leaving me a dowry of a *thousand pounds*?'

'No sum was mentioned, but Mackillin would have a fair idea of your worth. Some men would have leapt at the offer but Mackillin can't be bought.'

'You mean he doesn't want to marry a merchant's daughter now he is a lord,' she snapped.

'He never said that,' said Jack sharply.

Her eyes glistened with angry tears as she remembered the times she had spent in Mackillin's company. She had grown to like him and had changed her opinion of the kind of man she had believed him to be when first she set eyes on him. She had believed that he had found her comely and enjoyed her company, but it seemed she was wrong because, if that was so, then he would have changed his mind about refusing her father's offer and could have wooed her before broaching the subject. The truth was that he did not want her for his wife. 'I cannot bear any more.' Her voice was just a thread of sound. 'I'm going inside. I don't ever want to see Mackillin again.'

Chapter Six

An hour later Cicely sat at the table with her brothers. Having decided to leave it to Robbie to interrogate the prisoner, they were now discussing their father's will. She had calmed down somewhat after it had occurred to her that Mackillin would have hardly discussed her father's offer with her when he knew that she was intent on marrying Diccon.

'So what do we do?' asked Matt. 'We know the will Husthwaite has is a forgery, but where's the genuine one?'

'Destroyed, probably,' murmured Cicely, trying to concentrate on the matter in hand.

Jack said, 'Perhaps Owain has a copy of the will. He and Father were not only friends, but related by marriage, so that would make it a real possibility.'

'Then he will have to be informed of his death—and soon as possible,' said Matt.

Cicely stared at him, thinking that her brother's features had taken on a new maturity since their father's death and the threat to his own life. She sighed. He was too young to take on the heavy responsibility thrust on him by their father's murder. If Diccon was here he could have helped him. She decided to speak her thoughts. 'You're both needed here. I will go and visit the ap Rowans. Hopefully they will have had word of Diccon. I must speak with him.'

The twins stared at her and shook their heads. 'You can't,' said Matt. 'We can't spare anyone to accompany you and you cannot go alone.'

Cicely gripped her hands together until the knuckles showed white. 'Of course I can. If you two hadn't been born, I'd have inherited and made all the decisions despite being a woman.'

Jack frowned. 'But we *were* born, so Matt makes the decisions until we know whom Father has appointed as our guardian. You couldn't possibly make the journey across the Pennines on your own. You're a woman and it's too dangerous.'

'I have a plan,' she said with a smile.

'What sort of plan?' asked Matt, his eyes alight with curiosity.

Cicely leaned forward. 'I'll go in disguise and take Tom with me.'

'Tom!' Jack shook his head. 'I'm sure he would

do his best to protect you, but he's no Mackillin. Besides, Matt needs him here.'

'Then you come with me,' she said persuasively. 'All the goods Father purchased for his clients have not arrived yet. A couple of days is all it will take us to reach Merebury—you will not lose much time.'

Matt spoke up. 'How can you ask that of Jack when he's still having trouble with his arm? He can't possibly ride all that way.'

Cicely sighed. 'I beg pardon. I wasn't thinking. I have to go alone and I'll go in disguise.'

Matt muttered something in an undertone and shook his head.

'What sort of disguise?' asked Jack.

'I'll borrow some of your clothes and folk will believe me a youth,' she said lightly.

Matt's expression was horrified. 'It's not seemly for you to dress as a boy!'

'Why should I care about what is seemly?' she cried, suddenly feeling quite desperate to get away. 'I'm unlikely to meet anyone I know on the road. I must find out what's happened to Diccon and Kate will most likely know where he is…and as you have said, if he can't help us, then Owain needs to know about Father's death so he can.'

'When you put your case like that, I understand why you feel it's imperative that you go,' said Jack, drumming his fingers on the table, 'but it would be best to wait until Matt can hire more men. Also, have you considered that Owain might not be in favour of you marrying Diccon once he knows Father was against it?'

She had not thought of that and was at first dismayed, but then said, 'Why should he be against his own brother-in-law? He is fond of Diccon and knows my dowry will be of use to him when the troubles between York and Lancaster are settled.'

'Of course Diccon would like your money,' said Matt, pouring ale into his and his twin's cups. 'Perhaps that's why he wants to marry you. He knows that he can do what he wants and you'll still be here waiting. Probably he hasn't forgotten the way you looked at him with sheep eyes from the moment you met him at old Mistress Moore's house in Liverpool.'

Cicely flushed with anger. 'I did not! And I do not believe he asked me to marry him because he wants my dowry. He loves me and I love him,' she said firmly.

'They love each other,' said Matt, rolling his eyes. 'Since when has love got aught to do with marriage? Father and Mother certainly didn't love each other or he wouldn't have spent so much time away from her.'

Cicely could not argue with that, but still felt she

had to speak up for love between husbands and wives. 'He loved our stepmother…and Kate and Owain love each other.'

Jack gazed across at his brother. 'I wouldn't argue with that. Have you seen the way they look at each other when they've been parted for a few days? I've seen them kiss, properly kiss, not just a peck on the cheek.'

'So they love each other,' said Matt, taking a swig of his ale. He looked thoughtful. 'Truthfully, if Cicely isn't going to wed Mackillin, then I think she shouldn't marry anyone at the moment. We need her here. It's I who should be thinking of taking a wife. She could instruct my bride in how our household is organised and help with our children.'

Cicely decided not to take Matt's words seriously. 'You are but fifteen, brother, and there is no rush for you to produce an heir. You have Jack.'

Jack smiled faintly. 'She's right, brother. You don't want to be shackled yet. You've got enough to think about right now stepping into Father's shoes.'

'Of course I'm right,' said Cicely firmly, rising from the table. 'I'm going to my bedchamber. I have things to do.'

'You rest, Cissie,' said Jack. 'We can decide later what to do about informing Owain of Father's death.'

She nodded as if she was in agreement and left the hall. Upstairs in her chamber she sat on her bed, wishing she could have asked her father why he had offered her to Mackillin. Tears filled her eyes because, of course, she could not ask aught of her father in this life. She took a kerchief from her pocket and wiped her eyes. As she did so, she caught sight of her reflection in the polished metal mirror on the wall. What she saw caused her to start and then she clasped her crucifix and did her best to look pious. Why should she not pretend to be a nun? Surely she would be safe from attack if men believed her to belong to a religious order? Dressed in her mourning garb and with every strand of hair concealed, she could surely pass as such.

She began to give serious thought to making the journey alone to Merebury Manor in Lancashire. What if the weather changed and it snowed again? She could get lost and never be found; even the packhorses who crossed the Pennines travelled in trains. But the weather was clement at the moment and looked set to remain so for several days. She did not have to follow the trails the packhorses took along the ridges of the high fells. She could take the road to Skipton and, if she didn't reach there before nightfall today, then she would seek shelter at Bolton Priory. If all went well it would take her probably two days, maybe three, to reach Merebury Manor.

She decided to leave immediately and packed a few items needful for the journey, including a weapon that she had not practised with since last autumn. Then she went into her father's bedchamber and found writing implements and paper and wrote a message for her brothers, which she placed on her pillow. After that she made sure all her hair was hidden beneath white veiling and topped it with a black veil. Her fingers clutched her crucifix and she prayed the slight disguise would work. Without returning to the hall, she left the house by the kitchen door.

As Cicely saddled up her horse, she thought of Mackillin, wondering if he had news of Husthwaite. Perhaps the Scottish lord was even now making the journey to Kingston-on-Hull and thence to Scotland. No doubt he would wed a Scottish lady and forget that he had ever met a lass called Cicely Milburn. She determined to put him out of her mind.

Mackillin's expression was grim as he rode past the stone knight carved in the rock face, seemingly standing guard betwixt a bridge and what was obviously a wayside shrine to our Lady. He was not looking forward to giving Cicely and the twins the news that Husthwaite had not only managed to reach Knaresborough, but had departed for an unknown destination. He accepted that information as meaning the clerk could be anywhere, so the sooner Cicely and the twins were warned of this, the better.

He made good time, arriving back at Milburn Manor by early afternoon. His disappointment was keen when he entered the hall to find only Matt, his steward, Tom and Tabitha. They appeared to be in the middle of a heated exchange.

'What's wrong?' he asked, striding towards them.

'Mackillin!' exclaimed Matt, looking relieved to see him. 'You'll never guess what's happened?'

'Husthwaite's been here?'

'No!' Matt dismissed the two men and asked Tabitha to bring food and mulled ale for their visitor.

Mackillin sensed a nervousness in the youth, who had changed his clothes and was now wearing a black surcoat of fine linsey-woolsey and black hose. 'It's Cissie. She's taken herself off to the ap Rowans to tell them of Father's death and see what information she can glean from our stepsister, Kate, about Diccon.'

Mackillin froze. 'When was this?'

He grimaced. 'Only God knows. Before the midday meal for sure. Tabitha went in search of her and found a note on her bed. I was out in the fields, so Jack sent her to tell me. I returned to find he'd taken one of the horses. He's hoping to catch up with her before she gets too far.'

'Courageous, but foolish,' said Mackillin, fearful for them both.

'I know. That arm's still giving him trouble,' muttered Matt.

Mackillin pulled himself together and told the youth what he'd discovered about Husthwaite in Knaresborough.

Matt's jaw clenched. 'You think it's possible that he's returned here and might have seen her leave?'

'Maybe,' rasped Mackillin, removing a gauntlet and rubbing his perspiring face with it. 'Let's hope not. Where's Robbie?'

'Probably in the kitchen with Martha. What are you going to do?'

'Go after them, of course.'

Tabitha chose that moment to appear with a jug of ale and was followed by Robbie.

Mackillin said immediately, 'How's the head?'

'Still hurts, but I've felt worse.'

'Good. I need you to do something for me. If I don't return here with Jack and Mistress Cicely by tomorrow, I want you to go to Kingston-on-Hull and take a message to Angus.'

Robbie frowned. 'Has this to do with what King James demanded of you?'

'Aye.' Mackillin drew his groom aside and told

him exactly what he was to do when he reached the port. Then Mackillin turned to Matt. 'I'll need a fresh horse and directions.'

'I'll have Tom escort you to the road that leads to Skipton,' said Matt, and hurried away.

A frustrated Cicely rested her aching back against the trunk of a tree and stared at Jack. 'You shouldn't have come after me.' Her journey was not going according to plan. A fox had shot across the road and her horse had bolted. Unfortunately it had stumbled over a huge clump of grass and she had been thrown. Now her horse was lame and she ached all over.

Exasperated and in pain, Jack said, 'Why don't you give up, Cissie? I know we won't make it back home tonight, but Bolton Priory is but a short distance away. We could seek shelter there and then return home in the morning.'

Cicely knew his words made sense, but she wanted to go on. Perhaps it was selfish of her but she felt the need of her stepsister's council. Kate had been kindness itself to her from the day they had met and Cicely knew she could trust her to give her wise advice concerning Diccon. She must continue with her journey. Pushing herself away from the tree trunk, she went over to Jack's horse and placed a hand on its neck.

'I have a better idea. Why don't you ride pillion and I'll take the reins of your horse? You could rest your arm that way and we may still reach Skipton. What's the point of going back when we've come so far?'

He shook his head and said in a vexed voice, 'Father used to say you had plenty of sense, but your wits seemed to have gone begging today. We can send a messenger to Owain and Kate once we've hired more men.'

Cicely dropped her hand. 'Why did you not say that earlier?'

'Because I didn't think of it. Another matter I haven't broached with you is…' He hesitated.

'What?'

'The struggle between the Lancastrians and Yorkists is not over. Matt told me that the queen is already gathering her forces to march on London to rescue the king.'

'Husthwaite mentioned something about this, but I'd forgotten,' she said, dismayed.

'Apparently the Duke of York is dead and his heir, Edward, will surely want to avenge his death. We don't want to get caught up in their fight, Cissie.'

She curled her hands into fists. 'But Diccon will be involved in it. I must try and see him. If he knows Father is dead, then he might change his mind once he realises we need him here in Yorkshire.'

Jack frowned. 'I don't think you have a hope of getting him away from Edward right now, Cissie. Fortune and glory are what Diccon wants.'

She turned on him. 'What is wrong with that? But he might put aside his ambitions once he knows Father is dead. I'm going on, but if you feel you cannot, then you stay at Bolton Abbey. I will walk on to Skipton leading my horse and hire a fresh one in the morning.'

Jack shook his head. 'I can't allow it.'

Cicely smiled at him tenderly. 'Give up, love. Accept I will do this and return home.' She glanced back the way they had come and stiffened as she saw a rider in the distance. Instantly, she reached for the bow and quiver of arrows concealed beneath one of her saddlebags. 'Someone's coming! He looks a mighty big fellow.'

'What are you doing?' demanded Jack, watching her string her bow and take an arrow from its quiver. 'I never considered you'd think of taking your bow with you.'

'Well, I did and you know I hit the target as many times as Matt.'

'Aye. That made him really mad.' Jack drew his sword. 'I tell you now, though, you won't hit that rider at this distance. You should get off the road and conceal yourself.'

'It's a waste of time. He must have seen us by

now. I'll wait until he gets closer and only let fly if I believe he's a threat to us.' Cicely's eyes narrowed as she gauged the distance. Then her heart performed an odd little dance as she realised the identity of the rider. 'I don't believe it,' she murmured, lowering her bow.

'It's Mackillin,' said Jack, his face lighting up. 'By all that's holy, he must have ridden like the wind to catch up with us.'

'He has no right to follow me,' she said, even as she admired his horsemanship and her heart raced at the sight of his rugged features.

He pulled on the reins and his horse came to a snorting halt a yard or so from them. His gold-brown eyes with their facets of green were questioning as he gazed down at Cicely in her black and white garb. 'You would pierce me with an arrow, lass?'

'Not as soon as I realised who you were.' She unstrung her bow.

'I'm glad you haven't lost your wits altogether, lass, and at least thought to arm yourself. I presume you know how to use it?'

'Of course. I used to practise at the butts on a Sunday after Mass in case the marauding Scots ever reached this far south again.' Her tone was light.

He smiled. 'I'm impressed, although your arrows wouldn't do much good against cannon.'

'I don't remember ever visualising them carrying cannon,' she said. 'Claymores and battleaxes were what I had in mind.'

'I suppose you thought you'd shoot at them from that tower of yours?'

'Yes.'

'Did you visualise what could happen to you making such a journey as this one travelling alone, even with a bow and arrows?'

'Of course, but I didn't realise I needed your approval for my actions, my lord.'

'Did I say you did?' he said, dismounting. 'But admit that you've acted foolishly.'

Two spots of colour appeared high on her cheeks. 'I will not. You might be a Scottish lord, but you are not my guardian or my husband, or in a position to give me orders or criticise what I do.'

'You need someone to take you in hand,' he said, taking a step towards her.

She stood her ground. 'Well, it's not going to be you, is it? You turned down my father's offer.'

Mackillin's eyes darkened and he glanced up at Jack. 'What did I tell you?'

The youth said, 'Sorry, Mackillin, but I told Matt and he let it out. I should have kept my mouth shut.'

Cicely was annoyed with both of them. 'Why, when it involved me? I can't understand Father. He would have done better sending me his love with his dying breath than offer me as a reward.' To her annoyance she felt that urge to cry, thinking of her father, and turned her back on them, not wanting them to see her weakness.

Almost instantly her shoulders were seized and she was spun round to face Mackillin. 'How can you doubt your father loved you?' he said softly. 'His last thoughts were of you.'

The moment was fraught with emotion and she had difficulty saying what was in her mind. 'It hurts me that Father and I parted in anger when he refused to give his permission for Diccon and I to be betrothed. I do not want to believe that in offering me to you that he was punishing me for setting my will against his.'

Mackillin sighed heavily. 'I'd have thought you knew your father better than that.'

She shrugged. 'The ways of men are often difficult for a woman to understand. Now, of your courtesy, will you release me?'

He made no move to do so, but touched the muddy graze on her cheek with the back of his hand. 'What happened to you? Were you thrown?'

'Aye,' she replied. 'A fox frightened my horse and now she is lame.'

Mackillin's stern features softened. 'Why are you so set on placing your life in danger?'

'I am not,' she protested. 'But sometimes we all have to do what we feel compelled to do.'

'Could you not wait until Diccon proved himself worthy and came seeking you?'

She met his gaze squarely. 'I've done enough sitting at home, waiting to know my fate. Can you, as a man, comprehend a woman's feelings?'

'I admire your courage, lass. Of course I can understand your impatience, but it was foolish of you to set out alone on such a quest.' His hand slid down her arm to clasp her fingers and squeeze them gently before releasing them.

He turned to Jack and said sternly. 'As for you—admirable as it is that you followed your sister—I did not save your life for you to risk it. You'd be in serious trouble if you drew a sword in her defence and had to fight for more than a few minutes.'

Jack nodded. 'I know. But you don't have a sister, Mackillin, so you can't understand a brother's feelings. I had to chase after her.'

Mackillin scratched the back of his neck and said ruefully, 'I must accept your rebuke. Now tell me—do you feel fit enough to continue with this journey?'

Sister and brother stared at him. 'Why do you ask?' queried Jack, a gleam in his eye. 'My arm is giving me some trouble and I would return home, only Cissie is determined to carry on, even if she doesn't find Diccon, as we need to inform the ap Rowans about Father. If you could perhaps act as her protector, then I would be content to stay at Bolton Abbey and ride for home on the morrow.'

Cicely protested but Mackillin indicated with a wave of his hand that she be quiet and scrutinised Jack's face, remembering how keen the lad was on there being a match between him and Cissie. He wished he could oblige him, but it was out of the question. He was not going to place her in a compromising position. She must really love Diccon if she was prepared to risk making such a journey alone.

'I think not, Jack. But if you feel able to ride pillion on *my* horse, then I will willingly make this journey to the ap Rowans with you both. Your sister can ride your mount.'

Jack stared at him and then grinned. 'If you insist, Mackillin. I'll do what you say.'

'Oh, I do, laddie. Your sister needs a chaperon as well as a protector.'

'No, you can't want to go with us,' said Cicely, feeling quite breathless at the thought of spending a couple more days in Mackillin's company. 'You have to return to Scotland.'

Mackillin smiled in a friendly manner. 'Aye, I do. But Scotland will have to wait. I cannot have you risking your life by setting out alone when Husthwaite is at large and could have followed you.'

Her eyes widened. 'You know this for certain?'

'Aye. His exact whereabouts are unknown to me, but I don't doubt he will want to try to punish us both in some way for thwarting his plans. So what say you? If you feel you'd rather not have my company, we will spend the night in Bolton Abbey and return to Milburn Manor in the morning.'

Jack glanced at his sister. 'Well? I say let's be on our way before it gets dark. We could be in Clitheroe by tomorrow evening, and reach Merebury Manor by noon the following day.'

'I agree.' Cicely was relieved that her brother was coming with them. Obviously, even with Jack present, it would be necessary for her to keep her distance from Mackillin. There must be no opportunity for dalliance between them. She could not deny that he had a certain attraction for her. As for his reasoning… A thought occurred to her.

'What if you're wrong and Husthwaite has other accomplices, and they try to rescue my kinsman who is held prisoner?'

His eyes narrowed in thought. 'I deem it highly unlikely. As I said I believe it's you and I whom he'll want to punish. I honestly believe Matt's life is no longer in danger.' There was silence but for the sound of the wind and the shifting of the horses. 'Well?' Mackillin gazed down into Cicely's dirt-smeared face. 'Do we go on?'

She nodded.

* * *

It was dusk by the time they reached Skipton. They made their way along Sheep Street and into the High Street, at the conjunction of which stood a cross and stocks. Ahead of them lay a castle enclosed by a moat.

'Who dwells here?' asked Mackillin.

An exhausted Cicely glanced at him, still scarcely able to believe that they were making this journey together. 'Lord Clifford. He is for the queen, so is most likely with her host.'

He nodded and thought no more of the matter for he had spotted an inn and pointed it out. Immediately Jack offered to go inside and enquire of two bedchambers. 'Father's known in this town and your accent mightn't go down well here, Mackillin. The Scots are still regarded as enemies in this place and we're not looking for trouble, are we?'

Mackillin agreed. He dismounted and held up his arms to Cicely. She placed her hands on his shoulders and was instantly aware of the strength of his muscles. Reminded of the kisses they had shared in the snow that day, she knew that she must not behave in any way that could be misconstrued as seductive. She held herself stiffly; as soon as he set her feet on the ground, she moved away from him. Her back was aching and she could not wait to lie down. No doubt he felt the same, having ridden to Knaresborough and back to her home and then on to here.

Fortunately, Jack did not keep them waiting long, but he was frowning when he came over to them. 'The innkeeper has only one bedchamber available.'

'Then Cissie must have it. I'll see to the horses. Take your sister inside, Jack.'

'But where will you two sleep?' asked Cicely.

He smiled. 'We'll find somewhere.'

Cicely had no choice but to accept what he said. She entered the inn with her brother and saw men drinking ale in an overcrowded tap room. A woman of middle years hurried over to them and introduced herself as the innkeeper's wife. Cicely vaguely remembered meeting her before. She shook her hand and was soon ushered into a small private parlour.

A fire burned in a wall grate and immediately Cicely went over to it and removed her gloves and held her cold hands out to the blaze.

'That's right, Mistress Milburn, you warm yourself, whilst I prepare the bedchamber. I was so sorry to hear about your father. He'll be sadly missed.'

Cicely thanked her for her commiserations. 'My stepsister and stepbrother don't know of his death, so we're on our way to tell them. We've been travelling for hours.'

'Then you'll be glad of a rest and to get some hot food down you,' said the innkeeper's wife, placing a cushion on a chair.

Jack whispered in Cicely's ear. 'I'll leave you to the good wife's ministrations and go and see how Mackillin's getting on with the horses.'

She nodded and watched him leave the room, hoping neither would be long. The woman chattered to her about the weather, but soon left her alone to see to their supper.

Cicely's mind wandered over the happenings of the day, thinking that it had not turned out at all as she had expected. She pondered over Mackillin's decision to follow her and Jack and wondered how it would be between his lordship and Diccon if they were to meet at Merebury. Her eyelids drooped and a yawn escaped her and then another. She decided that perhaps it would be best not to worry about such a meeting; sitting down, she soon fell asleep.

Mackillin entered the parlour, carrying their baggage. Seeing Cicely asleep in front of the fire, he felt a peculiar sensation in his chest. She looked so defenceless that he wanted to scoop her up in his arms and sit down with her in his lap and soothe away her anxieties. He knew that he must not carry on thinking in such a way or his resolve to keep her at arm's length would soon weaken. He had to steel his will and think of something else.

For instance—how could she ever have believed she could stay alone at an inn such as this one and remain inviolate? He placed his bedding in a corner by the fire and then shook her gently awake. Just in time, for there came a knock on the door and the innkeeper's wife's shrill voice informed them that she had their supper.

Cicely gazed up at Mackillin from drowsy eyes and smiled. 'Am I dreaming?' she asked.

'Nay, love,' he said unthinkingly.

She blinked at him and then hurriedly got to her feet as the door opened to reveal not only Jack but the innkeeper's wife as well. 'I need to wash my hands and face,' said Cicely, wondering if she had imagined those words.

'Is the bedchamber ready for my sister?' asked Jack.

'Aye,' said the woman, gazing up at Mackillin in astonishment as he took the tray from her. 'I'll show Mistress Milburn the way.'

Cicely seized hold of her baggage and hurried from the parlour. Had he called her love? If he had done so, then what had he meant by it? Perhaps for a moment he had thought her someone else? Maybe a Scottish lass who waited up north for his return. Such tenderness had filled her with warmth, so it would be best if she told herself that he had forgotten whom he was talking to and the endearment was intended for someone else.

She followed the woman upstairs and along a short, narrow passage with two doors opening off it. One of them was standing ajar and she was shown inside. There was naught of note to admire, but she told the woman the room was extremely fine before dismissing her. Then she unpacked the little she needed to make her toilet. Afterwards, feeling refreshed, she hurried downstairs, intending offering the use of her bedchamber to Mackillin and Jack for their toilet.

Mackillin was sitting in front of the fire, but a frowning Jack sat at the table. 'What's the matter?' enquired Cicely. 'I was about to ask if either you or Mackillin would like to use my bedchamber to refresh yourselves.'

'That is kind of you, Mistress Cicely, but we washed in a bucket of water drawn from the well,' said Mackillin.

'Oh,' she said, wondering why he had resorted to calling her Mistress Cicely again.

Jack rose and pulled out a chair from the table for her. 'I'd forgotten it's Lent.'

'Lent?' So had she.

Mackillin came over to them and, lifting the jug, he poured ale into three cups. She thanked him and took a drink before picking up her spoon and scrutinising the bowl of food in front of her. She sniffed it, thinking that since her father's death and being snowed in with Mackillin, she seemed to have lost all sense of time. She dipped the spoon into the concoction in the bowl and swirled it around, peering at the shapes barely visible in the candlelight.

'Have you tasted it?' She glanced at her brother and then Mackillin and thought she caught a glint of humour in his eyes and could not resist returning his smile.

'It's onion soup,' said Jack with distaste.

She shook her head. 'It's a Lenten stew, so most likely there's bread, milk, wine and honey as well as onions. The dish we make at home has almonds in it, but I can't imagine the innkeeper's wife being able to afford such a luxury.'

Jack sighed. 'Hopefully, there's a second course.'

'Eat up, brother, and stop moaning,' she teased.

'It's all right for you, Cissie, but we men have bigger frames to fill,' said Jack.

She almost said, *You men, Jack?* but Mackillin winked at her and so she kept quiet. Suddenly she felt shy of him. Perhaps it was because he *was* so big and seemed to dwarf the parlour. She kept her eyes lowered and gave her full attention to her meal. A day spent in the fresh air had sharpened her appetite and she ate every morsel of the stew. Fortunately for Jack, they had no sooner finished that course than the innkeeper's wife appeared with a fish dish. It was followed by the local white crumbly cheese and a crusty loaf, which was served with a flagon of mead—brewed, she guessed, by the monks of Bolton Priory. It was extremely palatable and the ache in Cicely's back seemed to lessen. After the meal was cleared away, she felt content to sit in front of the fire, sipping another cup of mead. Jack excused himself and said he wouldn't be long. For some reason she felt compelled to ask Mackillin about his family.

'Unfortunately I am my mother's only child,' he said turning his cup between his hands. 'I was told she miscarried a couple of times before giving birth to me. My paternal grandmother blamed the miscarriages on her Englishness, saying her blood was weak.'

'Your poor mother. Surely she deserved sympathy, not condemnation,' said Cicely, astounded by such maliciousness.

He smiled faintly. 'My mother could give as good as she got. My grandmother resented her, though, because she was young and lovely, according to my father. I remember her dancing round the hall with me when the old woman died. Father was just as relieved because both women used to berate him if he dared to defend one against the other. There were many quarrels when I was a lad. My stepbrothers would have their say, as well, taking every opportunity to make my life unpleasant. But this was all years ago before I went to live with my English kin for a while.'

'So you're half-English. You must have been very unhappy.'

'Often, but I had to make the best of it. Fortunately my father was in agreement to my spending part of the time at Alnwick. The castle's a great brooding place, but it was there I learnt to read and speak Latin and French and to improve my swordplay and to dance.'

'Dance?'

He smiled. 'I can see that you cannot imagine my dancing.'

She blushed faintly and changed the subject. 'So is your mother alone in your keep now?'

He shook his head. 'She has the daughter of an old friend for company, as well as the servants and those men who survived the fight that took the lives of my father and half-brothers. If they had not been killed, I would not be the Mackillin.'

She hesitated before daring to say, 'So when you return to your Scottish home you'll take a Scottish wife?'

'Aye.'

'Have you a lady in mind?'

He hesitated, but before he could speak hurrying

footsteps signalled Jack's return. At any other time Cicely would have been relieved to have his company so as to ease any constraint between herself and Mackillin, but not at that moment. Perhaps she would never get the opportunity again to have Mackillin's answer to such an impertinent question.

Seemingly unaware that his arrival might not be welcome, Jack pulled up a chair next to his sister. 'I was just thinking I'm glad to be going to the ap Rowans. I'll be able to speak to Owain about my future as a merchant venturer.' He turned to Mackillin. 'What will you do about your ship once you settle in Scotland?'

Mackillin yawned. 'That is something I do not need to think about right now. I deem it's time for bed if we're to make an early start in the morning.'

Cicely decided it was a waste of time trying to return to the matter of the identity of Mackillin's probable bride, so agreed. 'Where will you two sleep?'

'Here in the parlour,' said Jack. 'No need to worry about us, Cissie.'

She smiled and bid them goodnight and went upstairs to her bedchamber. As she undressed, she thought of what Jack had said about Mackillin's ship. Despite her father having travelled much, she, herself, had never sailed across the sea and would like to think she'd enjoy the experience. That night she dreamed of being held in Mackillin's arms as his ship carried them to a far distant shore.

Chapter Seven

Cicely was dreaming that Mackillin was being taken away from her. She clung to him, calling to those who held him prisoner to let him go. Then a knocking began to disturb her dreams and proved so persistent that she tore herself from her sleep and lay there, trying to force her eyes open, wondering about the meaning behind her dream and who it was making such a noise. Then a familiar voice called her name—it was Mackillin, and, within seconds, the events of the previous day came flooding back. She climbed out of bed.

She was stiff, but managed to walk over to the door without much difficulty and open it. She was glad that she had slept in her kirtle. He looked cheerfully wide awake. His hair was damp, causing her to wonder if he had sluiced himself in a water trough. Whatever he had done, he looked good enough to kiss again. She shook her head to try to rid herself of such a notion.

'Time to get up and be on our way, lass,' he said. 'You've been dead to the world. I've asked the good wife to pack us some bread and smoked fish to eat on the journey.'

'I'll be with you soon,' said Cicely, puzzling over why he should need to pick up his sleeping roll from the floor outside her door.

'I'll go and saddle up and see you downstairs as soon as you're ready. Jack's in the parlour breaking his fast,' said Mackillin.

She thanked him absently and closed the door. As she washed and dressed, she wondered if he had slept outside her bedchamber. She felt quite odd, thinking that he might have been only a few feet away from her whilst she slept.

Yet such feelings could not last once she was up and about. The ground was white with frost, but the sun was shining and the road was protected from the cruellest of weather by the surrounding fells. For a while they travelled at a brisk gallop and it was a relief to her when she saw a long-ridged hill in the distance to their right.

Jack pointed it out to Mackillin. 'That's Pendle hill. Doesn't look far, does it, as the crow flies? Clitheroe lies the other side of the hill. I reckon it would be quicker going across country,' he added.

Mackillin glanced at Cicely, a question in his eyes. 'It probably is the quickest way, as long as we don't wander into a bog by mistake,' she said.

Mackillin's gaze measured the distance to the distinctively shaped hill. He could see flashes of light reflecting the sun on what he presumed was frozen water on the moor that lay between them and the hill. The terrain reminded him of the untamed expanses of the Border country. 'Have you crossed that way before, Jack?' he asked.

He nodded. 'With Father. If it was not such a clear day and there was a chance of mist, then I would say don't risk it, but all we have to do is to keep Pendle hill in our sights.'

'Then let us not waste any more time,' said Mackillin with a smile, urging his horse from the road.

Unfortunately the first track they followed petered out and they had to seek another to avoid a mere because the sun had melted its icy surface. Another path was soon found, but at times they had to ride over tussocky wasteland. As the day wore on they occasionally had to backtrack to avoid marshy ground. They paused only briefly to eat some of the bread and fish and drink ale before forging ahead again.

The sun was sinking low in the sky by the time they reached the outlying slopes of Pendle hill. In its shadow the grass was still hoary with frost and in front of them lay an expanse of marshy ground.

Cicely shivered in the freezing air, thinking that the journey so far had taken them much longer than estimated and hoped Mackillin was not vexed with them for suggesting this route.

Her brother must have been thinking the same thing because he apologised to Mackillin. 'Father made it seem so easy when last I came this way with him.'

'We're here now, so let's not worry,' said Mackillin, dismounting.

He picked his way to the edge of the marshy area and what he saw there lifted his spirits. 'We should be able to cross, the ground is still iced over and should be firm enough to take our weight.'

He hurried back to the horses and looked up at Cicely, noticing her face was pinched with cold and that she drooped in the saddle. He marvelled that not a word of complaint had passed her lips. He smiled up at her. 'We'll soon find shelter. You stay on the horse.' He looked up at Jack. 'You can get down and lead my mount. I'll go on ahead and test the ground.'

Jack did as ordered and, taking the reins of Mackillin's horse, followed him. Cicely drew alongside her brother, watching his lordship take out his sword and try the ground with the point of the blade.

It appeared to make little impression, so he walked on and kept testing the ground. They followed him and at last they were on safe ground. Ahead lay a wood.

'How far do the trees stretch?' asked Mackillin of Jack.

'Two hours' journey maybe.'

Mackillin looked up at the darkening sky and Cicely guessed what he was thinking. It would be nightfall within the hour. She noticed that he still clasped his sword and wondered if he feared there were outlaws hiding in the forest. She thought that they would have to be mad to do so in this weather, but hopefully there might be a woodcutter's hut or a charcoal burner's cottage. The horses' heads were bowed with weariness as they entered the trees. Dead leaves muffled any sound as they picked their way gingerly to avoid roots spread across their path. Cicely thought of the songs sung by travelling musicians about Robin of the Hood and his merry men living in the greenwood, robbing the rich to feed the poor. She smiled inwardly, questioning whether such a hero had ever existed. But surely there must be friendly folk who would give a Christian welcome to three weary travellers in this forest of Pendle?

They had been moving stealthily for a while, when the trees opened on to a clearing and there, a hundred feet or so in front of them, was a hut with a lean-to attached. She was not going to allow herself to hope too quickly and glanced down at Mackillin, a question in her eyes. Dusk had deepened and she could barely read his expression but guessed his feelings must be similar to hers—they were going to have to spend the night here.

'It appears deserted,' said Jack, dismounting. 'I'll take a closer look.'

Before either of them could say 'wait,' he sprinted across to the hut.

'There's no one inside,' he called.

Mackillin dismounted and helped Cicely to the ground. She swayed against him and he put his arm round her and half-carried her to the hut. Jack had already opened the door and vanished inside. Now he looked out of the single-window opening with its shutters askew. He signalled to them, then went back to the door and held it wide and waved them inside.

'It's no fine hall, but at least we'll have a roof over our heads for tonight,' he said.

'You two stay here,' said Mackillin. 'I'll fetch the baggage.'

She was only too happy to do as he said and entered the hut and tried to make out shapes in the darkness. She tripped over a circle of stones in the centre of the earthen floor and realised it was a primitive fireplace. The atmosphere struck chill, but better to have some shelter than sleep in the open on such a freezing night. Her eyes were becoming accustomed to the dimness and she noticed what appeared to be a wide ledge running the length of a wall. On closer inspection she noticed a space beneath it and discovered what felt like logs and kindling.

'Have you seen this, Jack?' she asked.

There was no answer and she realised he must have gone outside to help Mackillin. As soon as his lordship reappeared with the baggage she told him of her discovery.

'Well done!'

'You do have a tinderbox?' she asked.

His teeth gleamed whitely in the gloom. 'Never travel without one. A fire's essential even in hot countries when out in the wilds.'

She showed him where everything was and helped carry over the makings of the fire. Then she sat on the ledge out of the way, gazing at the dark crouching shape that was Mackillin. She imagined his lips pressed tightly together and his eyebrows knotted with concentration as he attempted to conjure up light and warmth for the three of them. She could even picture him in the role of one of those primitive men who had lived in caves performing the same magic. He would have worn animal skins and so would his woman. She would have roasted the wild animals or fish he caught. Afterwards they would have slept on furs in each other's arms for comfort and warmth. She felt a ripple of sensation in the pit of her stomach and ran her tongue around her dry mouth. She mustn't allow her thoughts to stray in that direction. Thank God for Jack's presence.

She heard Mackillin give a grunt of satisfaction and soon the kindling was cracking and popping and a scent of pine filled the small room. She watched as he lit a stub of candle and could see his face clearly. He looked in her direction and smiled. She felt happiness ripple through her and, astonished by its depth, got up from the ledge to fetch more wood, so he would not see it shining in her face.

Mackillin placed the candle on a blob of melted wax on the crude table that was there and she resumed her position on the ledge. The smoke spiralled its way upwards into the dark thatch of the roof and through a hole there. Even so, some of it weaved its way round the room and she coughed.

He glanced over at her. 'The remains of the food are in my pack. There's also a couple of flasks, one of water and one of whisky. I'll try to fasten that broken shutter. We won't be able to keep a fire burning all night and it'll be freezing towards dawn.'

She watched him disappear outside and went over to his pack and found the food and drink. When he returned he was accompanied by Jack and had a cord in his hand. She sat on the ledge, watching his strong hands drag the broken shutter towards him. Jack held it shut whilst Mackillin tied it up as best he could. How skilful those large hands were, thought Cicely, not the least bit soft and white like she had imagined a lord's to be. It was only when he had completed his task that he looked her way. 'The food and whisky?'

'Here,' she said, picking them up from the ledge beside her.

Jack took them from her and he passed them to Mackillin. That done, his lordship came and sat beside her. 'You've no tasted whisky?' he asked.

She shook her head. 'Is it like mead?'

'It's not sweet, but it lights a fire as it goes down the throat and burns nicely in the belly. Too much and it gives you a thirst and a head fit to burst.'

'Then I'll not touch it,' she said with a light laugh.

He grinned. 'A dram won't do you any harm if you have a drink of water with it. Besides, I've not enough *aqua vitae* in my flask to give any of us a bad head.'

'*Aqua vitae!* Doesn't that mean water of life?' asked Jack.

'Glad you know your Latin, laddie,' said Mackillin, unscrewing the top of one of the leather flasks. 'Taste it and see, lass.'

She hesitated, but the challenging light in his eyes caused her to reach out a hand and take the flask. Cautiously she took a mouthful and felt the cold liquid trickle on her tongue. Then she gasped as it slid to the back of her throat and down her gullet, warming a path to her belly. She would have taken another gulp if he had not removed the flask from her hand. 'Not too much at once when you're not used to it and on an empty stomach,' he admonished. Taking a swig from the flask, he closed his eyes and then opened them again and smiled. 'Now food and water.'

Mackillin handed the flask to Jack. 'A mouthful, Jack. That's all I have.'

Jack thanked him and took only a sip.

When it came to the food there wasn't much of that either. Cicely would have given his lordship and her brother the bulk of the food, but Mackillin insisted on equal shares. They all ate the food slowly, savouring every mouthful. Jack sat on the ledge with his back against the wall and closed his eyes.

Suddenly Mackillin touched Cicely's chin with the tip of his finger and then held out the digit to her. She spotted the crumb of fish and found herself remembering, when the twins were being weaned, how her mother would soften meat for them by chewing it before offering it to them on her finger. Sometimes the babies would bite her finger with their tiny teeth and her mother would squeak like a mouse and Cicely would laugh. She felt a smile start inside her and attempted to lick the crumb off his finger, but it escaped her and she sucked it up. It gave her an odd thrill, and when she looked up at him she saw that he was gazing at her from beneath drooping eyelids.

'When I was a lad I used to creep through the long grass to the edge of Loch Trool and tickle trout. I liked it best in the early morning when I had the loch to myself. Sometimes there would be mist on the water and there was a different kind of magic about the place then. I was always hungry in those days, so I'd struggle to get a fire going and cook a couple of trout out there in the open.'

'I'd like a trout right now,' said Cicely, lowering her gaze and fiddling with the girdle about her waist. 'The loch you mentioned—is it a pretty place?'

'Aye. I deem it so…although there's those from the Highlands who'd claim their lochs are grander. I do not care about that—for me there's no finer place to be on a spring morning when the bluebells are blooming and the eagles are soaring above the crags. Even Robbie Bruce, the greatest king Scotland ever had, is said to have spent time there, finding sanctuary in a cave whilst hiding from his enemies.'

She forced her eyes open. 'By enemies, you mean the English?'

'Och! Not only the English, Cissie. He had enemies aplenty in Scotland. When they wouldn't accept him as king, he killed them.'

She shivered and drew her cloak closer about her. 'I would not like to move in royal circles. It's not safe.'

'Aye, 'tis not,' he said heavily.

He forced himself to his feet and fetched his sleeping gear and placed pallet and blanket on the ledge beside her. 'You can use these. I'll do well enough with my cloak by the fire.'

She shook her head. 'It's kind of you, but I have my cloak and will be warm enough.'

He frowned. 'Don't argue with me, woman. I saw your face earlier. That kind of cold seeps into the bones and I don't want you catching a chill.'

'I'll be all right,' she whispered, glancing at her brother who appeared to have fallen asleep. 'Anyway, I need to go outside.'

Without more ado she got up and hurried out of the hut. The cold took her breath away and she glanced towards the trees that creaked eerily in the wind. An owl hooted, scaring the life out of her. She wanted to rush back inside where Mackillin waited and it was safe. Instead, she wasted no time scuttling behind the lean-to where the horses huddled together for warmth. After relieving herself, she wiped her hands on the wet grass and hurried back to the entrance where she found Mackillin waiting outside the door. She was touched that he had kept watch and was reminded of that morning when he had picked up his bedding roll from outside her bedchamber. He ushered her inside and then his gaze swept the clearing before closing the door.

He was aware of Cicely's eyes on him as he shot the bolt. Then she lay on the pallet he had rolled out on the ledge, thanked him, and wrapped her cloak round her and closed her eyes. He sat on the floor and put another log on the fire. The heat released the resin in the wood and it hissed, flaring up and lighting the room and filling it with that scent of pine once more. 'That smell brings back memories,' he said softly.

'Of your childhood?' she murmured.

'Of my travels. When I bought my own ship I journeyed into the hinterland of foreign lands and slept under the stars. We'd keep a fire burning through the night to ward off wolves and bears.'

She could imagine him making some makeshift shelter near a stream or river and living off the land, and thought it could be a great adventure in the right company. 'I always longed to travel and see how other people live,' she said wistfully.

A faint smile lightened his face. 'Some of the

most interesting places I've seen are those I never intended visiting.'

'You mean you got lost.'

'Aye. Fortunately I always found my way again.'

She prayed they would have no trouble finding the right way on the morrow. She would have liked to have heard more about his travels, but she could feel herself drifting into sleep.

But for Mackillin sleep would not come. He could not stop thinking about her, imagining the feel of her in his arms. At last he rose and placed the last of the logs on the fire. From the sound of their steady breathing she and Jack were both asleep. He made his way to the ledge, but could see little of her. She had wrapped herself completely in her cloak. He reached out with a gentle hand and touched her head. She did not stir and, with a sigh, he returned to the fire and curled himself up on the floor, praying that sleep would take him.

It was the scream that woke him. Instantly he reached for his sword. The room was pitch black for the fire had burnt itself out and so had the candle. 'Wha-what's that noise?' asked Jack, roused from sleep.

'Wolves and men's fearsome faces hidden amongst the trees,' responded Cicely, starting upright.

'There's no wolves here, Cissie,' said Mackillin. 'You're having a nightmare.'

'I know I must be, but it was still frightening,' she said. 'Sorry to wake you.'

'It doesn't matter,' said Mackillin. 'I've had many a bad dream in my time.' Impulsively he made his way over to her in the darkness and sat beside her.

'That is you, Mackillin?' she asked, sensing him close by.

'Aye.'

'The dream felt so real.' Her fear was abating.

'I've heard it said that there are no wolves left in England,' murmured Mackillin.

'But there are men who are savage and would devour a woman, such as Husthwaite and my northern kin,' whispered Cicely. 'I thought you were one such when I first set eyes on you, but now I know better. Tell me—are there wolves still in Scotland?'

'Possibly. But they avoid the places of men.'

'I'm glad of that. I would like to see this Loch Trool you spoke of,' she said sleepily.

'That would mean your visiting Scotland.'

'I know.' Her head rested against his shoulder.

He could feel the outline of her breast touching his arm and had difficulty restraining himself from bringing up his other hand and caressing its rounded softness. The thought of kissing its rosy peak aroused him and he knew he must move away, otherwise the temptation might prove too great. 'You're safe. Now go back to sleep. We've got to be up early in the morning.'

'Of course. You're right.' She yawned and gathered her cloak around her.

He moved away from the ledge and curled up on the floor and closed his eyes. When he slept it was to dream that Cicely was being torn from his arms by a man in a wolf's mask and he couldn't do anything to prevent it because his hands were tied and he had no idea of where he was.

When he woke again it was still dark. He yawned and stretched, wondering how long it was to dawn. Then he noticed a faint lifting of the darkness around the shutter and beneath the door.

Silently he got to his feet and, taking his leather flask, went over to the door. Carefully, he drew back the bolt and went outside. The wind had dropped and the first faint rays of the sun were slanting between the trees, dispelling the gloomy atmosphere of the previous night. He went and checked on the horses before scouting around the immediate area and was relieved that the only tracks he found were those of woodland animals. He discovered a stream a short distance away and filled his flask with fresh water and returned to the hut. As he entered Cicely started awake and reached for her knife, but then she saw it was Mackillin and smiled.

Her smile was one of such sweetness that his breath caught in his throat. He had to clear it before he offered his flask. 'Fresh water. We're going to have to make a move soon.'

She thanked him, drank some of the water and rose from the ledge.

Jack woke suddenly and gazed at the pair of them. 'Is it time to get up?' he asked.

'Aye,' said Mackillin.

Jack's eyes went from one to the other, but he could not gauge from their behaviour how they had spent the rest of the night after the disturbance. He watched his sister fold Mackillin's pallet and hand it to him. Then she smiled at her brother and said, 'Hurry up.'

Soon they were riding in the opposite direction to the rising sun. There were few signs of human habitation, but they did come upon a man setting traps for rabbits. They paused to ask him for directions to Clitheroe and had to repeat themselves several times because he appeared not to understand what they were saying. Eventually he went with them and in no time at all they arrived in the town.

Mackillin gazed along the high street towards the castle on a limestone crag. 'Which lord lives in that castle?'

Neither Jack nor Cicely knew. 'Whoever it is, his allegiance will be to King Henry for this is Lancaster country,' said Jack. 'After Mother died, Father brought us this way to his aunt's house. He put in some orders for fustian cloth while we were here.'

'I remember it well,' said Cicely, glancing at Mackillin. 'Father's sister had taken care of us whilst he was in Europe. When he returned she told him that he had to find us a new mother as she was planning to marry again. So my father found himself a new wife.'

'Diccon's mother?'

'Aye,' she murmured. 'We met the Fletchers in Liverpool in company with Owain ap Rowan. I was ten summers old. Diccon was five years older and fair of hair and face. He was kind to me. Within weeks our parents were wed and Diccon came to live with us for a while.'

She fell silent, thinking that it had not been until she was fifteen that he had seen her as a potential bride, months after his mother had died. It had been Christmastide and they had been playing Hoodman's Bluff. He had kissed her. At the time she had believed all her dreams would come true. Never had she suspected that one day he would be so rash as to become involved in the quarrels of York and Lancaster. He had spoken only once to her about not wanting to depend on her father's provision for them both. So he really was fighting for fortune and glory as Jack had suggested.

They lingered in Clitheroe only long enough to eat some cheese patties washed down with ale and then they set out along the old Roman road that led to Ribchester, and so they made good time.

In less than two hours the church of the market town of Preston could be seen and after crossing the River Ribble, Jack told Mackillin that they had less than seven leagues to go. It was mid-afternoon when they reached the summit of Parbold hill. There they rested the horses and stretched their legs. Cicely walked the short distance to where the south-west Lancashire plain fell away below her, stretching to the horizon where the sun reflected off the Irish sea.

Mackillin came and stood beside her. 'It's a fine view,' said Cicely, his arm brushing her shoulder. She was aware of that thrill she felt whenever he touched her and marvelled at it. To try and get it out of her mind, she said, 'Have you ever been to Ireland?'

'Once or twice to the north of the island.'

'Father said that except for the trade in cattle and horses it has naught to recommend it. That it rains a lot and so there's plenty of bogs and the mist is inclined to linger past noon and that's why legends of monsters and magic come from there. I admit I would still like to go and see for myself,' she said softly.

He glanced at her, noticing that the breeze had brought colour to her cheeks. She looked even lovelier than the first time he had met her.

'Perhaps one day Diccon could take you there,' he suggested, his eyes darkening. 'Edward, whom he follows, has lands in the south of Ireland. If the Yorkists win this struggle, then no doubt Diccon will be rewarded.'

She paled. 'Whoever wins the coming battle, I fear many men will die. Shall we go on now?'

He nodded, wishing he had not mentioned Diccon's name.

It was early evening when they turned off the road in the direction of Merebury. A couple of men were ploughing a field and watched Mackillin, Jack and Cicely as they passed. In the near distance could be seen a sandstone house and outbuildings. As they drew closer, Mackillin commented on the number of horses out in the fields.

'Remember, we told you that Owain breeds horses and sells them,' said Cicely. 'I do hope he's here,' she added fervently.

Dogs began to bark and the front door of the house opened and a woman appeared. From a barn two men came hurrying out. She was armed with a stave and one of the men held a bow and was fixing an arrow to the string; the other carried a pitchfork.

Cicely recognised her stepsister and called out, 'Kate, it's me, Cissie. Jack is with me and also a friend of Father's, Lord Mackillin.'

Kate, flaxen-haired and wearing a green gown, lowered her stave and indicated to the bowman to hold his fire. 'Cissie, is that really you?' she said, approaching the riders. 'I did not look to see you here until late spring, but you are always welcome.' She looked Mackillin up and down as if she could not quite accept he was of noble birth. 'A lord and a friend of Nat's, you say?'

He smiled faintly, seeing a woman of maybe twenty-seven summers. She was not as pretty as Cicely, but there was something appealing about her wide-set eyes and dainty nose. He could tell she was still on her guard despite Cicely's introduction of him.

'What brings you here, my lord?' she asked.

'Cissie and Jack needed an escort and I volunteered, Mistress ap Rowan,' he answered. 'Is your husband here?'

Cicely slid from her horse and went over to Kate. 'We bring sad tidings about Father,' she said, her voice breaking. 'He is dead.'

The stave slipped from Kate's fingers and she

held out her arms to her stepsister. 'Oh, my dear Cissie!' Kate's eyes filled with tears and she engulfed her in an embrace.

Mackillin turned away, moved by such naked emotion, and caught Jack's gaze on him. His face was tight with pain. Instantly Mackillin dismounted, and stood by in case the youth needed help to dismount but Jack managed to get down unaided.

'Shall we leave the women to comfort each other?' murmured Mackillin. 'If one of these men could show us the stables, we can see to the horses.'

'I can do that, Mackillin,' said Jack. But despite his offer one of the men came over to them. Jack greeted him like a friend and spoke of their journey whilst Mackillin removed the baggage. The man said he would see to the horses, so his lordship, noticing the two women had gone inside the house, followed them.

By the time he entered the hall Cicely and Kate were sitting over by the fireplace. A young woman sat on a settle with a boy and a girl, one each side of her, and a smaller child on her lap. The elder two appeared to be listening intently to what she was saying, but the youngest was wriggling as if it wanted to be up and about.

'The ap Rowan children,' said Jack, coming up behind Mackillin. 'I wonder where Owain is?'

Kate must have heard the question because her head turned and she looked in their direction. 'There you are, Jack…and my lord. Come over and warm yourself by the fire. Cissie has been telling me what happened in Bruges.' She stretched out a hand towards his lordship. 'I see we have much to thank you for, Mackillin.'

He shrugged deprecatingly. 'I only wish I could have saved Nat's life and spared Jack an injured arm.'

Kate turned to her stepbrother. 'Cissie mentioned how much pain it causes you.'

'It's improving,' Jack said. 'Naught to make a fuss about.'

'Good. You said you wish to see Owain. Unfortunately he's not here.'

'Is he at Rowan Manor?' asked Jack.

'He sent word to me ten days ago that he and Hal were having to deliver horses to my Stanley kinsmen at Nether Alderley. They are to join the queen's host as it travels south.'

Mackillin and Cicely exchanged glances. 'I presume then that you know of the battle that took place near Wakefield,' said Mackillin.

'Aye,' said Kate. 'My kinsman Sir Thomas informed me of it. Fortunately Owain has promised me by all we hold sacred that he will return home once he has fulfilled his obligation to Sir Thomas by supplying him with a dozen war horses. He will not fight. The horses will be his contribution to Henry's cause.'

'That must be of a great relief to you. When do you expect him?'

'He's bound to stay at Rowan Manor a few days before returning to Merebury, so hopefully next week. If your need to speak to him is urgent, then I would advise you to spend the night here and in the morning ride to Rowan. If you set out early you will reach there the next day.'

He thanked her with a smile. 'We will do as you say.'

'What of Diccon?' asked Cicely. 'Where is he?'

There was a wary expression on Kate's face. 'Later, Cissie. Let the news he is safe suffice. Now take your ease, all of you. If you will excuse me, I will order refreshments,' she added and hurried away.

Chapter Eight

Jack drew closer to the fire and Mackillin walked over to Cicely. He was unable to resist saying, 'So his sister has had word from Diccon or possibly she has seen him.'

Cicely said lightly, 'Better that she should hear from him than both of us worry.'

'Do you think he is here now?' murmured Mackillin. 'The way Mistress ap Rowan armed herself when she heard riders at her door causes me to wonder if she was expecting trouble.'

'Perhaps you should ask her if you are worried,' suggested Cicely.

'My interest in Master Fletcher is purely on your behalf,' he said, resting a hand on the back of her chair, and lowered his head so his mouth hovered near her ear. 'For her to know he is safe makes me wonder if he is in the vicinity. Maybe she has concealed him somewhere, because this area is a Lancastrian stronghold.'

'Diccon grew up here, so I doubt if anyone would betray him. At least, I hope not,' she murmured, wondering if it was possible that she would soon see Diccon. She felt a lift of the heart at the thought of setting eyes on him, but wondered what his feelings would be once he knew that she had been escorted here by a Scottish reiver.

Before she could think any more on the matter, the door opened and Kate entered, accompanied by a couple of serving men carrying trays. They placed them on the table and she dismissed them and poured the wine herself. Mackillin and Cicely strolled over to the table and she handed them a cup each. 'It's a rioja from Spain. Nat had it delivered only last year. I find it hard to believe that we will never see him again in this world.' Kate's face was sad.

'Nat had a gift for friendship,' said Mackillin, a faint smile of reminiscence playing about his well-formed mouth.

'He was a kind man and made my mother very happy.' Kate's voice quivered.

'She made him happy, too,' said Cicely.

'And we were very fond of her,' said Jack, helping himself to a drink. 'This despite her calling Matt and me *imps of Satan,*' he added with a wry smile.

'Let us drink a toast to Nat's memory,' said Mackillin, raising his cup. 'May he always live in our hearts.'

The others echoed his sentiments.

Cicely took a deep draught of the red wine and, when she felt more in control of her emotions, said, 'Please, Kate, tell me—is Diccon hiding somewhere near about?'

Startled, Kate spilt drops of wine on her green gown. She made a distressed sound. 'Now look what you made me do, Cissie.'

'I beg pardon. It's just that Mackillin wondered…'

'Then wonder no longer, lord,' interrupted Kate, darting him a frowning look from her fine eyes. 'Diccon was here and he did consider making the journey north, but made no mention of definitely doing so.'

Cicely was disappointed and asked, 'Where has he been all this time?'

Kate bid them be seated and joined them by the fire. 'He spent Christmas at Ludlow Castle in the company of Edward of York and those young men who have pledged their allegiance to his cause.'

Cicely frowned. 'It is as we feared. Still, he surely could have asked to be excused for Christmas? He must have known Father would have tried to be home for the festive season.'

'I asked him almost the same question because

Rowan is only two days' journey from Ludlow and we were spending the festive season there,' said Kate, 'but he did not give me an answer that I found satisfactory. He chases a dream and it worries me that it will cost him his life.'

Cicely paled and her throat tightened with fear for him and she took a sip of her wine to ease it. Mackillin looked at her with concern and was angry with Diccon. 'He must know what he is doing and will have trained with his comrades-in-arms. As for Edward…whilst in Calais he asked many questions of veteran soldiers guarding the port and its surrounding area. No doubt he knows what he is about.'

Cicely's expression lightened. 'My thanks, Mackillin, you have reminded me about what Father said about Edward being more aware than the king that trade overseas has been difficult for English merchants. It was of concern to Father that the king took so little interest and seemed to regard merchants only as a means to borrow money.'

Jack nodded. 'He spoke to me of it, but his loyalty was still with the king.' He turned his blue eyes to his lordship as if for affirmation.

Mackillin nodded. 'Once Nat's allegiance was given, it was for life.'

Cicely turned to Kate and murmured, 'Did Diccon give you a message for me?'

'He sent his love to you all.'

Cicely was aware of Mackillin looking in her direction and felt her humiliation was complete. It hurt that Diccon had not spoken of her specifically. Had he changed his mind about wishing to marry her? She had to get out of here and be alone. 'I wonder, Kate, if you could show me where I'm sleeping and if I could have some hot water? I'm filthy after the journey.'

'Of course, Cissie.' Kate smiled and rose to her feet. 'I thought you might like to share my bed, seeing as how Owain is away. We'll be able to talk and it'll be warmer than sleeping alone at this time of year.'

'Of course.'

Kate turned to his lordship. 'If you have finished your wine, Mackillin, I could show you to a bedchamber at the same time.'

He thanked her and drained his drinking vessel, wondering if her reason for having Cicely sleep with her was to make certain she was safe from him. No doubt she, too, was puzzled by Nat's choice of a Border reiver for a friend. He watched her speak to Jack, who smiled and nodded before she turned to him and Cicely. 'If you'll follow me, my lord.'

The three adults went upstairs together and Mackillin was shown into the best guest bedchamber. 'I've already given orders for hot water to be brought up, so hopefully all is ready for you,' said Kate, gazing up at him. 'Supper will be served within the hour, if that suits your lordship?'

'I look forward to breaking bread with you,' he said, inclining his head. With a brief glance in Cicely's direction, he closed the door.

Kate linked her arm through her stepsister's and hurried her along the passage. 'I have not told you all about Diccon. He was still here two hours ago, but we quarrelled and he stormed out. I accused him of sadly neglecting you and the twins since our mother's death. I told him that he should stop following Edward and visit you. Then he told me something that amazed me.' She paused and said with concern, 'Tell me it is not true, Cissie, that you and he made a secret pact to marry? It will not do, you know. I am aware that you have worshipped him since you first set eyes on him, but your father spoke to Owain and I only a year ago, when I mentioned your feelings towards my half-brother, and he said that he would never countenance such a match.'

Cicely came to a halt and faced her. 'Do I not know this? Father told me exactly what he thought of the notion. Still, I love Diccon and want to wed him.'

Kate squeezed Cicely's arm and said quietly, 'But

is it the kind of love a woman feels for a man? How do you see your life with him? Would you face danger to be at his side, knowing that you would rather die than live without him?'

'I have never thought of our married life being like that,' said Cicely honestly. 'I only dreamed of his living with us at Milburn and of us all being happy together as a family. I like children and I presumed they would come after we wed.'

'You do not know my brother well if you think he would settle for a domestic life at Milburn. Diccon's ambition is such that if he survives the next battle and Edward is victorious, then he will want to spend more time at court than at home to get what he wants.' Kate's blue eyes were worried. 'Mingling in royal circles is dangerous. You would be lonely and never have a moment's peace and that is not the life your father wanted for you.'

Cicely gasped. 'How could Father speak of my wanting a life without worry? Did he care about my mother when he went on his travels? Was not his life as a merchant venturer just as dangerous as the one you speak of for Diccon?'

'Aye. But your mother and father did not marry for love. When he married my mother, he gave up travelling for her sake.'

Cicely knew this to be true. 'He was lost after she died and that is why he could not settle at home,' she said sadly. 'You're right. They truly loved each other, just as you and Owain love each other.'

Kate's face softened. 'Aye. Love changes all. Life is uncertain and it can be short. Loving someone means you want to spend as much time together as one can. When children come along it is not always possible. When Owain is away as he is now, my heart longs for him.' She put a hand to her breast. 'It is like a constant pain. Has your heart ached for my brother in such a way?'

Cicely could not honestly say that her longing for Diccon was an actual pain. 'I need time to think. I need to see him.'

'Of course you do,' said Kate, biting her lower lip. 'Perhaps I should not have said all I have, but I want the best for both of you and I fear that you both might settle for second best. Owain believed that Nat had someone else in mind for you to marry.'

Cicely decided to tell her about Nat's last words. 'Father offered me to Mackillin with his dying breath, but he refused his offer.'

Kate's eyes widened. 'You surprise me. I must say—Scottish or not—Mackillin is a fine figure of a man. Your father must have known him for some time. Did Mackillin tell you he turned you down?'

'No. Jack told Matt and he let it slip. Mackillin did not wish me to know of it.'

'Did he say why he refused your father's offer?'

'Of course not. But most likely he wants a Scottish bride.' Cicely's voice was terse. She walked on.

No more was said until they had reached Kate's bedchamber and she opened the door and they went inside 'Tell me more about how you came to be here with Mackillin,' said Kate.

Cicely did not immediately answer because she was pondering what Kate had said about love, thinking that she would prefer to spend her life at the side of her husband and face danger with him than to be expected to sit at home with her sewing or be about her household tasks. She walked across the candlelit room and sank onto the bed and eased off her boots.

'I set off alone. Jack caught up with me and then Mackillin found us both. There's a horrible toad of a man called Husthwaite. He forged Father's will and was determined to force me into marriage. Mackillin saved me from that fate and knocked him down. Then he escaped and Mackillin feared for us. Because he saved Jack's life he feels responsible for him. He has kissed me and I enjoyed it very much. I have wondered how this can be if I truly love Diccon.'

Kate stared at her hard. 'He acts like a man who has a fancy for you and cares about your safety.'

Cicely rubbed the small of her back, which ached

after having been in the saddle for so long. 'Perhaps. Although it cannot be the kind of love you speak of which makes a man want to marry a maid even if it's not sensible and he believes her to love another.'

Kate said softly, 'Perhaps his feelings go deeper than you think and he's fighting against them. Maybe he questions if he has made the right decision in not accepting your father's offer. I suggest for the moment you put all thought of suitors out of your mind. Rest. You may have your pick of what is in my chest and armoire if you wish to change your raiment. I must oversee supper.' She opened the door and left her alone.

Cicely tried to do as Kate had said and stop thinking about the two men. She slipped off the bed and removed her garments and washed all over. Then she delved into Kate's chest and found some clean undergarments and put them on before going over to the large armoire and opening the door. She searched through the gowns and surcoats there and eventually drew out a simple dark blue gown of woollen cloth. If she had not been in mourning, she might have been tempted by a gown made from fabric from a roll that she remembered her father shipping over from a mercer in Italy. The silk weavers in places such as Florence and Genoa had copied those fabrics originally made and brought overland from the Orient. It was a vivid green and she had one similar at home.

She loosened the fastenings on the blue gown and pulled it over her head. Then she drew the ribands on the front of the bodice tight again. It had a scooped neckline that revealed an expanse of cleavage; the sleeves were long and came to points at her wrists. She ran her hands over the fabric, revelling in the warmth of the wool and the gown's snug fit. How she wished she could see her reflection in a mirror, but there was only a small oval looking glass on the wall. She undid her braids and, reaching for a comb, began to untangle her hair. It was then she heard a sound at the door and turned to see a man standing in the doorway.

Mackillin removed his boots and stripped to the waist. He washed his upper torso before realising there was no drying cloth on the washstand. He frowned and wondered whether the serving wench was late bringing one and had left it on the chest outside. He opened the door and stepped into the passage and saw that his assumption was correct. He picked up the cloth and was about to close the door when he heard footsteps. Curiously, he peered round the door jamb and saw a young man coming in his direction.

Swiftly Mackillin pulled the door so that it was

only slightly ajar and waited until he had passed. Then he slipped out of the bedchamber and followed him, rubbing his upper body dry as he did so. He draped the drying cloth over his shoulders and padded after the man until he stopped outside a bedchamber. He watched him open the door and go inside. Then he heard an exclamation and, recognising Cicely's voice, sped over to the door, only to have it shut in his face. He hesitated to burst into the bedchamber, but decided to remain outside in case Cicely should have need of him. At least that was part of his reason.

Cicely stared at the bearded and flaxen-haired man standing in the doorway. For a second she did not recognise him due to the beard; then she realised who it was and dropped the comb. 'Diccon!'

He looked astounded. 'Cissie! I was expecting to see Kate.'

'She's downstairs. She said you'd left.'

'I did, but knew I could not go without making up our quarrel.' He ran a hand through his hair. 'But what are you doing here? You should be at Milburn.'

She felt a sinking in her stomach. 'Are you not pleased to see me?'

'Of course I am.' He forced a smile and strode over to her. Placing his hands on her shoulders, he bent his head and kissed her lightly on the lips.

As kisses went it did not make her pulse race and he released her almost immediately. 'It's just that these are dangerous times.'

'I'm aware of the risk, but it's months since I've seen you and there's something I had to tell you—also I was concerned about your safety.'

He reddened. 'I meant to send a messenger, but I was short of funds. Besides, I've been that busy, I—'

'Given little thought to me,' she murmured, her hurt compounded by the way in which he had rcleased her so swiftly.

'That's not true, Cissie.' His eyes glinted with annoyance. 'I have thought of you often.'

'As I have you, but there's little pleasure for me in waiting and waiting and not hearing from you for months.'

'I really am sorry.' He sighed and scrubbed his beard with his knuckles. 'You've changed, Cissie. You never used to complain about anything.'

She felt her temper rising. 'I don't mean to sound as if I'm harping on about your not getting in touch, but since your mother died, I've had to take on new responsibilities and I could have—'

He interrupted her. 'I'm sure you cope very well.'

'I do my best, but I miss your mother and would that you were home.'

A shadow darkened his blue-grey eyes. 'I miss

her, too, and pray God the day will come when I can provide you with a better home.' He lifted her hand and kissed it before drawing her into his arms and pressing his lips to hers. She waited, but felt no thrill tingle through her veins and her spirits sank even further. It was pleasant enough to be kissed by him, but could not compare with the feelings Mackillin's kisses had roused in her. In truth, she felt slightly uncomfortable and was glad when the kiss ended.

Diccon gazed down at her with a faint smile. 'Aye, you're no longer a girl.'

She freed herself and with a trembling hand picked up the comb and began to tidy her hair. 'I have something to tell you.'

He peered into her face. 'What is it? You look sad.'

'It's Father.'

Diccon tensed. 'Is he here? I'll tell you now, Cissie, he will be willing to give me your hand once he hears my news.'

Tears pricked the back of her eyes. 'No, he will not—he is dead.'

'What!' Diccon stared at her as if he did not believe her.

'It's true,' she said in a low voice. 'He was murdered in Bruges. Jack brought us the news on St Hilary's Day. I so wished you could have been with us.' Agitated, she began to comb her hair with long sweeps of her arm. 'I had such need of you then, but I could not even send you a message because I did not know where you were.'

'I've already said I'm sorry.' His face was fixed.

Cicely thought of Mackillin escorting her brother all the way home from Bruges because he had made a promise to her dying father. 'You could have come yourself.'

He walked over to the window and gazed out. 'I was about the king's business, so it was out of the question. I am sorry about your father's death. I was fond of him despite our differences.'

'Thank you.' She softened towards him. 'It grieves me that you could not have made up your quarrel before he died.'

'So do I, but it's too late now for regrets.' Diccon turned and gazed at her. 'I will make it up to you. When you hear my news and what the king has promised me, you will understand.'

'You mentioned the king before. I don't understand, I thought you were against King Henry.'

Diccon smiled. 'Not Henry, silly, but the real king. King Edward the Fourth.'

She frowned. 'Henry *is* the real king.'

Diccon shook his head. 'No longer, Cissie. Listen to what I have to say and you will be convinced by the rightness of his cause.'

She had no desire to hear about the conflict between York and Lancaster, was hurt that he had so quickly moved on from what was a tragedy in her life to the Yorkists' cause. 'Go on.' Her voice was cool.

He did not appear to notice, but instead seemed to be gazing into the distance, almost as if she was not there. 'Since Edward received the news of his father's and brother's deaths, he has been rallying men along the Welsh Marches. He was intent on joining forces with the Earl of Warwick to defend London from the queen's host when he learnt of a great army of Lancastrians to his rear in Wales.' Diccon paused as if for effect.

She resumed combing her hair. 'So who was victorious?'

Diccon ignored the question, but said in a hushed voice, 'Before the battle Edward received a sign from God.'

Her eyes narrowed. 'A sign from God?'

'Aye. That's what I said. Don't interrupt, Cissie.' He smiled as if to soften his rebuke. 'Three suns rising through the early morning mist. Edward took it for a good omen, saying that his father had left three sons, Edward, George and Richard, and God was telling him they would be victorious. What do you think of that?'

'I presume he won the battle.' She began to braid her hair.

Diccon's eyes shone. 'Edward achieved a great victory at Mortimer's Cross and afterwards declared himself King of England.'

Cicely was astounded. 'He has dared to go that far?'

'Aye. I am convinced that God will give him complete victory.' He took a deep breath. 'I must be there in his company throughout the coming conflicts. He has promised me a knighthood and a manor of my own when he is crowned in London. I am on my way now to rejoin his host.' He came back over to her and said seriously, 'You must not fear for me. I will return, I am certain of it. It is my destiny.'

Cicely could not think what to say in the light of his conviction, but one thing was for sure—she was no longer willing to sit at home and wait for his return, whenever that might be. If that was so, was it purely because she no longer loved him as a sweetheart? 'I pray you are right. Tell me, why did you come here if you intend rejoining Edward's host so soon?'

He grimaced. 'I received a slight wound and sought Kate's ministrations. Also, I wanted my family to know that I wasn't following a hopeless dream. I only wish your father could have lived to see Edward's star and mine in the ascendant.'

Cicely could understand his reasoning, but his

words still saddened her. Their marrying and living at Milburn was just a dream. Her father had been more perceptive than she had given him credit for when he had refused his permission for their betrothal. 'I also wish it, but it is too late now.' All the time they had been talking, she had been braiding her hair and now tied a plait off with a black riband. 'Anyway, you need not concern yourself about mine and the twins' safety. We've had a protector, Mackillin. You might remember him.'

Diccon swore under his breath and then begged her pardon. 'I remember him, all right. He owned a ship and Nat had known him since he was a youth. A reckless type, but a good man to have by your side in a fight.'

Cicely smiled. 'I would agree. I was glad of his sword when my kinsmen would have slain my family and acquiesced in my abduction from Milburn.'

Diccon gaped at her. 'You jest! How did that come about?'

'It is too long a tale to tell.'

Diccon frowned. 'Have you questioned what Mackillin's intentions are in helping you? Perhaps he has an eye to your dowry. I suggest you be on your guard in his company. Your father told me that he is a younger son, and just like me he has to make his own way in the world.'

Cicely almost told him the truth about Mackillin

being the new lord of Killin, but instead she kissed Diccon's cheek; a chaste kiss, a sisterly kiss. 'You must not worry about me. I can take care of myself. You must follow your own star, as you've just said—it's your destiny. I wish you God speed and that all goes well with you.'

'I sense a rebuke in those words, but I will not take you up on them now.' He drew her close and hugged her. 'Forgive me for leaving you so soon, but I must find Kate and ask her forgiveness.'

She nodded, knowing for certain now where her heart lay, but what good it would do her, she could only hazard a guess.

As Diccon opened the door, Mackillin slipped inside a nearby chamber and waited until he had passed. He hated the notion that during the silences in the snatches of conversation he had heard, Diccon and Cicely might have been locked in a passionate embrace. The depth and strength of his feelings said much and he was unsure what to do about them. Once Diccon had passed, he stepped out of the chamber and was about to return to his bedchamber when the other door opened again and Cicely stepped into the passage.

Cicely felt the blood rush to her cheeks at the sight of Mackillin and, involuntarily, her eyes lowered their gaze to his bare chest and the curling hairs that ran in a V to the waist of his hose. She did not allow her eyes to linger on the bulge below, but hastily lifted them to the scar beneath his collarbone. She wanted to touch it, press her lips against it. She had to shake her head to rid herself of the notion.

'What are you doing here, my lord?' she asked. 'Are you lost?'

Mackillin had had a few seconds to come up with an answer, but doubted it would sound convincing. 'I had no drying cloth—hearing footsteps, I thought it was the wench bringing one. I was correct in that, but then I saw the back of a man and I had it in mind that he could be an enemy, so I followed him.'

Her brows knit. 'You did not recognise him?'

'I told you I was behind him.' Mackillin did not know why he was so reluctant to admit having suspected the man's identity.

'Why did you not knock on this door when you followed him here?' She rat-tatted on the wood behind her.

'You did not scream.'

'But you saw him enter this bedchamber.' The colour in her cheeks deepened. 'I hope you did not think…'

'That you had a lover?'

She gasped. 'What kind of woman do you think

I am? The man was Diccon Fletcher, my step-brother. There was no need for you to concern yourself for my safety.'

'Does that mean Master Fletcher will escort you to Rowan Manor and then home to Yorkshire?' asked Mackillin, a mocking light in his hazel eyes. 'Somehow I do not believe that is likely.'

She realised then that most likely he had overheard part of her conversation with Diccon. 'Eavesdroppers, Lord Mackillin, are despicable,' she said with icy disdain.

'I would not always agree with you there,' he said smoothly. 'Now if you will excuse me, I'll go and finish my toilet.' Without another word he turned and left her.

She gazed after him, wondering what he had made of the conversation between herself and Diccon. Obviously he knew that she could not depend on her stepbrother to protect her. Cicely remembered how she had been almost dizzy with delight two years ago when Diccon had smiled at her as if he was seeing her for the first time. Now she only longed for Mackillin's kisses. Was she fickle or was it as she now believed—that the nature of her love for Diccon was not that of a woman for a man? But did he still wish to marry her? He was no longer passionate about her, that was for certain.

Not for the first time she wondered why her father

had offered her to Mackillin. Had his knowledge of his lordship been such that he had believed him to be the right husband for her? She remembered her first sight of Mackillin and how she had called him a barbarian. He had looked so wild that she had been scared of him at first. Yet still his touch had thrilled her. Then she had discovered he was not a savage at all. She came to a decision. She needed to pray for God's will and his guidance for the three of them.

Cicely entered the hall to see Kate playing with her children. As she watched her stepsister lift her younger son into her arms and smile down at the elder, Gareth, who was tooting on a wooden whistle, she felt affection for them all.

'She has two fine lads and a lass who will break men's hearts one day,' said Mackillin from behind her. Cicely whirled round to face him, thinking he must have moved fast and dressed quickly, to be here so soon. She saw admiration and some other emotion flame in his hazel eyes. 'I know your father thought the same of you when you were a child,' he added.

'He spoke often of me to you?' she asked.

'He was very fond of you and always wanted what was best for your happiness and safety. That was why he would not take you on his travels. The life of a merchant venturer can be a dangerous one as you must know.'

She nodded, adding, 'But one can die in one's home. A fall down the stairs, a broken neck.' She shrugged. 'I would rather he had allowed me to take that risk.' Before Mackillin could comment on her remarks, Cicely's stepniece came skipping up to her.

Mackillin watched as she spoke to the girl. A fierce ache made itself felt in the region of his heart and he wondered what it would have been like between himself and Cissie if they had met in happier circumstances. He imagined them being introduced at a feast where there was dancing. Maybe a wedding at his kinsman's house in France, where they could have laughed and sang and there was no possibility of them being parted, never to see the other again. He knew then what kind of future he wanted, but needed to give it more thought.

Cicely glanced at him and was surprised at the yearning she saw in his face. 'Do you like children, Mackillin?' she asked.

'Aye.' For a moment in his mind's eye he could imagine the begetting of such children with her and felt a hot melting sensation in the pit of his stomach.

'You'll want sons,' she murmured, as if to herself.

'And daughters,' he said, wanting to bury himself into her. It was amazing how the dark blue of the gown seemed to have altered the blue of her eyes, so that they appeared mysteriously deep like twin pools that a man could drown himself in.

For her part, Cicely was considering how wondrously fulfilling it would be to bear Mackillin's children and raise them together to be courageous and caring of others, to have fun with them and to show them so many wonderful things in life. A wistful sigh escaped her.

'What is it? What are you thinking of?' he asked, wondering if she was thinking of Diccon Fletcher.

She knew that she could scarcely tell the truth, so when her eyes rested on Gareth, she said, 'About children and music. Do you like music, Mackillin?'

He was not convinced she was telling him the exact truth, but decided to go along with her chosen subject matter. 'I deem we have spoken a little about music before,' he drawled.

'Aye!' Her eyes danced. 'When Jack unpacked the lute for Anna. What a pity I did not think of bringing it with me. She lives at Rowan Manor and we could have brightened her day with such a gift.'

'It is indeed a pity.'

'What about singing?'

He grinned, showing even teeth. 'I'm certainly not a man to inflict punishment on folk for whom I have a fondness. I would like to hear you sing, though. You have a pretty voice.'

She laughed. 'If you flatter me much more, I might just begin to believe you.'

'Believe me when I say that you are beautiful,' he said rashly.

His admiring stare brought a flush to her cheeks and she stared at him with her lips slightly parted. He wanted to kiss her. If they had been alone, he damn well would have kissed her. But what was he thinking of? He needed to consider carefully the pros and cons of a marriage between them. Nat might have considered it an excellent notion, but then he had not known about his being the Mackillin before he had died. He needed to see Cicely safely to Rowan Manor before making any decision.

Chapter Nine

'Can't I go to Rowan, Mama?' asked Gareth, his dark hair so like his father's.

They were standing outside in the stable yard.

'Nay, love. They must make haste,' said Kate briskly. 'Later in spring, we will all go to Yorkshire. Will that not be a treat?'

Gareth beamed up at Cicely. 'Aye. When the twins are together they play japes and make me laugh.'

'Then God willing we will see you soon,' said Cicely and kissed him.

She accepted the stable lad's help into the saddle and watched as Jack mounted a gelding from the ap Rowans' stable. Both beasts waited patiently for Mackillin as he came across the yard, leading his horse. He caught Cicely's gaze, but had no smile for her; rather his expression was dour. Her spirits plummeted. Was he already regretting the compliments he had paid her last evening and the enjoyment spent with Kate and her children? Not only had they played music and sang, but Mackillin had told then such interesting tales of his travels in Egypt that he had held them spellbound. He had also been patient with Gareth when the lad had begged him to draw pictures of a camel and a pyramid. Now it seemed he had put all that aside. She wondered if he was thinking of Diccon and whether he had heard her and Kate discussing him. She watched him thank Kate for her hospitality and then he swung himself up into the saddle. She wondered if he was wishing himself already in Scotland.

But returning to Scotland was far from Mackillin's thoughts. His mind was concentrated on what he should do once he reached Rowan Manor. Should he speak to its master about Nat's dying words and what he knew of Diccon's plans? Seeing Cicely in the company of Kate and her children, he had questioned whether she could be happy living in the Scottish Border country far away from her home and family.

They all raised a hand in farewell and Jack led the way out of the yard towards the road that would take them to Liverpool. They would have to stay the night in the port and in the morning cross the Mersey on the ferry—for which they would have to pay a toll to the priory at Birkenhead on the other side. Cicely and Mackillin were not alone in having decisions to make; Jack also was pondering on his future since hearing all the news about Diccon. He was convinced more than ever that he was not the right husband for his sister. Since hearing his father's dying words, Jack had been convinced that his own future was linked with Mackillin's and that of his sister. He would have to be blind not to be aware of the yearning in Cicely's and Mackillin's eyes when they did not realise they were being watched. If either did not speak to Owain about Nat's dying wish, then he would do so himself. He felt that the happiness of all of them was dependant on it.

The journey passed without aught of note happening.

The following day when Rowan Manor came into view, the sun was reflecting off its windows and turning its sandstone walls a warm shade of dusky pink. Two men stood in conversation at the entrance to the stable yard. Thankfully, Cicely recognised Owain and his youngest brother, Hal, and called out to them. Their heads turned and, after the barest start of surprise, both men hastened towards them.

Cicely glanced at Mackillin and murmured, 'The

dark-haired man is Owain and the younger one with flaxen hair is his brother, Hal.'

Mackillin nodded, vaguely recognising Owain ap Rowan. He was relieved to find him at home and now made himself known. 'I'm Lord Rory Mackillin, Master ap Rowan. I don't know if you remember me but I, too, was a friend of Nat Milburn.'

Owain shot him a swift estimating look before his gaze passed on to the black-clad Jack and returned to the sombrely gowned Cicely. 'You say *was*—does this mean what I have feared and my dear friend is dead?'

Cicely felt the tears prick the back of her eyes. 'Aye. Your fears have substance. Father is dead.'

He reached up a hand and covered the one she held out to him with his long, strong fingers. 'I'm so sorry, Cissie. I have been uneasy since receiving no courier from Nat in the last three months. What happened to him?'

It was Jack who replied. 'He was murdered in Bruges by one of our northern kinsmen. If it had not been for Mackillin, I would have perished, too.' He dismounted swiftly and added purely for Owain's ears, 'He saved my life and Father offered him Cicely's hand in marriage as a reward. He has refused, but I think they have a growing attachment to each other.'

Owain did not appear as startled as Jack might have expected, but rested a hand on the youth's shoulder and murmured, 'Calm yourself. I will deal with this matter.'

Owain's expression was grave as he looked up at Mackillin. 'I recall seeing you in Nat's company in Calais when we were both much younger. You were no lord then.'

'That is true.' Mackillin dismounted and held out a hand to Owain. 'These are sad times, Master ap Rowan. We are all in need of your counsel.'

A flicker of surprise passed over Owain's face. 'I will do all that is in my power to help you.'

He turned to his brother, who was assisting Cicely to dismount. 'Hal, if you and Jack could see to the horses? But first make your bow to Lord Mackillin.'

Hal nodded, inclined his head in his lordship's direction and then, with a wink at Cicely, excused himself.

She turned to Owain, wondering what Jack had said to him, but was too polite to ask. Instead she enquired after his housekeeper. 'Is Mistress Carver within?'

He smiled warmly at her. 'Aye. You go on ahead and inform her that we have company. She is to prepare bedchambers for the three of you. Hal and Jack can bring the baggage in later. I must just have a word with Lord Mackillin.'

She thanked him, thinking that no doubt Owain would want more details of her father's death. She climbed the steps into the hall. Inside all was hustle and bustle. Obviously preparations were being made for the evening meal. Cicely's eyes scanned the hall and she saw a veiled grey-haired woman bending down and scolding an auburn-haired girl of some eight summers. Instantly she recognised the housekeeper and Owain's half-sister, Anna, and hurried over to them. 'Mrs Carver!' she called.

The woman turned and stared at her in amazement. 'Mistress Cicely, I did not look to see you here until later in the year.'

Cicely returned the regard of the woman who had served the ap Rowans since Owain was a small boy. 'I know you weren't expecting us but I am here with sad news. My father is dead.'

The housekeeper looked dismayed. 'Oh, my dear, I am so sorry. He was such a kind and generous man and will be sadly missed by the master and mistress.'

'It is, indeed, a grave loss for us all. Fortunately, we have good friends. One such is Lord Mackillin, who is with us and is to stay the night. The master said you are to prepare a suitable bedchamber for his lordship. I presume I will stay in the usual guest chamber I have when here?'

'Aye, mistress. A lord, you say?' She pursed her

lips. 'I know the very chamber for him. Sir Thomas Stanley slept there when last he visited with us.'

Cicely smiled. 'Of course, you aren't the least put out at entertaining a lord. Owain has done business with lords and earls for many a year, due to his belonging to one of the most successful horse-breeding families in the country.'

'That is true. I will see to it immediately.'

Cicely thanked her. Noticing that Anna had gone over to the fireplace, she followed her over. The girl gave her a penetrating stare from vivid green eyes. 'I remember you. Are you not Kate's stepsister?'

'I am.' Cicely held out her hands to the fire and smiled down at her.

'You have twin brothers.'

Cicely agreed that was indeed true. 'Jack is with me.'

Anna's dimpled face lit up. 'I would not know which one is Jack because your brothers are alike as peas in a pod. If only one of them had an interesting scar on his face or a strawberry mark on the back of a hand, then I could tell the difference between them.'

'That would be helpful,' said Cicely. 'I remember thinking when they were born that Mother should tie different-coloured ribands about their ankle or wrist.'

'Not in their hair, though.' Anna's eyes danced.

'At least I know that the one I speak to today is Jack. Where is he?'

'Helping Hal stable the horses.'

Anna's smile faded. 'Hal makes me cross. He speaks of my mother in a way that is not proper, saying that she was a witch.'

Cicely recalled snatches of conversation that she had overheard between her stepmother and Kate. 'That is, indeed, wrong of him. Have you spoken to Owain about this?'

'Aye, and he tells Hal that he should not speak ill of the dead and that there are no such persons as witches.'

'Then you must take notice of what Owain says.'

Anna pulled a droll face. 'I do. Yet a part of me wishes there were witches and I was one so I could cast a spell on Hal and turn him into a toad.'

Cicely laughed. 'That is not kind.'

'What is this about witches and toads?' asked a voice behind them.

Cicely whirled round and saw Mackillin and Owain standing there. She smiled. 'If you heard enough to mention witches and toads, then I think you know. I suggest that Anna goes in search of Jack. He will have more interesting tales to tell her so that she will forget witches and toads. He has visited many interesting places since last he was here.'

Anna's eyes lit up. 'I will go immediately in search of him. It can be so dull here during the winter, especially when the children are at Merebury.' With a wave of her hand, she skipped from the hall.

'An interesting girl,' said Cicely, gazing at the two men as they drew closer to the fire. She doubted that they would have had any time yet to discuss her father's death and its consequences at any length.

Owain grimaced. 'She's a handful, just like her mother. Do you have any sisters, Mackillin?'

'No. And I felt the lack when Jack rebuked me for scolding him for following after Mistress Cicely a few days ago,' he said ruefully. 'He has courage, but a streak of recklessness when it comes to feeling the need to save his sister from her own folly.'

Cicely said indignantly, 'I think I've admitted already that I was foolish in setting out alone—you don't have to remind me of it again, my lord.'

'That wasn't my intention.' He smiled warmly down at her. 'I was just confessing my own lack of a brother's need to protect a sister.'

'I, too, never had a sister, but Anna's mother was for a while as one to me and my brothers and I felt that need,' said Owain.

'So Anna's mother was…your…'

'Stepmother.' Owain's voice was terse. 'Her

parents died when she was only young and when she was old enough to realise that there was no relationship between us at all, she decided to marry my father.'

Mackillin apologised for being so inquisitive. 'I did not mean…'

Owain forced a smile. 'It is of no matter. But I'm sure you found out for yourself that when a parent marries more than once and there are children from two different mothers or fathers involved it can cause problems.'

'Aye,' agreed Mackillin heavily.

The two men moved away so that Cicely could hear only the murmur of their voices. She so wanted it to be true that it was as Kate had said and Mackillin was fighting his feelings for her. But there was no chance of her discovering if that was true and he was speaking of it to Owain. She drew closer to the fire and as the heat from the burning logs penetrated her clothing and warmed her chilled body, she mulled over the events of the last few days. She realised that, despite the discomfort of travel, she had gained so much from spending time in Mackillin's company. If sadly naught else came from their relationship, she knew that she would always be glad that she had met him.

It was at that point in her deliberations she became

aware of a pungent odour and realised with horror that the smell was coming from her black gown. A smouldering brand had dropped from the fire and set her skirt alight. Swiftly she patted it out with her gloved hands and then stared in dismay at the ruined fabric. It was easy for her to imagine what the men would say if they knew how careless she had been for her safety by standing too close to the fire. Without delay she must go in search of Mistress Carver to borrow another gown. She hurried from the hall, scarcely aware of the two men's eyes upon her. She found the housekeeper in one of the bedchambers and told her what had happened. 'Is there a dark-coloured gown anywhere that I could borrow?'

The housekeeper looked pensive and then gave a sharp nod. 'Right at the end of the passage where your bedchamber is, there's a small room that seldom gets used. Inside there's a chest full of clothes that have been discarded. I'm certain that the gown worn by Mistress Anna's mother after the old master died is still in there.'

Cicely thanked her. Then, following the housekeeper's instructions, she found both the room and the chest. When she lifted the lid a strong smell of lavender assailed her nostrils and she saw that the chest was brimming with clothes. She put down the candleholder and began to drag them out so she could have a proper look at them. As she did so, lavender bags scattered on to the floor. Amongst the essentially feminine garments, there were also hose, breeches, leather jerkins, shirts, surcoat and hats. All too small now, she deemed, for the ap Rowan brothers, of which there were three. She wondered why they had not given them away. Maybe it was simply because the clothes had been forgotten about. At last she found what she was looking for and held the black gown against her; the length was perfect. She fingered the fabric and decided that Anna's mother must have had expensive tastes. It was normally only the nobility that wore velvet.

Placing the gown on a chair, she piled all the other garments back inside the chest. Then, picking up the garment and the candle, she left the room.

Mackillin was wondering why Cicely had hurried from the hall. Was she annoyed with him for what he had said earlier? At least he knew she was not being ogled by that bold-eyed brother of his host. He scowled at the memory.

'Perhaps you'd like to tell me the details of Nat's murder whilst your bedchamber is being prepared, your lordship,' said Owain, interrupting his guest's reverie.

'Call me Mackillin,' he said, following his host

over to the fireplace where a covered pan now stood on the hearth.

Owain wasted no time filling two tankards from the pan. He handed one to Mackillin and waved him to a carved oak chair with a seat cushion that stood close to the fire. He waited until he was seated before sitting down opposite him. 'Your good health, Mackillin.'

The spicy smell of nutmeg and cinnamon filled his lordship's nostrils. 'And yours, ap Rowan.' Mackillin took a deep draught of the mulled ale. It was a good brew and he decided he was not going to drink it in haste, but savour the flavour. Cradling the tankard in his strong hands, he began his tale.

'As Jack said, it happened in Bruges. Nat was unaware that I had recently learnt that my father and half-brothers had been killed, that I had inherited the title and my mother wanted me home. She's English, a Percy, and it was to her family I was sent after one of my half-brothers tried to kill me in my youth. For this reason alone I knew my inheriting the title would not be popular with some of my Scottish neighbours. Raids over the border are still common despite England and Scotland supposedly living in peace, but raids between neighbours also can be frequent at times.' He paused to quaff a mouthful of ale. 'I need allies and I decided to marry a Mistress Mary Armstrong, a biddable maid, whom I have known a long time.'

Owain's expression was thoughtful. 'I presume you have a good reason for telling me all of this?'

Mackillin nodded. 'I'm so eager to explain to you the reasoning behind my thinking that perhaps I have started on the wrong foot.'

Owain said, 'Tell me now about Nat's murder.'

Mackillin nodded and began the story with when he had heard the cry for help and how he had found Nat fatally wounded on the ground whilst Jack was hard pressed trying to defend himself from the attack of two assassins, whilst a third seemed bent on robbing the dying man. He spoke of Nat offering him Cicely as a reward for his accompanying Jack home.

Owain's blue eyes were intent on Mackillin's frowning face. 'And what was your answer?'

'I refused. I did not need a reward for helping a dying friend.' His brows knitted and he tapped a fingernail against the tankard. 'But I had not seen Cicely then and now…'

'You have changed your mind?'

Mackillin nodded.

Owain was quiet a moment, but then said, 'Tell me the rest.'

So Mackillin brought Owain completely up to date with all that had happened to the twins and Cicely since the time he had arrived at Milburn Manor. There was a pause after he had finished and then Owain leaned forward and said in a low voice, aware of the servants bustling around them. 'Do you believe she has formed an attachment to you? If so, then you must speak to Cissie of your change of heart.'

'No. Not yet,' Mackillin said firmly. 'I do believe she is not indifferent to me, but I cannot risk her life by taking her to Scotland with me. I must make Killin as safe as I can before I speak of my feelings.'

Owain frowned. 'I understand your reasoning. But what if she believes you do not care enough for her? Does she already know of your intention to take a Scottish bride?'

'Jack knows and—I might have mentioned it to her,' he said with a grimace.

'Then you can only blame yourself if, believing you do not want her and Diccon survives the battle that lies ahead then, she does something foolish out of desperation and runs away with him.'

'I have thought of that, but I consider Cissie a lass of good sense—most of the time.' He smiled faintly.

Owain raised an eyebrow, but did not ask Mackillin to elucidate further. 'I can tell you that Nat spoke of the pair of you to me. He wanted to help you some more after you repaid the loan he forwarded to you to buy your ship and the house in Kirkcudbright.'

'It is true I do not like being in any man's debt,

but I am not completely without funds these days, Master ap Rowan.'

Owain smiled. 'I am glad to hear of this. As you must know by now, Nat was deeply concerned for Cissie once her stepmother died. He was not happy about her infatuation with my brother-in-law and truly believed you and his only daughter could be happy together. Cissie has a goodly sum of money for a dowry, which could be of great use to you despite any funds you might have.'

'I would not marry her for her money,' protested Mackillin, putting down his tankard, so that ale splashed onto the hearth.

'I am glad you feel like that, but you must allow her to feel that she is of great worth to you. You are a lord and she is a merchant's daughter—there are those who would regard your marrying her as beneath you.'

Mackillin agreed. 'My mother is a proud woman, but she will accept my decision or leave my house.'

'Then I must leave it to you to make the next move when you are ready,' said Owain. 'I do stand guardian to Nat's children now he is dead. I also have a copy of his will, as did the older Husthwaite. This nephew of his most likely saw it and so will know I hold that position.' He topped up their tankards. 'If you are not prepared to marry Cissie just yet, then I will go with her and Jack to Milburn

Manor and sort matters out there. I will take armed men with me, so you need not fear for their safety.'

Mackillin thanked him.

Owain hesitated. 'Does Mary Armstrong's family have any expectations of your marrying her?'

'Aye. Mary lodges with my mother while her father answers the king of Scotland's summons to help free Henry of England.'

'I presume you were also summoned?'

'I was, but I am still undecided about whether I should answer the summons. I do not wish to disobey my king but I have made no vow of allegiance to him. Also, I feel I have no part to play in the dispute between the Houses of Lancaster and York.'

Owain was about to explain to him why it was important to Scotland that its fighting men support King Henry when a slight cough caused them both to look up.

Mistress Carver smiled at them both. 'I beg pardon for interrupting your conversation. My lord, your bedchamber is prepared and hot water made ready for you to wash.'

Mackillin's craggy face lit up and he placed his empty tankard on the hearth and rose to his feet. 'If you will excuse me, ap Rowan, I would not have this good wife's labours wasted by allowing the water to cool.'

'Of course not, Mackillin. You go ahead. I will speak to you later,' said Owain.

His lordship picked up his pack and followed the housekeeper upstairs.

The conversation at the supper table between the adults was desultory; most of the talking was left to Anna, who was prattling on to Jack about music and horses and how she wished she could go with him next time he sailed to the Continent. Cicely was hard put to speak at all, unable to stop thinking about being parted from Mackillin. She avoided looking in his direction and so had to accept the attentions of Hal, who sat beside her and whispered nonsense in her ear. As the wine loosened his tongue even further, he burst into song with lines about a swain worshipping the ground his love walked on, and likening Cicely's eyes to the blue sky and her lips to cherries. It was a relief when Owain told him to stop his caterwauling. Hal adopted an injured expression and gave his attention to the food set before him.

As it was, both Cicely and Mackillin found the rest of the conversation enlightening. Owain told them that even if the Lancastrians were to win the forthcoming battle and King Henry was freed, some doubted if he was fit to rule. 'The Stanleys' spies say that many more men are rallying to Edward's banner as they truly believe he has as much right to the throne of England as Henry's heir. That is why the queen has asked for aid from Scotland. It is rumoured that the seven-year-old Prince of Wales and a sister of King James are to be betrothed.'

Cicely and Mackillin exchanged swift glances. 'So there could be an alliance between Scotland and England at last,' said his lordship, his rugged features lighting up. 'Now that is something worth fighting for. Lasting peace between our countries is long overdue. Perhaps I should have second thoughts about my king's command,' he muttered. 'It could bring peace to the borders of our two countries.'

Owain stared at him hard. 'It will only happen if the Lancastrians rescue the king. The Stanleys and their adherents will head south-east through the heart of England where they have kin and there are many Lancastrian supporters. They will meet up with the queen and her Scottish allies either close to Stoke or Northampton. If you are of a mind to obey your king's summons after all, then I will write down directions for you, Mackillin. I'll also provide you with a better mount than the one you have in appreciation of what you did for Nat and his family.'

'That's generous of you,' said Mackillin, taken aback.

'So was the service you performed,' said Owain gravely.

Cicely did not like what she was hearing and her stomach churned with dread. What if Mackillin was killed in the battle? She could not bear the thought. She remembered a tournament she had attended in Knaresborough and the manner of the weapons wielded to inflict injury on one's opponent; they were truly horrific. Would there be physicians nearby to tend the wounded in the coming battle? She had no notion of this, remembering only that Diccon had come to Kate to have his wound tended. Who would look after Mackillin if he was hurt? It was one of a woman's tasks to have knowledge of simples and herbal medicine, so she could care for the various ailments and common injuries that happened in a family. If only she could be of help to Mackillin if the need arose.

Yet she had no doubt that he would say that the battlefield was no place for a woman. She stilled her racing thoughts and listened intently to the conversation between Owain and Mackillin about towns and people and the likelihood of the place where the battle would happen; a plan began to form in her mind.

Not long after, Cicely excused herself, claiming to be exhausted and in need of her bed. It was not far from the truth. With a heavily beating heart, she gazed across the table at Mackillin and knew she had to sound convincing when she bid him farewell. 'I pray that God will grant you a safe journey and deliverance from the conflict ahead, Mackillin, if you should decide to go and fight.' She could scarcely control the tremor in her voice.

He rose to his feet and could do no more than reach for her hand and lift it to his lips. 'I appreciate your prayers. No doubt I will be gone before you rise in the morning. May our Saviour keep you in His care.' He pressed another kiss on her wrist before reluctantly releasing her hand.

Cicely echoed his words before turning and hurrying from the hall. Once upstairs, she went to the bedchamber containing the chest of clothes and removed several garments from its depths. Then she returned to her bedchamber.

Hours later she did not know what it was that started her awake, but she was grateful for whatever reason because the room was filling with the pearly light of dawn. She climbed out of bed and dressed in a set of the youth's clothes she had taken from the chest and concealed her hair beneath a hat. She picked up her saddlebag and her bow and quiver and left the bedchamber.

Once downstairs she made her way to the kitchen and was relieved to find that the cook was not yet up and making bread for the day ahead. She found some food in the pantry and wrapped it in a napkin and then she quit the house and made her way to the stables. It was getting lighter by the minute, so she wasted no time saddling her horse and mounting. Then she turned its head towards the path that led to the highway and urged the beast into a trot. She had no idea how long the wait might be before Mackillin set out on his journey, but she knew the perfect place to conceal herself until he passed by; then she would follow him.

Chapter Ten

He was being followed. Mackillin had spent too many years in places where his life had depended on his being alert to danger from drunken sailors, footpads and his own kin not to be aware of it. At first he'd thought it could be Husthwaite, knowing that he was aware that Owain ap Rowan was Cicely's and the twins' guardian now, and had traced him to the manor near Chester. But he had seen no sign of the man, only having noticed a youth in Uttoxeter, whom he remembered catching sight of in Stoke and Nantwich. He did not consider the lad a threat in himself because he certainly couldn't equal Mackillin if it came to a fight; but it was possible he could be another man's spy. Perhaps he should slow his pace and let the rider on his tail catch up with him, then he could ask where he was bound.

But to Mackillin's annoyance the youth had overtaken him at speed when he had slowed down and had soon vanished in the distance. Despite this Mackillin did not drop his guard, considering the lad might have just gone on ahead to lay a trap for him. Even so, he relaxed enough to think of Cicely and wish that he had thought to ask of her some small token to take into battle with him; a kerchief or hair ribbon on which her scent lingered. It would make him feel close to her, just a breath away. He rode for a while, planning how the future he desired for both of them could come about.

Suddenly he was roused from his reverie by an altercation on the road ahead. A cart had overturned and crockery lay scattered on the ground. Some had not broken and a boy was intent on picking up platters and bowls and cups. Two men were in heated debate whilst a woman and youth bent over a horse that lay on the ground. Some wayfarers had stopped to watch what was going on, whilst others skirted the obstacle presented by the horse and cart and hurried on by. Mackillin noticed a horse cropping the grass beside the road and gave the youth a keen scrutiny.

Convinced this was no trap, he dismounted and went over to where the woman and youth hovered by the horse. He saw that the horse was little more than skin and bone and had breathed its last. He caught the words 'knacker's yard in Leicester' and asked if there was aught he could do to help.

The woman stared up at him with fear in her eyes and shook her head. The youth darted him a look from beneath the rolled brim of his hat and mumbled, 'I've offered her a lift into Leicester, my lord. Yous be on your way, thankin' yer kindly.'

Mackillin had seen enough of the lad's face to give him pause for thought, but he nodded and strode back to the stallion that Owain had gifted him and swung up into the saddle. He was convinced the youth was the one who had been tailing him and also felt there was something vaguely familiar about him. At the moment he could not remember why that should be, but was certain he would remember sooner or later. He determined to keep a watch out for him in Leicester.

Cicely eased aching shoulders and wished she could turn off the woman's chatter; it appeared she was not only upset by the death of the horse but also Mackillin's appearance on the scene. She had spoken of a great army marching down the old road, bringing with them wild men from Scotland. She had seen several for herself with their rude bare legs and long tangled hair and beards. She had heard them speak in a like tongue similar to the one who had spoken to her earlier and feared there were more of them to come. It was rumoured they were performing unspeakable acts as they advanced and she was terrified of being raped and having her throat cut.

Cicely could have assured her that she was perfectly safe from such violation at the hands of Mackillin, but she had barely recovered herself from that brief encounter with him. Fortunately he seemed not to have recognised her and that gave her hope. She had no doubt that she would be able to track him down in Leicester on this second evening of the journey south.

The sun had disappeared by the time they entered Leicester and the woman asked to be set down in the market square. At Cicely's request, she directed her to the nearest inn. After tying up her horse outside, Cicely entered the building but, to her dismay, the host could only offer her a place in a communal sleeping chamber. As it was getting dark, and she felt too weary to go looking elsewhere, she paid her money and went outside to tend to her horse.

She was in the act of untying her beast to take it to the stables when a hand grasped her shoulder and a voice said, 'You've been following me, laddie, and I want to know why.'

Cicely dropped the reins in fright as she was spun round. She told herself to keep calm and lowered her eyes to the ground after a swift look at

Mackillin's stern features. 'I don't know what you mean, my lord,' she said in a gruff voice.

'I noticed back on the road you called me *lord.* Why give me that title, unless you know who I am?'

'You—you've the bearing of a lord,' she said with inspiration, remembering to deepen her voice and not look at him.

He laughed. 'You speak false. You know who I am. Is it that you are a younger member of the Milburns' kin up north? Have you been ordered to follow me and report back to your elders concerning my movements? Well, I'll soon put an end to your game by taking you to the sheriff,' he threatened.

As his grip tightened on her shoulder, she cried, 'Take heed and unhand me. You talk like a Scotsman and he'd throw you into the dungeons and leave you there to rot if you were to do that.'

He looked amused. 'You dare to threaten me, lad?'

'Aye,' she replied boldly. 'Anyway, you're mistaken, my lord, I'm not whom you think I am.'

At the change in the pitch of his captive's voice Mackillin's hazel eyes blazed. 'It's not possible. You can't be…'

She heard him catch his breath and her heart quickened its beat as he seized her chin and tilted up her face. Fixed by his shocked gaze, she felt the colour rise in her cheeks, but remained silent.

'Cissie!' he hissed. 'Why are you dressed as a lad? What are you doing here? Do you not know that two women were once arrested in Durham for dressing in male garb? They could shave your head and dress you in sackcloth and parade you through the streets.'

'You're trying to frighten me,' she said in a trembling voice.

'You're damn well right I am.' He glowered at her. 'I don't suppose ap Rowan knows you've followed me?'

'Of course he doesn't! Like you he would have prevented me from doing so.'

'Then who does know? Jack?'

'And have him risk his life following after us?' said Cicely indignantly, brushing aside his hand. 'I care for him more than you think.'

Mackillin almost exploded. 'You little fool! Did it not occur to you that you were putting your own life in danger?' He seized her by the shoulders and shook her, dislodging her hat so that her braids uncoiled and fell down her back.

'Now, see what you have done!' she exclaimed, horrified in case anyone else might have penetrated her disguise. Wrenching herself free, she picked up her hat and quickly shoved her hair back inside it.

She looked about her and noticed two men across the street. Thankfully they appeared not to have noticed what happened. Then a shutter banged above them and she glanced up, but could not see anyone. 'Thank the Trinity that no one saw me,' she muttered.

Mackillin took hold of her a little less forcibly and brought her close to him. 'You don't mean to persist in this role of a boy? It's not seemly,' he said in a sibilant whisper.

'Who is to know but you and I?' she questioned softly. 'You're not going to tell anyone, are you? As you've said in the past, I can hardly travel about on my own as a woman.'

He counted to ten and reined in his anger. 'Don't you care that ap Rowan might think I've abducted you?'

She laughed shortly and then her eyes hardened. 'Why should he believe that when it must be obvious to him that your thoughts are purely on doing your king's will? He would know that you wouldn't risk my life by taking me with you.'

He felt a need to count to ten once more. 'You always have an answer! Well, I will not allow you to travel any further south. In the morning, I'll find a respectable married couple to accompany you north,' he said firmly.

Dismayed, she stepped back and eyed him from

top to toe. 'No! You can't. Besides, no respectable couple would pass the time of day with you. One look would be enough for them to go running for the sheriff.'

His scowl deepened and he brought his face close to hers. 'That's as maybe, my pretty boy,' he growled. 'But I tell you now that, even if I have to tie you up, I will keep you out of trouble.'

She paled. 'Bind me, then. But where do you intend leaving me while you go on with your journey? Will you toss me up in a hayloft in the stables and forget about me?'

A gleam of amusement lit his eyes. 'Now that's a fine notion. Trouble is that I can't forget you. I'd have to pay someone to feed and water you and I haven't that much coin on me.'

She smiled. 'That is a shame. I do believe we've reached stalemate, my lord.'

'We have indeed, but I have a question to ask of you. Why have you followed me?'

She shrugged and her fine eyes wore a serious expression. 'I cannot tell you. You would consider me more foolish than no doubt you already do.'

He had a sudden terrible thought that perhaps she was following him because she believed he would lead her to the battlefield where she would find Diccon Fletcher. 'You're right. The battlefield is no place for a woman,' he said harshly. 'You will return home. Do you hear me?'

She was chilled by the coldness of his demeanour.

'I hear you, my lord. Now, if you'll permit?' she said tartly, tilting her chin. 'I need to stable my horse.'

He grabbed her by the arm. 'I'm not letting you out of my sight.'

Her eyes flashed blue fire. 'You'll have to because there are certain matters a woman needs to attend to without the presence of a man. I have that need now.'

He released her. 'I'll see to your horse. You do what you must and I will join you inside. Tomorrow, you return north.'

She did not speak, but watched him lead her horse away before going inside the inn. There was no way she would do what he ordered. He was not her keeper. She would ask the innkeeper for bread and cheese and then seek her pallet in the chamber upstairs so she did not have to speak to him. Then she would decide what to do later. God willing Mackillin would not be sleeping in the same chamber as herself. In case he was, she must conceal herself completely.

Mackillin was annoyed and worried when he returned to find no sign of Cicely downstairs. He described her youthful appearance to the innkeeper, but received a suspicious look so said no more and walked away. Not knowing which room she was in meant that he could not go barging into all of them in search of her and drag her out. The mood she was in, God only knew what she might do. So he ate his supper and then went up to the communal sleeping chamber. There were several people already there, but all appeared to be asleep. He was of a mind to inspect each one, but after being firmly rounded on by a man with a bushy black beard, he decided to wait until morning as a couple of other sleepers had complained about the noise. He stretched himself on his pallet as close to the door as he could get and determined to stay awake all night if need be. If Cicely tried to sneak out of the building so as to avoid him, then he would surely hear her.

So he lay there listening to every creak, murmur, snore, the patter of tiny feet in the thatch overhead, as well as the occasional footfall. He thought of Cicely dressed as a boy and by then had calmed down enough to reluctantly admit that she had some spirit. With such a lass at his side, what couldn't they face together? He imagined her in his arms, then drifted into slumber.

Mackillin started awake. What hour was it? He gazed about the room and heard a man shifting in his sleep. Then there came a cough and a snore. He lay down again, but the screech of a bolt being drawn below was loud enough in the silence to cause him to rise from his pallet. He rolled up his bedding and placed it in his saddlebag, then crossed the short distance to the door and opened it. He caught the sound of footsteps below. Perhaps it was the innkeeper, but maybe it was Cicely? Deciding he could take no chances, he headed for the stairs.

The moon was a silver discus in the pearly sky when Cicely hurried across the cobbled yard and into the stable. She wasted no time saddling up her horse and leading it over to a mounting block. Soon she was out in the street and riding for the road south. So intent was she on looking for a place to conceal herself until Mackillin came by that at first she did not hear the drumming of hooves to her rear. The moment she became aware that there was a rider or riders behind her, she left the road. It might not be Mackillin and even if it was, she did not want him catching up with her yet again.

She rode through the undergrowth to the trees a short distance away, determined to stay in hiding until whoever it was had passed. Despite the rising sun it was cold waiting there, so she pulled her hat further down over her ears and drew her cloak closer about her. A rider came into view and she reeled with shock as she recognised a man that she had hoped never to see again.

To her horror he left the road and appeared to be heading straight towards her. What was Husthwaite doing here? How had he known where to find her? No time to give more thought to such questions. Her heart thudded in her chest as she reached for her bow. Then, to her amazement, he dismounted. She watched him take something from his saddlebag and do something with it before moving stealthily through the undergrowth nearer to the road. She realised that he could not have seen her. It was then she heard the sound of another rider approaching. The next moment Mackillin came into view. Instantly Cicely realised what her enemy was about and she rode from out of the trees, removing an arrow from its quiver as she did so.

Mackillin's head turned in her direction. At the same time Husthwaite raised his weapon and there was a bang. The noise so startled her horse that she had difficulty controlling it and dropped the arrow. Then everything seemed to happen fast. She saw Husthwaite coming towards her with a murderous expression on his face and a dagger in his hand. Then there was the thundering of hooves and she saw Mackillin riding towards them. The man must have suddenly realised what was happening because he flung the dagger at her before swerving and running for the trees. The dagger glanced harmlessly off her gloved hand. She caught sight of Husthwaite's terrified face and then Mackillin passed her, but was too late to rein in his horse. The stallion trampled the man beneath its hooves.

She stared aghast at the scene, but then Mackillin managed to pull back his horse and calm it. They dismounted almost simultaneously and hurried over to where Husthwaite lay. It was obvious that he was fatally wounded, but his eyes were still open and he was mouthing curses upon them.

'How did you know where to find me?' demanded Mackillin.

Husthwaite did not answer, but panted, 'You'll rue the day you interfered in my plans. My—my accomplices know…you—you are heading south. You….will…die a horrible…death.' His head fell back and for several seconds there was no sound but the wind in the trees.

Mackillin stood up and looked across at Cicely. Her face was ashen, but she stood as straight as a rod. 'Who do you think he meant by his accomplices? Other members of my kin?' she asked.

'Possibly. Do you think he recognised you?'

Cicely shrugged. 'I thought at first he had done so, but it was you he was intent on killing. What was that weapon he aimed at you? The bang frightened my horse and drew his attention to me.'

Mackillin's relief on finding her safe was taking its toll on his emotions. 'He could have killed you, little fool, but as it is you saved my life!' he snapped. 'I only wish you'd stayed at the inn and waited for me.'

She fixed him with a faint smile. 'If I'd done that, then he might have killed one or the other of us. As it is, I've proved my usefulness and I will not be sent back home.'

There was a baffled expression in his eyes. 'I've never met a lass like you. I hate it that you put your life in danger.'

She warmed to his words. 'Then allow me to ride with you,' she pleaded. 'I am not the only one prepared to put their life in danger.'

He took off his hat and ran a hand through his hair. 'The battlefield is no place for a woman, Cissie. You might want to find Diccon, but you will see such horrors that it will turn your stomach and cause you to swoon. You, yourself, could be killed.'

She supposed that she should not have been surprised by his mention of Diccon. 'You're mistaken. Remember the time you vanquished one of my kinsmen at Milburn?'

'That has naught to do with this. I admire your bravery, but I cannot allow you to endanger your life further, Cissie,' he said earnestly.

She was disappointed by his words and felt a

lump rise in her throat. She looked away quickly, then thought to search for the arrow she had dropped. An idea occurred to her. 'Do you not think that it could be just as dangerous for me to return north whilst an army is on the march than to continue south? There are bound to be deserters with plunder heading back north. If you will not allow me to go to the battlefield, then at least let me go with you as close to it as I can?'

Her words gave him cause for thought. Most Scotsmen didn't like to travel far from their homeland into enemy territory. With the queen having given them leave to plunder the Yorkist lands, most likely it was as Cicely said and some were heading home, having filled their packs with booty.

'All right,' he said abruptly. 'I will allow that, but you must do exactly what I tell you when the time comes for us to part.'

Relieved that that was not to be just yet, Cicely agreed.

Mackillin was vexed that she should have put him in such a difficult position, and his tone was more curt than he intended when next he spoke. 'Let's be on our way. The sooner King Henry is free, the sooner we can all go home.' He did not immediately mount his horse, but walked back the way he had come. Suddenly he bent down, then straightened with a weapon in his hand.

'What is it?' asked Cicely, walking over to him.

Mackillin smiled. 'I suspected it was a hackbut and I was right. It shoots lead shot as well as arrows. I wager there's a bag of shot in his saddlebag.'

'So that's what caused the bang. It looks fearsome.' She gazed at the weapon, noticing its trigger.

'Aye,' he said grimly, wondering where Husthwaite had come by such a weapon. 'Could prove useful, though. If I had time, I'd show you how to use it.' He placed it in one of the saddlebags and then searched those belonging to Husthwaite and removed that which he had hoped to find.

'What do we do with his body?' asked Cicely, watching him stow away the bag of shot. 'However much I despise him, I do not feel it is right to leave him here for the wild animals and birds to pick his bones.'

Mackillin glanced to where Husthwaite's horse tore at a patch of grass; although touching the man was distasteful to him, he hoisted the body on to the back of the horse and tied it there. Then he whacked the animal's rump and sent it on its way, wishing he could have squeezed some information out of Husthwaite before he had died. It would have been useful to know how he had known where to find them and glean information about his accomplices. Too late now. He would just have to be even more on his guard.

Mackillin helped Cicely into the saddle and then mounted his own steed and headed for the road. He deemed it was going to be a difficult journey. They were both silent as they rode further south. Cicely would have liked to hold back time so she could keep him with her longer, but Mackillin now wanted to rush ahead and have the battle behind him. He was so determined to live that he refused to contemplate his own death.

Once past Northampton, they discovered the forces of Lancashire were well ahead of them; also from the same peddler they learnt that the Yorkist forces led by the Earl of Warwick were camped in the vicinity of St Albans. A penny gained Mackillin the further information that the earl was fortifying his position with ditches, barricades and nets sewn with nails that could cripple and bring down the horses of the enemy.

'What of the young Edward of York—have you heard aught of his host heading this way?' enquired Cicely.

The peddler shook his head. 'No sign of him. It's rumoured that he and his army are still a good number of leagues away to the west the other side of the Cotswolds.'

Cicely glanced at Mackillin. 'Does that mean his army will not be in time to fight in the coming battle, you think?'

He shrugged broad shoulders and turned back to the peddler. 'You mentioned the Lancastrians—where exactly did you see them?'

'Marching towards Dunstable.'

'How far is that?' asked Cicely.

The man shrugged and Mackillin handed him a groat. 'I doubt you'll get there before nightfall, sirs,' he said. Nevertheless, when asked directions, he set them on the right road.

Mackillin made the decision to part from Cicely at Dunstable. When they came to the town, it was to discover that the queen's forces had wiped out the small Yorkist garrison and, having left a small detachment of Lancastrians in the town, the rest of the army had departed, intent on marching through the night to surprise the Yorkists at St Albans.

'Then I must do the same,' said Mackillin, after they parted from the soldier who had given them that information. 'You will stay here, Cissie, and await my coming. I doubt Diccon will be numbered amongst Warwick's army.'

She agreed, wanting to say that she didn't give a groat for Diccon, but that was not true. She loved him like a brother, but Mackillin in the fashion of a woman caring for her lover. The muscles of her face quivered as she tried to control her emotions and she reached up a hand and touched Mackillin. 'You will promise me you will take care?'

He was touched by her words and impulsively drew her into his embrace. 'Aye, I promise. And you must give me your word to not be foolish.'

She had no intention of doing what he asked, but instead said, 'There you go again, calling me a fool, my lord.'

'Forgive me,' he said hoarsely and kissed her.

Afterwards she wondered what it was she was supposed to forgive him. He was about to leave the stable when she stayed him with a hand. 'Wait!'

He stared at her, watching as she lifted the long chain that held the crucifix that had been her mother's from about her neck. 'Wear this and may it protect you.'

As he took the precious gift from her there was a brightness in his hazel eyes. He placed the chain about his neck so that the crucifix hung beneath his clothing against his skin. Then he took both her hands and kissed her fingers.

'Fare thee well, sweet Cissie, until we meet again.'

'Aye, till we meet again,' she whispered.

He climbed on to his stallion and she went to the entrance of the stable with him and stood watching until he disappeared in the moonlight. She felt a few flakes of snow land on her cheek and hoped they were not the forerunners of a blizzard, then she returned to her horse. She needed to consider her next step. There was no doubt in her mind that

Mackillin was right in saying the battlefield was no place for a woman; even so she could not spend the days to come anxiously waiting to know if he was alive or not. She would rest awhile here in the straw, close to her horse, then she would ride for St Albans and pray God she would have the courage to go where the fighting was and do what she could to help the injured whilst at the same time looking out for Mackillin.

She had thought sleep would evade her, but, physically and emotionally exhausted, she went out like a snuffed candle.

She woke to the sound of a voice and realised it was coming from the other side of the partition dividing her horse's stall from the next. She got up and saw a figure dressed in a woollen brown habit and a large brimmed hat. Man or woman, it was leading a horse out of the building.

'Where are you going to at this time of night?' asked Cicely, rubbing the sleep from her eyes.

The figure started and turned and looked at her. 'It'll soon be morning and battle will be joined,' it said in a squeaky voice. 'You're not from hereabouts, young master. Are you one of them?'

'I'm not with the armies, if that's what you mean,' said Cicely, following out the old person, 'so there's no need to fear me.'

'Am's not scared. The Saviour looks after His own. I'm off to tend the wounded and dying. It's the task He's given me to pay penance for my many sins.'

Cicely now saw that there was a wagon outside and watched in astonishment as the aged figure backed the horse between the shafts. She had an idea. 'May I come with you?' she asked.

'For what purpose?'

'To assist you in tending the wounded. Will you be allowed on the battlefield?' queried Cicely.

'They'll be too busy trying to kill each other to stop me. So either join me now or get out of my way, young master. I have work to do.'

Cicely went back inside the stable and took up her saddlebag and bow and quiver of arrows before eventually leading out her horse. 'I've visited the sick and helped my stepmother tend the injured on my father's manor in the past,' she said conversationally, 'so hopefully I will be of some help to you.'

The ancient nodded. 'Let's pray so. Although they would not have been the kind of injuries sustained in battle, hacking, slashing, stabbing and cutting. Fighting is a bloody business, young master.'

Cicely quailed at the images the words conjured up, but she stiffened her backbone. 'If there's any man we can save, I can help lift him into the wagon if he needs carting somewhere else.'

'Agreed. Now, let's not waste any more time. Climb up beside me and let's be on our way.'

Cicely tied her horse to the back of the wagon and then sat beside her newfound companion. She wondered if Mackillin had already reached St Albans and was preparing for battle. She realised that the pace the wagon would travel could mean that by the time they arrived in the town, he could already be fighting for his life. She felt a deep sense of urgency and prayed that he would survive.

It was getting dark and there appeared to be few men about as Cicely rode past tents flapping in the biting wind. She had yet to find Mackillin and felt sick at heart, scared stiff that he might be dead. The clashing of weapons and the screams and shouts of men came to her on the wind, so, despite the pain in her arm, where an arrow had whistled through her sleeve grazing her skin, she gave her horse its head. The ancient hung on behind her.

The wagon had lost a wheel and they'd had to leave it behind. Cicely had thought her companion would have given up when that happened and been satisfied with what they'd done to help those dying in the streets of St Albans, where there'd been hand-to-hand fighting, but she, for it turned out that strange figure in the stables was a woman, had refused to do so. Cicely had barely been able to control her tears as they had attempted to ease the pain of the battle's victims, whilst thinking all the time that Mackillin could be suffering in like manner. But to find him when there was so much confusion was difficult and there were so many in need of their care. All she could do was to hold him constantly in her prayers; that she had done whilst tending the suffering. The groans and screams of the dying still echoed in her ears, but there were holy men and women tending them now, so she had come in search of Mackillin because the Lancastrians had won the battle in the town.

'There, there! See, see!' The crone pointed a scrawny arm in the direction of a ridge.

The slopes were dotted with fleeing men, pursued by horsemen. As the two women drew closer, they could make out some men still fighting. It was then Cicely spotted Mackillin. If he'd ever been given a helmet, then he had lost it for he was bare-headed. Also he was on foot, involved in close combat, so she could only presume that his horse had been killed from under him. Her heart was in her mouth as she watched the two men slogging it out with sword and axe. Then she saw Mackillin give what proved to be the decisive blow to his enemy because the man fell. Only then did she cry out Mackillin's name.

He looked up in the gathering gloom and could scarcely believe his eyes when he saw Cicely. He watched as she brought a leg over the horse's neck and slid to the ground, only for her legs to buckle. He swore and hurried over to her and dragged her upright.

'Can't you ever do as you're told?' he rasped, shaking her.

'I had to come,' she said in a tremulous voice, clinging to his arm. 'I told you once before I'd had enough of waiting.'

He ran a hand over his bloodied and dirty face. 'I have seen no sign of Diccon. I presume Edward's forces did not arrive, so there was no need for you to worry about him.'

'I wasn't worrying about him. It was you I was concerned about.'

For a moment they stared at each other and then he smiled. 'The battle is as good as over and I deem the Lancastrians are the victors on this field. Shall we go?'

'You mean it really is over? I can stop worrying?' There was a tremor in her voice.

'I certainly hope so.' A sense of euphoria overrode the common emotions he always felt after a fight, but he kept it under control and said in a mild tone, 'Let's away from here. The stallion ap Rowan gave me is dead and I grieve its passing, but he fought well and no doubt saved my life many a time.' Mackillin wiped his bloodstained sword on the grass and then put it away. 'You disobeyed me. I don't know what Master ap Rowan and your brothers are going to say about this. I can only hope for the sake of the future we might have that none of them believes I encouraged you.'

She was tempted to ask, What future is that? But at that moment the ancient shrilled, 'Help me down and then you can be gone.'

They both looked up at the old person who held out her arms. Mackillin rolled his eyes in Cicely's direction before obeying the crone's summons and lifting her from the horse. She shooed them away and bent over the man on the ground.

Cicely hesitated. 'I should help her.'

Mackillin drew her away and growled, 'No. You have done enough. This time obey me, Cissie.'

After the scenes of suffering she had seen that day, she did as he said. As he helped her up on to the horse, she winced.

'What is it?' he asked anxiously. 'Are you hurt?'

'It's but a graze,' she answered, biting her lip.

He glowered at her. 'I knew you shouldn't have come. I'll have a look at it as soon as I can.'

He retrieved his saddlebags and threw them over the horse and climbed up behind her. He took the reins in one hand and held her with the other. She leaned back against the wall of his chest with a great sigh of relief as he urged the horse into a walk. The battle was over and she thanked God and St George that they had both survived.

Chapter Eleven

Cicely could see flaming torches flickering ahead in the gloom.

'Did any of the men from Killin join the fight?' she asked.

'I found a small number and they told me that others of their company had deserted a day or so ago.' She sensed rather than saw his frown.

'You hold yourself responsible for not being with them?'

'Aye. Although that's not to say they would have pledged me their loyalty,' replied Mackillin frankly. 'Most do not know me well and my half-brothers would not have painted me in bright colours.'

'So you're likely to have trouble with them as well as your enemies when you return to Scotland?' asked Cicely.

He shrugged. 'Who is to say? There are men here who will vouch for my bravery—but let us forget such matters for now.' His arm tightened about her waist and he breathed in her familiar scent; he felt warmed by the feel of the softness of her body against his and exulted that they were together. In that moment he wanted only to find a place where they could be alone, rest and enjoy each other's company. He shut an ear to that inner voice that warned that temptation lay in that direction. After such an arduous day that had brought victory to the Lancastrians, he felt a need to celebrate in some way.

They came to the next field where the tents were pitched. In the short time since Cicely had traversed the ground it was now filling with men. In the torchlight she noticed a woman and a small boy surrounded by several men in plate armour. The lady was of stately bearing and wore a gold circlet on her head.

'She must be the queen,' whispered Cicely, glancing up into Mackillin's weary face.

Almost as if she had heard her words, the lady looked in their direction and there was a questioning expression on her face. Suddenly Cicely remembered the garb she wore and instantly sat up and ensured that there was now a gap between her body and that of Mackillin. She felt him withdraw his arm and knew that he had made the same error of forgetting she was dressed in the guise of a youth. It would not do for her Majesty to guess that she was a woman.

The queen said something in an aside in French to one of the men beside her and he turned and addressed Mackillin. 'Who are you and who is this youth?'

He thought swiftly and answered in French. 'I am Lord Rory Mackillin and this is my young cousin. He has fought bravely and was wounded in the fight. I need lodgings where I can tend his wound.'

The queen's face lit up. 'You speak my language well, Lord Mackillin. Dismount, I would speak with you.'

He obeyed and bowed before her. 'It is an honour to meet your Majesty.'

She inclined her head. 'I have heard of you. Your kinsman, our Earl of Northumberland, spoke of your having spent time in Angers at my father's court.'

Mackillin straightened and smiled. 'Aye. We conversed on all manner of subjects. He is a noble ruler.'

Her hard eyes gleamed. 'We must talk more of this. In the meantime lodgings will be found for you in the town. It is possible I can make use of you.'

Mackillin did not like the sound of that, but said politely, 'I am at your service.'

'C'est bien!' She offered him her hand to kiss. He touched it lightly with his lips and then stepped back and bowed again. She turned to those about

her and spoke in fractured English. 'Lord Mackillin will be treated with all courtesy. Lodgings must be found for him and his kinsman in the town.'

She turned away as a man in plate armour came hurrying towards her. He bowed and, given leave to speak, said in English, 'Majesty, Warwick has fled and we have found the king.'

Queen Margaret's hand fluttered to her breast and a delighted smile lit her face. 'Take us to him.'

The queen, her son and her retinue hurried away, leaving only one man behind. He turned to his lordship and said, 'Meet me at the entrance to the abbey in an hour's time and I will tell you where your lodgings will be situated. There will be plenty of room in the town now the Yorkist traitors have fled.' He did not wait for a response from Mackillin, but went rushing after the queen.

'So the king is recovered and his army is victorious, so we can go home on the morrow,' said Cicely, relieved.

Mackillin frowned. 'The queen thinks she can make use of me. I might have to stay a little longer.'

Cicely felt a sinking at her heart, remembering their conversation at Merebury about the danger of involving oneself in the affairs of royalty. 'So that is what she said when the pair of you spoke in French?'

He nodded and took hold of the horse's reins and

stroked its nose. 'I told her that you were my cousin and had fought bravely in the battle.'

'A *male* cousin, I presume?' she muttered, longing to rid herself of male attire, now it had served its purpose, but now she could see no way of doing so until she left the town. The thought appalled her.

'I left it to her to make that presumption,' he said softly.

'Did you give me a name?' Her tone was tart. She was beginning to feel light-headed with hunger, thirst and exhaustion; also her wounded arm throbbed.

'It was not necessary but if you are to continue as a youth then we'll have to choose one for you.' He grimaced, moving away from the animal's head, and suggested that she move into pillion position.

She raised her eyebrows and shifted backwards on the horse. 'Perhaps I will take my father's name,' she suggested.

Mackillin thought about that as he climbed into the saddle. 'I'm sure he'd be proud of your doing so. I have wondered why neither of the twins were named for him.'

'There was a boy born before me called Nathaniel, but he died in infancy.' She gripped the back of his belt as he set the horse in motion.

'Well, Nathaniel,' murmured Mackillin, 'as long

as no one suspects your true identity, you should escape notice if those enemies Husthwaite mentioned are in the vicinity. But perhaps I should send a courier to Owain ap Rowan to inform him that you are safe and give him news of the battle.'

She felt a sinking of her spirits, knowing that Owain had every right to be furious with her. 'You will send one of your men?'

'Aye.' He wondered if she should accompany him but decided to ignore that voice of common sense, wanting to have her with him for a little while longer before he returned to Scotland and sorted out his affairs. 'In the meantime let us forget Lancaster and York and think of food and wine and taking our ease,' said Mackillin, staring ahead through the dusk now they were away from the lights of the torches and riding towards the town.

Cicely had no argument with what he said and her spirits, which had drooped before at the thought of facing Owain, now soared. She, too, wanted to forget the horrors of the day.

Mackillin placed the baggage in the corner of the bedchamber and gazed about him. 'It's not as sumptuous as the guest chamber at Milburn Manor, but even so…'

'They've done you proud, my lord,' said Cicely, gratified but also apprehensive and excited as she gazed about the room that the queen's administrator had informed them was at his lordship's disposal. The house was of a decent size but they were having to share it with several knights. Candlelight gleamed on the shining oak of the chest, armoire and that of the bedposts, as well as the surface of the water in an enormous tub—the previous owner of the house must have been an extremely large man. She wondered who had ordered that to be filled and told herself that no wonder her emotions were in turmoil.

'The task the queen has for you must be one of importance. Perhaps dangerous, even?' she murmured in an attempt to take her mind off the bed. Were they expected to share that as well?

'The queen mightn't have any real purpose in mind,' said Mackillin, removing clean garments from his saddlebag, as well as the hackbut and the bag of lead shot he had taken from Husthwaite's saddlebag. 'She might have been feeling generous because I mentioned talking to her father whilst in France.'

'I see.' A thought occurred to Cicely as she, too, removed a change of clothing from her own baggage. 'You say that the battlefield is not the place for a woman and yet the queen was there amongst her captains.'

'But she did not take part in the fighting, but

watched at a distance. Queen Margaret might be a determined and desperate woman, but she does not take up arms herself. Even so, she is a dangerous woman and I would have you out of here if I suspected your disguise was penetrated. A lass disguised as a lad is not an act that queen or king would countenance, so both of us must needs be careful when in company,' he warned.

'Yet there are women who wear breeches when out riding,' said Cicely with a tilt of the chin. 'I am certain Father told me that Henry II's wife, Queen Eleanor of Aquitaine, did so.'

He said mildly, 'I wonder what other stories Nat has told you, although I must admit that my mother has done so when necessary.'

'Of course,' murmured Cicely, 'a queen and a lady can escape stricture that a merchant's daughter will not.'

His face softened as he saw the concern his words had roused. 'You must not worry. It should be simple enough to slip away from here if need be. For now let's put aside all thought of danger and think only of taking our ease.' His gaze shifted to the tub.

Cicely felt the colour rise in her cheeks. 'You—you will bathe?'

His smile was quizzical. 'Aye, lass. But I'm much dirtier than you and it will take me longer to get out of this mail shirt than it will for you to remove your garments. At least I don't have plate armour, which would require Robbie's help if he was here. You use the water first.'

She murmured her thanks whilst wondering where exactly she should undress. There was no screen behind which to conceal herself. Her gaze took in the damasked blue-and-green curtains that hung around the bed. Perhaps she could hide herself behind them? Yet how foolish was that thought if she was to make use of the tub? What did he expect of her? Could she ask him to turn his back? Her stomach rumbled—she had eaten only a crust that day—and she wondered if she could refuse to bathe and just wash her hands and face in the water. Surely an evening meal would be served soon. Yet how wonderful it would be to slip into the tub and feel the water's heat soothing her aching body.

Suddenly she remembered that in her saddlebag was a jar of soft soap that she had made the previous autumn. She removed it, glanced at Mackillin and saw with relief that he had his back to her. She placed the jar on one of the drying cloths on a nearby stool and suddenly felt a pain shoot up her arm and gasped.

He turned immediately and said with concern, 'Is it your arm? Does it hurt? You must allow me to tend it.' He had removed the old-fashioned chain mail and stood before her in a padded jupon and hose.

She caught the gleam of the silver chain holding her crucifix and was pleased that he wore it next to his skin. 'I'm all right. It was the other arm that hurt. Probably with using it so much to lift the wounded.'

He frowned. 'You should not have been performing such tasks. Do you need help to undress? Should I send for a serving woman?'

Cicely promptly said, 'Now that would be foolish if we are to keep my real identity secret.'

A groan escaped him and he put a hand to his head. 'How right you are, Cissie. Stupid of me. Then there is only myself to offer you assistance.' He stared at her.

She was lost for words, but then the warmth in his eyes reassured her somewhat and her trepidation drained away, although she still felt shy at the thought of his seeing her in a state of undress.

'You permit?' he asked.

She nodded, her heart increased its beat and she felt slightly breathless as he began to unbutton her surcoat. Perhaps she should try to enjoy the experience of not having to make the effort to undress herself. He eased the garment from her shoulders before relieving her of doublet and shirt. She had to admit it was pleasant to have someone's assistance when one was feeling weary. She stood before him in her chemise which was tucked into a pair of breeches. He took her left arm and inspected the bloodied graze on the skin and frowned. 'It looks nasty. You should have had that ancient tend it immediately.'

Cicely said sadly, 'There were many men in far worse straits than I. The water will clean it and I have a jar of salve in my saddlebag.'

'Then into the water with you.' He lifted her off her feet and up into his arms.

She clung to him, aware of his tremendous strength. 'What are you doing, my lord? Not only do I not wish to be dropped into the water from a great height, but I will dirty it if I go in wearing these breeches.'

'I admit they are filthy,' he agreed with a wry smile, lowering her to the floor.

She said awkwardly, 'Perhaps you'd like to turn your back whilst I…'

'If that's what you wish, sweet lass, I will do what you say.' He turned from her to place another log on the fire and hoped she realised how difficult this situation was for him. He would have liked to have whipped the breeches from her and made love to her.

Swiftly she disposed of the brown woollen breeches, but kept on her chemise and lowered herself into the water after opening the jar of soap. She kept her eyes on his lordship's back whilst she washed herself. Then she immersed herself up to her neck in the warm water and closed her eyes. It was bliss and she felt as if she was drifting on a sea of warm contentment.

There came a splash and it was as if she was being lifted on a wave. A voice whispered against her ear. 'Perhaps you'd like me to wash your back? If so, I suggest you remove *this*.' She was aware of a tug on her chemise and, gasping, roused herself. She clutched a wet fold of the fabric and, forcing her eyes open, saw a pair of muscular thighs and weatherbeaten knees enclosing her hips and legs as if in an embrace. For a moment she could not believe what she was feeling and seeing. Mackillin was in the tub with her! She let out a shriek.

'Don't be afeared, lass,' he said soothingly. 'You looked so restful that I didn't want to disturb you, but time is passing and I needed to bathe.'

'But you are disturbing me,' she retorted, clinging to her chemise. 'I will get out and you can have the tub to yourself.'

'Not just yet,' said Mackillin. Having given way to his baser instincts, he intended going a little further. Pushing her wet hair out of the way, he tickled the nape of her neck with his tongue.

She found it so delightful that she almost did not demure. 'You should not do that,' she murmured.

'You can't be comfortable in this wet chemise,' he said, kissing her ear.

She swallowed. 'I—I did not mind it until y-you drew my attention to it.'

'And now?' he said, turning her head slightly so that he could look into her face and watch her expression.

'I'm aware that it's clammy and…' She lowered her eyes, realising that perhaps those words were encouraging him to believe that she wanted him to remove it.

'You'd be better rid of it?' he asked, his eyes twinkling in such a way that she decided to fight him no longer.

'I'm not answering that,' she said on a tiny laugh, but released her hold on the fabric.

He lifted the wet garment over her head and dropped it at their feet. Drawing her against him, he cupped her breasts in his strong hands and freed a contented sigh. She was utterly confounded and thrilled at the same time by an even more delightful sense of pleasure. Something firm brushed against the secret place between the top of her thighs and she started up instantly in shock. Was he completely naked, too? Dear Mother of God, how did she ever confess this to the priest? But then all thought of confession and conviction of mortal sin went out of her head as his fingers caressed her nipples. She moaned and rubbed herself against him. She felt something jerk upright beneath her.

'You're playing with fire, my sweet honey,' he said with a hoarse laugh.

'But I did not do anything. You are to blame, Mackillin. Anyhow, I didn't know one could create fire in water.' Her voice was breathless. To have such power over him made her suddenly feel marvellous and she was tempted to behave recklessly. Seizing hold of the sides of the tub she swooshed in the water, laughing as she did so. He laughed with her, kneading her breasts before teasing her nipples with fingers that were surprisingly sensitive, rousing that melting sensation in her loins again. He pressed hard up against her and gasped in her ear. 'Do you realise if we carry on like this I will not be able to resist you—is that what you want?'

It had been such fun and she had not wanted to stop, but now… 'Why did you have to ask me? Why?' she asked, almost savagely.

'Because you once called me a barbarian and I would not force you against your will.' He was astounded that she did not understand his reasoning. 'I am no saint, but I have never forced a woman. I've been fond of several, but never wished—' He stopped abruptly because he had been about to say *to possess and share my life with any but you.* Why had he had to remember that he had to make Killin safe for her before he could take her as his wife?

'What do you wish?' she asked, confused by his silence and sudden lack of movement.

'I cannot tell you,' he muttered, disentangling his legs from beneath hers.

Her disappointment burst like a bubble inside her. 'You deem I'm a wanton,' she cried. 'I should not have allowed myself to forget that you need a Scottish bride. I know that you desire me, but I should not have encouraged you to surrender to that desire.'

'Don't blame yourself,' he growled. 'I needed little encouragement. The trouble is that you're too damned comely to resist. Especially after the rigors of the last few days.'

She turned and knelt between his hunched legs. Water dripped from her hair and breasts as she gazed into his unshaven face. 'What are we to do?'

The water dripped on his naked chest and for a moment he could not speak and then he managed to say, 'Get out of this tub for a start.'

She nodded and stood up. For an instant she loomed over him. The breath caught in his throat as he viewed her from that position and then she climbed out of the tub. He watched her dry herself and then take a jar of salve from her saddlebag and spread some on her grazed arm, managing by using her teeth to fasten a strip of cloth round it. He took a deep breath and ducked his head beneath the water, thinking a cold dip in a river would have been more appropriate to cool his ardour at that moment.

A knock sounded at the door and a voice informed them that supper would be served within the hour. He began to wash himself and was out of the tub in time to see Cicely pulling on a clean pair of breeches. 'Don't forget,' she said in a cool voice. 'I am your cousin Nathaniel.'

'So d'you think we'll begin the march on London tomorrow, Lord Mackillin?' asked the young knight, seated across the table from Mackillin and Cicely.

'I don't know the minds of your king and queen or those of their captains,' answered Mackillin, dipping his greasy fingers in a fingerbowl.

'I doubt it will be on the morrow,' growled a burly man a couple of feet away. 'The sensible move would be for the king and queen to head for London and get safely behind the walls of the Tower before it's too late. The citizens will have heard of our Scottish allies' deeds and be trembling in their beds.'

Cicely glanced at Mackillin and remembered the first time she had set eyes on him and called him a barbarian. He had proved he was not and now she was wishing that she could ride with him to the Border as his wife.

'You consider it a possibility that the citizens of London will close their gates to its king and queen because of your allies?' said his lordship.

The older man hesitated. 'There are many Yorkist supporters inside the capital. Trade has suffered for years and it's said that the young Edward of York has sympathy with the merchants of the city and would bring stability to the country.'

There was a silence as the servants arrived to clear away the plates. A sweet cheese flan was served next with a full-bodied tawny wine. When conversation was resumed it was no longer of London and what the royal couple's plans might be, but was about armaments. Mackillin told them about the hackbut he had upstairs and the men showed an interest that Cicely did not feel. She offered to go upstairs and fetch it, thinking after she had done so that she would excuse herself and go to bed.

The tub had been removed and someone had placed more wood on the fire and there was a truckle bed a few feet from the larger bed. Most likely a servant had put it there—at least it answered the question she had asked herself earlier. She took the hackbut and bag of shot downstairs and then returned to the bedchamber.

Despite her weariness she felt restless and filled with a sense of foreboding. Instead of undressing and getting into bed, she stood a while, thinking of Husthwaite and his dying words. She wondered whether to suggest to Mackillin that she left here and went with his courier back up north in the morning. There seemed little point in extending the agony and temptation of being in his company when there was no future for them together.

As she slowly undressed, she considered how to frame the words, so they would sound right. The most sensible thing to do was never to see each other again, but she had trouble putting that suggestion into words.

Wearing just a shirt, she slid between the cold sheets of thc truckle bed and turned on her side to gaze at the fire. She blanked out all thought and her eyelids began to droop and soon she was asleep.

Not half an hour later, Mackillin opened the door and slipped inside the bedchamber before closing it quietly behind him and locking it. He placed the hackbut and bag of shot on a chair, then noticed the truckle bed and Cicely's humped shape and frowned. In the past he'd often slept on one and knew that when it came to comfort they left a lot to be desired.

He whispered her name, but there was no

response. Removing his shoes, he padded over to the bed and gazed down at the delicate features of her slumbering face. His mouth eased into a tender smile. He had been right to allow himself to be drawn into further conversation with their supper companions. He brushed her forehead with his lips before undressing down to his shirt. For a moment he clutched the crucifix she had given him and then he removed it and placed it on the chest. He pulled back the bedcovers before returning to the truckle bed and bending down. He slid his arms beneath her and lifted her up with the covers and all and carried her over to the larger bed. She stirred in his arms, but did not wake even when he placed her down and covered her with an extra blanket. Then he removed a couple of the blankets, and closing the bed curtains, went over to the truckle bed and lay down. He turned on his side and thought about those moments in the tub and what he needed to do. Then, weary with all that had taken place that day, he fell asleep.

Mackillin drew back the curtain and bent over the bed. Cicely stirred and opened her eyes. She pressed her eyelids tightly together and then forced them wide. 'You're safe. I was having a dream.' Suddenly she realised where she was and sat up. 'How did I come to be here?'

'I carried you. I thought you'd be more comfortable.'

She glanced at the other pillow, but saw no indention on it and said accusingly, 'You slept on the truckle bed, my lord?'

He nodded and smiled. 'What were you dreaming?'

She did not answer him, only saying, 'Why? You're so large. You must have been cramped.'

'It's of no importance.' He moved away to fetch her clothes and place them on the bed. 'Get dressed. I need to find out what plans are afoot and whether the queen and her captains will march on London today. Tell me, how is your arm this morning?'

'It still hurts a little, but it could be worse.'

He looked concerned. 'Can you manage to dress?'

She nodded. He moved away and she reached for the clothes she had taken from the chest at Rowan Manor and began to dress. It was as she was putting on her boots that she noticed her crucifix on the chest. She looked up at him. 'You're not wearing it?'

'It's yours and you must wear it now.' He picked up the crucifix and placed it about her neck, unable to resist kissing her nape. 'There, it's back where it belongs.'

She darted him a questioning look. When he was

silent and turned away, her fingers strayed to where his lips had touched her skin. She felt tears prick her eyes and blinked them back and said, 'I was thinking that perhaps—'

He looked over his shoulder and now his expression was dour and her heart sank. 'Later you can tell me your thoughts. Now let us break our fast.' Without another word he opened the door and led the way downstairs.

She'd hoped to speak of her plan over the breakfast table but, since they were not alone, this would have to wait. After the meal was over, he insisted on her accompanying him in his search for news. As they walked around the town, he stopped and spoke to several people. She was aware of curious eyes upon them and one man in particular stared at them both with anger in his eyes and whispered to his companion. Cicely pointed him out to Mackillin and was informed that the two men were Armstrongs and, if he was not mistaken, one was the father of Mary Armstrong, who was keeping his mother company at Killin.

'I'm surprised he did not come across and speak to you,' said Cicely, wondering about this Mary. She glanced towards the abbey where the two men lingered.

'It's of no importance,' said Mackillin shortly and

suggested that they return to the house for the midday meal.

It was then that the opportunity rose for her to bring up the matter of her returning north with his courier. She was flabbergasted when he calmly told her that he had already sent a courier to not only Milburn Manor but Merebury as well before she had got out of bed that morning.

'But it would have suited me fine to go straight home,' she said, further taken aback. 'Why could you not have roused me earlier and I would have gone with him?'

He glanced at the others sitting at the table and frowned her down. 'It suits me that you stay with me for now,' he said in a low voice.

'But why?' she whispered.

He took a deep draught from his cup of ale and then said in her ear. 'Think, lass. You might be dressed as a lad, but if the courier was to discover your true identity I cannot vouch for your safety.'

Her cheeks reddened. She had not considered this when she had come up with the notion of travelling in a stranger's company. Indeed, there had been times that day when she had completely forgotten the role she was playing. After begging his pardon she fell silent, wondering whether Mackillin had asked Owain to send someone to accompany her home.

* * *

By late afternoon Mackillin was still in the dark about the exact whereabouts of Edward of York and his army with presumably Diccon in its ranks, but envoys had arrived from London to speak to the queen. Apparently they had offered to open the city gates to her and the king if she would send her Scottish allies home. Some had already marched on the suburbs across the river and plundered the area.

By evening it was obvious to Mackillin that there would soon be no Scots left to dismiss. Loaded with booty, they were deserting in droves.

'Perhaps we should leave, too,' suggested Cicely, watching Mackillin load the hackbut with lead shot. They were in the bedchamber and it was an hour short to supper.

Mackillin nodded. 'We will go tomorrow.'

The words were no sooner out of his mouth than there came a knock on the door.

'Who is it?' he called, putting down the weapon.

'A messenger has come from the queen, who wishes to see you both,' shouted a man's voice.

Mackillin swore beneath his breath. 'I had hoped she had forgotten about us.' He reached for his sword and buckled it on.

Cicely whispered, 'What do you think she wants?'

'Can you tell me why the queen requests our company?' shouted Mackillin.

'It is no request, Lord Mackillin, it is an order, and if you don't wish to earn her disfavour then I would not delay,' came the voice from the other side of the door. 'She's already had two heads chopped off since we arrived here.'

'Tell her Majesty we shall be with her forthwith,' said Mackillin, eyes glinting with anger.

There was the sound of retreating footsteps.

Mackillin and Cicely stared at each other and then he reached out a hand and caressed her cheek. 'Pray God, all will be well. I should have done as you said and let you go with the courier.'

'It is too late for that now.' She did not know if her safety was an issue here at the moment. But surely she had not betrayed herself and revealed herself a woman to any one? She could only pray that the queen only wished to speak to Mackillin about her father, King René of Anjou, and Cicely's role was simply that of a listener.

Chapter Twelve

The royal couple were seated at table and servants were scurrying here and there with large salvers of food and jugs of wine and ale. Mackillin and Cicely bowed before the king and queen, aware not only of their scrutiny but that of numerous pairs of eyes upon them.

'You may rise, Lord Mackillin,' said King Henry, indicating that he do so with a fluttering, be-ringed white hand. His hair fell to beneath his ears and he had thin lips. 'Please, join us. The queen tells me you are not only from Scotland, but have recently spent time in France, where you spoke to her father in Angers.'

Mackillin straightened. 'That is true, sire.'

'You are also related to my Earl of Northumberland, so you are doubly welcome here. He tells us you have sailed the seas and done much travelling. Sit down with us. We would hear more from you.'

'That is kind of you, sire.' Mackillin felt relieved, but hoped it was not going to be a long evening.

The king turned to his wife and gave a sharp nod. Queen Margaret fixed her eyes upon Cicely. 'Lord Mackillin told us that you were his cousin, but did not tell us your name. What are you called, young master?' There was a derisive note in her voice.

Cicely squared her shoulders. 'My name is Nathaniel, your Majesty. Nathaniel Milburn. I am but a distant cousin to his lordship, but he has always shown me great kindness.'

A murmur rippled through the hall, but the king raised his hand and there was silence. 'Nathaniel Milburn, I seem to know that name.'

'You might remember my father, sire,' said Cicely, turning to him. 'He never wavered in his allegiance to you. He was a merchant venturer and proved his loyalty many times.'

'Ahhh!' The king smiled. 'I knew I knew his name. He was very generous with gifts of money. How is your father?'

Cicely cleared her throat. 'He is dead, your Majesty. Murdered in Bruges by members of our own family. If it had not been for Lord Mackillin, then my brother would have died also—and that is why I am here with his lordship now. I owe him my gratitude and loyalty.'

'Well said,' murmured the king. 'I am sorry to hear about your father.'

The queen nudged him with her elbow. 'This is all very interesting, but have you forgotten, my liege, the rumours that have come to our ears?'

King Henry looked baffled for a moment, then he tugged on his lip before saying, 'Are you certain your name is Nathaniel?' His voice was gruff. 'I find it hard to believe, but they are saying you are not a youth but a woman. I cannot see how this can be true, but…' He stopped as if uncertain how to continue.

Cicely's heart had begun to thud in her chest and she was lost for words. She looked at Mackillin for help and swiftly he responded with the words, 'Why should you believe these rumours, sire? Who started them? Let him stand before me and we will sort this out man to man.'

'No, no, no, no,' bumbled the king, fluttering his hands. 'I hate the sight of blood. I'll have no fighting in my court. Just tell me the truth, Mackillin. Is Master Nathaniel a wench or youth? On your word, mind you, or on holy writ.'

Mackillin opened his mouth, but before he could perjure himself, a voice shouted, 'I saw them together, saw how they looked at each other. Besides, I recognise her. She is Mistress Cicely Milburn, my kinswoman.'

'Who is that? Who is that who spoke up?' demanded the king.

No one answered, but there was a babble of voices and the queen turned to Cicely. 'Is this true? Are you Mistress Cicely Milburn?'

Cicely felt a peculiar calmness come over her and she removed her hat and allowed her braids to ripple down over her shoulders. 'Aye, it is true, your Majesty. I am she.'

The queen gasped and gripped the arms of the carved oak chair. 'You dare to admit this to me?'

Cicely was pale, but she held her head high. 'You would have me speak an untruth, your Majesty?'

'*Non, mais je...*' The queen seemed lost for further words, but then appeared to pull herself together and scowled at Cicely. 'It is not seemly that you should be dressed in such a fashion and share Lord Mackillin's bedchamber. It is against holy writ. You will need to be imprisoned and brought before the justice.'

'No! This would be wrong, your Majesty,' burst out Mackillin, starting forward.

'You dare to speak to me in such a tone?' said the queen, looking furious. 'I am the queen of England.'

'And I am a Scotsman, who has answered my own king's order to come to your husband's aid.' Mackillin bowed before her. 'Forgive my hotheadedness, but Mistress Cicely is a loyal servant of both your majesties, as was her father. I speak the truth to you now. Her father gave her to me to be my wife. We are betrothed.'

Cicely drew in her breath with a hiss. Did he realise what he was saying?

The queen would have spoken, but the king signalled her to be silent. 'But you are not wed to her yet, Mackillin, and it is not seemly that your betrothed dispenses with her feminine attire to wear that of a youth.'

Mackillin stood straight as a ramrod. 'No, sire, it is not. I left her behind in the north when I obeyed my king's command to fight for your freedom, but she followed me—and in this garb so as to escape notice on the road and the battlefield.' He inclined his chestnut head. 'I ask for your understanding and...your mercy.'

Cicely stared at him, marvelling at his honesty. She wondered what the royal couples' response would be and turned her attention to them.

The king returned her regard and muttered, 'Most unseemly, Mistress Milburn. We must do what is right here.' He turned to Mackillin. 'I suggest you marry Mistress Milburn immediately. Whether she is still a maid I know not, but her name is besmirched and, for her father's sake, my chaplain can perform the deed here and now.' He looked towards the cleric seated a few places up from him on the high table. The man's expression was disapproving and he seemed about to refuse, but the king said firmly, 'You must do this. Her father was a friend to us and Lord Mackillin has risked his life for our cause.'

'I will do as your Majesty insists, but…' The cleric stared at Cicely in distaste '…but surely this…maid will change into raiment more suitable for such an occasion.'

Cicely felt the blood rush to her cheeks. Should she be honest and say Mackillin did not wish to marry her? That he had refused her father's offer and was only saying that they were betrothed to save her face? Besides, she had no women's garments with her. Perhaps if she told them that, then the wedding might not take place. She did not want Mackillin marrying her because he was forced into doing so.

But she had delayed too long. The queen said, 'Take Mistress Milburn to my apartments and find her some feminine apparel to wear.'

Cicely turned to Mackillin. 'Is this really what you want?' she whispered.

'I could ask you the same question, but it would be pointless,' he answered in a low voice. 'I should have sent you home when I could, but now we have no choice but to do as the king says, otherwise we both might be thrown into prison.'

Her spirits plummeted. She had hoped he might

have said *yes! It was his dearest wish to make her his bride,* even if it were not true. Instead he was marrying her purely because it was a royal command. There was no chance for them to speak again as she was hurried from the hall by two of the queen's attendants and along a passage, around a corner and then along another passage. During that time not once did they speak to her.

They came to a large oak door guarded by men-at-arms, who obviously recognised the two women and allowed them to enter the rooms set aside for the king and queen. They were not as sumptuous as Cicely had expected royal apartments to be but, of course, these were their temporary quarters.

'Come, this way, Mistress Milburn,' said one of the ladies-in-waiting in a cold voice. She picked up a candle from a wooden tray near the door and lit it from one of the candles in a sconce in the passage. Then she set a flame to a four-branched candelabra and led Cicely across a small antechamber into a larger chamber where there were several chests and a couple of armoires. She lit more candles and tapped a chest.

'You are fortunate that those who lived here fled and left their belongings behind. There are several gowns in here. Do not dally, for their Majesties have more to do with their time than waste it on the likes of you.' She turned her back on her and left the chamber.

Cicely could feel anger burning inside her chest and would have given it utterance if it were not that she wanted out of the building as soon as possible. She would not allow that woman to make her feel guilty and ashamed. What did it matter what she wore? Wearing breeches did not turn her into an evil person. She lifted the lid and, reaching inside, brought out the first garment to hand. Holding part of the skirt close to the candle, she saw that its colour was green and the fabric was linen.

It suddenly occurred to her that this could be her wedding gown. Never had she imagined that it would be chosen in such a manner. Tears rolled down her cheeks. In her dreams she would have chosen primrose or turquoise silk such as her father might have brought back from Venice. But what did it matter now what she wore—Mackillin would not care. It might be true that he lusted after her body, but she was not the bride he would have chosen.

Still, they were to be wed and she would do her best to make him a good wife. And he would gain by marrying her. After all, it was her father's wish and her dowry would be of use to Mackillin.

She wasted no more time, but searched for a kirtle and then stripped off her youth's disguise and donned a cream woollen kirtle and gown of green. Then, carrying the candleholder, she left the chamber; her tread was light despite she was wearing boots.

The two women were talking in low voices, but stopped and turned when they heard her coming. They looked her up and down with disdain and one said, 'I hope his lordship knows what he's doing.'

The other one said, 'What does it matter? He's a Scottish lord and they don't count. Let's go. We're missing the feasting.'

She led the way. As Cicely followed her along the passage, trailed by the other attendant, she experienced a moment of panic and wanted to run away, but then she stiffened her backbone. She would pretend that she and Mackillin were marrying because they loved each other, not because of her reckless foolishness in dressing as a youth and following him. Then she remembered that this wedding was taking place due to the rumours started most probably by her Milburn kin. A faint smile lifted the corners of her mouth. No doubt he had not reckoned on King Henry remembering her father's name, so that instead of punishing her and Mackillin as he intended, his plan had backfired.

They had reached the hall and Cicely's heart increased its beat. Mackillin was talking to a man she recognised as his kinsman, Northumberland. She wondered what the earl thought of Mackillin being forced into marrying a merchant's daughter. Her arrival caused a sudden hush and for an instant the panic she had experienced earlier gripped her. Then

Mackillin turned and stared at her. A smile broke over his rugged features and her panic subsided as she walked towards him.

He took her hand and drew it through his arm. 'I know this is certainly not how Nat intended our wedding to be, but I'm certain he would be delighted that it is taking place,' he murmured against her ear.

'I agree,' she whispered, her hand trembling on his sleeve. 'But it seems odd that it should come about due to the deeds of our enemy.'

'His mistake. Northumberland tells me that he has seen him with the Armstrongs, but right now he has vanished.'

'What do you plan to do about them?' she whispered as he led her slowly towards the high table where the king and queen were seated. The priest awaited them.

'I'll ponder on that later. Look happy, sweet Cissie, as if you are a willing bride.'

If only he knew how willing she was to be his wife, she thought, and smiled as he had requested. She sank in a deep curtsy before the royal couple, her green skirts billowing about her. She was bid rise by the king, who smiled and rubbed his hands together. 'Now you look as God intended you to do, Mistress Milburn. Let us get on with the ceremony.'

With Mackillin's upper arm touching her

shoulder, she took a deep breath as they faced the cleric. She remembered the last wedding she had attended had been that of her father and stepmother and she had not forgotten the seriousness of the vows they had made. As the ceremony began she was again aware of all the eyes of the royal attendants and the Lancastrian lords, knights and servants upon them.

'I, Rory, take thee, Cicely, to be my wedded wife, to have and to hold, for fairer, for fouler, for better for worse, for richer for poorer, in sickness and in health, for this time forward, till death us do part, if holy church will it order…and thereto I plight thee my troth.'

Mackillin's words sounded loud in the hall and so binding that Cicely was filled with trepidation. There was no going back now. The priest muttered some words that she did not catch, but she guessed he was asking her to repeat them after him. She did not need him to tell her what to do in that cold voice of his, so hurried into speech. 'I, Cecily, take thee, Ma—' She corrected herself. 'Rory, to be my wedded husband, to have and to hold, for fairer or fouler, for better…for worse, for richer for poorer, in sickness and in health, to…be meek and obedient in bed and at board, for this time forward, till death us do part, if holy church will it order… and thereto I plight thee my troth.'

Relieved at having managed to make her vows with scarcely a fault, she was aware of Mackillin gazing down at her with a faint twinkle in his eyes. She told herself that all would be well as she watched him remove his signet ring from the little finger of his right hand. He took her left hand in his. 'With this ring I thee wed...and with my body I thee worship.'

She scarcely heard the next words because she was recalling those moments in the tub when they had been naked together and the thrilling excitement she had felt. Then she became aware that he was holding the ring over the tip of her thumb. 'In the name of the Father—' over her index finger '—in the name of the Son—' over her middle finger '—in the name of the Holy Ghost—' and finally he said, 'Amen' as he slipped the ring on her third finger. It was still warm from his hand and was slightly too large for her. She touched it as he bent his chestnut head and kissed her lightly on the lips. 'May God bless our union, Lady Mackillin,' he murmured.

'Aye, my lord,' she responded, feeling quite odd at being addressed by her new title.

'Try calling me Rory, wife,' he said in a good-humoured voice.

Ciccly felt a soaring in her spirit at his use of the word *wife*. It was going to take some getting used to, being his spouse; as for using his Christian name, so accustomed was she to addressing him as Mackillin that that might prove impossible. 'What do we do now?' she whispered, knowing that if their wedding was a normal one in church it would have been followed by a nuptial mass, but she doubted that would happen here.

'We did not have time to eat earlier, so perhaps we should eat, drink and be merry?' he suggested.

Before she could agree, the king beckoned them to come forwards. 'Lord and Lady Mackillin, we invite you to be seated.'

Mackillin thanked him and they both sat down where indicated. Bowls of creamy leek soup were placed before them and wine poured into cups. As Mackillin picked up his spoon, he glanced in the direction of his mother's cousin, Harry Percy, who had taught him swordplay at Alnwick Castle and received a mocking smile. Mackillin returned the smile before allowing his gaze to wander round the hall. He stilled suddenly as he recognised Sir Malcolm Armstrong, whose expression was ugly with fury.

Mackillin had little time to worry about him or to pay attention to his new wife now because the royal couple were eager to hear more of his time in France and of his travels. He was surprised by their interest, but came to the conclusion that perhaps they needed to be distracted from the decisions that would soon have to be made concerning their next step in the power struggle to rule England.

When at last they switched their attention to someone else and the meal came to an end, his kinsman signalled to him. Mackillin had hoped he and Cicely would be able to escape and return to their lodgings, but he could not ignore Northumberland, so he turned to his wife of a few hours. 'Hopefully, I will not be long. You will be all right here for a few minutes?'

'Is it possible that I excuse myself and return to our lodgings? The noise is giving me a megrim and I do not wish to be indisposed when—' She stopped abruptly, feeling the colour rise in her cheeks and realising the wine had freed her tongue too much.

A chuckle resonated in his deep chest. 'Whatever you wish, sweeting. I will speak to the king. I'm sure he will excuse you and have a man-at-arms escort you to the house.'

It was done as Mackillin requested and within minutes, he was making his way over to his kinsman, determined to keep their conversation brief. He was impatient to be alone with Cicely; it appeared to him that she was willing to consummate their union and he felt a stir of arousal at the thought. He would handle her tenderly, so as to reassure her that now they were wed his aim was to please her, but that he also wanted her safe. He was of a mind to escort her to Milburn Manor where she could gather her belongings together. She could remain there until Mackillin could have all made ready for his lady's arrival at Killin. He needed to check his defences and strengthen them if need be, as well as setting about forming other alliances rather than the one he had planned with Armstrong. His mother might be disappointed, but he had made no promises to her or Mary Armstrong.

'My congratulations, Rory,' said Northumberland, poking him gently in the ribs. 'I wager you never thought you'd be leaving here with a bride this even?'

It was obvious to Mackillin that his Grace had been imbibing freely of the excellent burgundy, for he had made a similar comment earlier. 'If that is all you wish to say to me, Harry, then I'll be on my way,' he said with a smile.

'Nay, coz, don't go rushing off yet.' The earl brought his mouth close to Mackillin's ear and muttered, 'But leave St Albans as soon as you can. We have delayed here long enough. The queen should have agreed to whatever the capital's citizens asked for immediately. Once inside the city, we could have taken the Tower and its artillery. Methinks now the Scots are deserting that she and the king will back off. I plan leaving on the morrow. I cannot risk my lands being unattended any longer. You and your bride can ride with us if you wish.'

Mackillin realised his kinsman was not as drunk as he appeared. 'Thanks for the offer. I accept.'

Northumberland said, 'Good. I will have my men call on you later.'

Mackillin thanked him and was about to take his leave when a man hobbled over to them. The earl introduced him as Sir Andrew Trollope, the great captain of the Lancastrian army who had ensured their victory and had been knighted on the battlefield for his efforts. Sir Andrew kept Mackillin talking for several minutes, but then he managed to make his escape.

His intention was to return to the house and pack his and Cicely's belongings ready for them to leave. But before packing there could be a short time for them to consummate their union. As he made his way along the footpath past the abbey and Ye Old Fighting Cocks inn, he smiled, imagining holding Cicely's body against his own, of kissing every inch of her. Then suddenly he felt a blow on the back of his head. He staggered and reached for his sword, but a second blow ensured he had no time to loosen it and he collapsed on to the ground.

* * *

Cicely twisted a strand of golden hair between her fingers as she paced the floor. It seemed an age since she had left Mackillin and she was anxious in case some terror had befallen him after her dream last night. If only he would come, then she would tell him of the nightmare. Suddenly she heard footsteps approaching and in her thankfulness did not listen properly or consider her own safety. Hurrying over to the door, she flung it open.

Instantly she attempted to close the door in the men's faces, one of whom she recognised. She only wondered for a second how he had escaped Milburn Manor as he wedged the door open by placing his foot in the gap. She backed away and, seeing the hackbut on the chest, picked it up and pointed it at him.

'Take one step nearer and I will fire,' she said.

The Milburn laughed. 'Fire away, girlie. I doubt Mistress Cicely Milburn would know how to use such a weapon.'

'Then you would be wrong,' she said, and fired.

At that distance it would have been impossible for Cicely to miss her target. The bang and the screech made by her kinsman was deafening. He clutched his face and the next moment sank to the floor. His accomplice, a murderous expression in his eyes, wrenched the hackbut from her hand and threw it aside. She tried to escape, but he seized her wounded arm and flung her over his shoulder. Kicking and screaming, she was carried out of the bedchamber. The smell of onions and stale sweat filled her nostrils as he took the stairs at breakneck speed, violently jolting her so that she thought she would vomit up her supper. She caught a glimpse of one of the servants lying in a pool of blood in the hall and was dizzy with fear. If only Mackillin would come, she thought. And where were the rest of the men who lodged in the house?

Outside, the cold air penetrated the linen sleeve of her gown, but she had no time to worry about catching a chill because she was tossed to another man. A cloak was flung over her head, blinding her. Then a rope bound the garment about her so that she could not move her arms. She heard the snorting of a horse and the clatter of hooves. She tried to claw her way upright, but her assailant slapped her down. She was flung on to a horse and someone mounted behind her. The horse began to move and, blinded by the cloak and sick with terror, she had no idea where they were taking her and feared she might never see her husband again.

'Milburn hit him too hard! I didn't want him dead, Jamie.'

The words seemed to be coming from the far end of a tunnel.

'He's not dead, Malcolm,' said an impatient voice. 'Look at his chest. He's still breathing. I've seen men in a stupor like this before and they've survived.'

'Aye, but others never come out of it,' rumbled the first voice.

Mackillin's head ached abominably and he seemed unable to move his limbs. He recognised the voices and wished he could remember how he had come here. He must have lowered his guard and was furious with himself. He wondered where Cissie was and felt a chill of fear.

'He'll be fine. All the Mackillins I've known have had hard heads.'

'What of his wife?'

'I've left her bound in one of the wagons and set a guard over her. Is it that yer wishing to see her now? She's a bonny lassie. Who's to know if we—?'

'Nay! You will not touch her,' snapped Malcolm. 'Even if this night I hadn't heard it from the king about her family's wealth, I had it from her kinsman that she's no common wench. I will demand from her guardian a ransom for her safe return.'

Wife! Were they talking about Cissie? Mackillin could remember sharing a bedchamber with her but had no recall of a wedding taking place. When had that happened? Somehow he had to free himself and rescue her.

'Milburn had been of a mind to keep her for himself, but he paid for presuming that because she was a lass, she was weak. He was as dead as a doornail in the blink of an eye,' said Jamie.

Brave lass, thought Mackillin, marvelling at her actions and wondering how Cissie had managed to kill her kinsman.

'If she wasn't worth a small fortune, I'd break her spirit,' drawled Malcolm. 'I'll need to get rid of her, so my daughter can wed Mackillin, but we'll get our hands on a ransom first.'

'So what are yer planning on doing with him once he weds your daughter? Milburn said he killed *his* kinsman for love of this wench and he wanted him dead.'

'I, too, had a brother, whose body I buried in St Albans,' rasped the Armstrong. 'But that had naught to do with him. Once he and Mary are married and there's a child on the way, I'll dispose of him because he'll be less trouble dead. His mother and I would rather he had never returned once we got rid of his father and his half-brothers, but those I hired to kill him failed in their task, so we had to change our plans.'

Mackillin could scarcely believe what he was hearing. He had known his mother hated his father, but that she could be in league with this man to destroy her husband and his sons, including himself, shocked him to the core.

'Why don't you just take his land?' asked Jamie.

'Because there are others, such as the Douglases, who would fight me for it. Better to make it legal, then there'll be no dispute over ownership. Mary will do as I tell her or suffer for it.'

Armstrong laughed in a way that infuriated Mackillin. He had to get free. Once he was, then he would cut their accused throats.

There was the sound of a chair being pushed back. 'We ride for the Border at first light. Mackillin can go in the wagon with the wench and booty. Just make sure they're tied up good and tight. Gag them, too. I don't want them talking to each other.'

Mackillin knew he had to pretend to be still unconscious, so went limp, allowing himself to be carried to the wagon where they held Cissie a prisoner.

Cicely turned her head as the canvas flap of the covered wagon was lifted and her mouth went dry as she looked at the man standing outside in the torch light. He was short of stature, but had huge shoulders and long arms; his hair and beard were black. She trembled beneath his lecherous dark beady eyes and longed for Mackillin, praying he would find her.

'Who are you?' she demanded with more confidence than she felt.

'Ma name's Jamie Armstrong,' he replied. 'Mebbe yer've heard of us Armstrongs, lassie?'

She shook her head, but her heart was pounding with fear. She wondered if she had been abducted to lure her husband into a trap, so this man could kill him.

He thrust his face into hers. 'Ye haven't answered me, lassie. Perhaps Mackillin didna tell yer that he's going to wed ma kinsman's daughter? I wager he made yer all kinds of promises to lure ye into his bed?'

'Then you'd be wrong,' she said stoutly. 'We were married before the king and queen of England and he will rescue me.'

Jamie grabbed her by the hair and she bit back a cry. 'No, he won't, lassie,' he hissed. 'He's being brought here but he's our prisoner and hasn't woken yet from the blow the man you killed dealt him. Perhaps he never will.'

She bit back a cry. 'Where is he? Let me see him.'

He laughed. 'You'll see him soon enough. If he dies—see it as a fit punishment on yer wicked ways. A lassie dressing as a laddie—now that's a sinful thing to do.'

'And what you do, is that not wicked? You have no

right to hurt Mackillin or to abduct me in this fashion.'

The laughter faded from his eyes. 'Just ye be thankful that yer kinsman told us yer worth more than half the booty we carry. Otherwise, I'd have to…' He did not finish, but his grip on her hair tightened and he rubbed his beard against her face. 'Who's to say that we'll hand you over once we've got our hands on your ransom?'

She felt a chill run down her spine and her mouth felt so dry that she could not speak. Jamie gave a humourless smile. 'That's shut you up.' His dark eyes surveyed her and then he bent his head towards hers. She averted her face, but even so her empty stomach heaved, for his breath was foul. 'You'll pay for that later,' he snapped, taking a narrow length of linen cloth and gagging her with it.

She retched and then managed a breath, watching him step aside with loathing in her eyes. Her expression altered as she saw a couple of men approaching, carrying the limp body of Mackillin. She wanted to cry out to him, but could only produce a strangled gasp and watch as they dumped him inside the wagon some distance away from her.

Mackillin waited until the men had gone before opening his eyes. His head throbbed, but he ignored the pain and peered about him. The light was dim, but he caught a muffled cry and his head swivelled in its direction. Then he saw Cicely and his heart lifted because she was staring straight at him; the relief in her blue orbs was such that he wondered what they had told her about him. She tried to speak, but he could not make out what she was trying to say. Even so he hazarded a guess that it was along the lines that she was glad to see him. He echoed her feelings, but would be happier if he could free them both soon. He needed something sharp. Surely amongst the booty stored in the wagon they might discover something to cut their bonds. But first he needed to rid them of their gags; they had to talk. He began to shuffle across the sacks, wincing as he jarred a knee on something square, one of its corners piercing the jute material of a sack.

The instant Cicely realised what he was doing, she attempted to throw herself towards him. She landed face down on something soft, but all the air was knocked out of her. For a moment she could not breathe, but before she could panic, a bristly chin nudged against the curve of hers and forced her head up. Mackillin's nose brushed hers and they were almost eyeball to eyeball. Then he drew back a little in order for her to catch her breath.

A little calmer now, she watched Mackillin's head loom towards hers. Then his parted lips were touching hers. It was a moment she would never forget for, despite the thrill of it, this was no simple kiss; somehow he managed to get his tongue out from beneath his gag and worm the fabric from her mouth and force it beneath her chin. Once that was done, it was so much easier for her to do the same for him, except she was able to use her teeth as well.

'That was some feat,' he murmured, before kissing her for real this time. It was of necessity not a long kiss, but even so she found it immensely satisfying. When they had to stop to draw breath, he whispered, 'Now let's see if we can find something to cut these bonds.'

She did not ask how they were to do that with their hands tied because he must surely know how difficult it would be without her saying so. They would just have to shuffle round and feel for a knife, or some such sharp implement; a piece of metal or glass that would do the trick. It was Cicely who found the chandelier half in, half out of a sack. Her fingers searched its metallic branches and discovered a design of what felt like fleur-de-lys, the points of which were sharp. 'Mackillin, over here,' she called in a low voice.

He did not hesitate, crawling towards her on his elbows and knees. She gripped his fingers and placed them on one of the metallic flowers. 'There's several of these. They might do the trick.'

'Well done, Cissie, let's get weakening these cords.'

They wasted no time and, although it was not easy because the metal tore their skin, at last some of the strands of hair and wool parted. Mackillin managed to get his hands free first and immediately tore apart the cord binding Cicely's wrists. She was aware of his sense of urgency as he bent over her legs and she bid him free himself first. He hesitated but she added, 'It makes sense, Mackillin. You're stronger than I am. If Armstrong was to come in the next few minutes, then it's best you get to him first.'

He nodded and set about the task of undoing the knots securing his ankles. Cicely began the job of getting rid of the cord that bound hers, breaking several fingernails in the attempt. She was almost free when there came a lightening of the darkness outside. Then she heard galloping horses and the shouts of men. 'I wonder what's happening,' she said, lifting her head.

'It sounds like an attack on the camp,' said Mackillin, alert.

They heard screams of pain and could see shadows moving outside. Suddenly there was a flash of light and a whooshing noise as the canvas roof of the wagon caught fire.

Chapter Thirteen

Cicely had no time to dwell on her fear because Mackillin seized her hand and dragged her to the rear opening. His arm went about her waist and he shouted, 'Jump!'

They leapt out of the wagon and landed on the grass. Men were fighting nearby; as the two looked around, they could see more men grappling with each other in deadly combat. 'What do we do?' she asked, still on her knees on the ground.

'I'd like to kill that cur who dared to touch you,' muttered Mackillin, gazing about him.

Cicely had no argument with that, but thought it might be sensible to try to escape and said so. Mackillin nodded vaguely and gazed about him. Then he began to crawl swiftly through the damp grass in the direction of another wagon. She wasted no time in following him and soon saw the reason why he was heading in that direction. A shadowy, squat figure was backing a horse between the shafts of the wagon. By the light of the fires and torches she recognised Jamie Armstrong.

'You have no weapon,' she whispered.

Mackillin made no sign of having heard her, but rose to his feet and dove in through the rear opening in the canvas hood, just as the wheels rumbled into motion. She followed him and did not waste time asking what he planned on doing. He reached out for her hand and raised it to his lips, before releasing it and crawling towards the front of the wagon.

She held her breath, scarcely able to make out his outline. Her fear for him was a tightness in her chest as she listened to the struggle taking place beyond her reach. There was a gurgling noise and the sound of something falling. Then Mackillin called to her. She was filled with thankfulness and hurried towards him. He had taken hold of the reins and she had almost reached him when a voice shouted, 'Where do you think you're going? Stop immediately!'

'Is that you, Harry?' called Mackillin in amazement.

'Rory, by all that's holy!' exclaimed the man on a large horse, carrying a flaming torch. 'We've been looking for you. One of my men called at the house and found two dead bodies. Then it was discovered you and your lady wife were missing. Afterwards

I learnt that Armstrong and his kin were also missing, so I became a mite suspicious.'

Mackillin felt a peculiar leap of the heart. 'My lady wife,' he murmured. 'So it's true.'

'Aye. Don't tell me you've forgotten already that you were wed at the king's bidding?' said his kinsman, smiling.

Mackillin glanced sidelong at Cicely and said softly, 'How could I forget?'

She did not speak, but only gazed at him, thankful that they were both still alive. Then Harry cleared his throat as the wagon was surrounded by horsemen. 'Time to get on the move,' he said.

'I presume these are your men, Harry?'

'Aye, although when I couldn't find you at first I thought I'd made a mistake. Then Jonah here spotted this wagon trundling away.'

Mackillin's smile was grim as he said, 'I appreciate your help. Armstrong's plan was to ransom Cissie and eventually to dispose of us both.' He decided to keep quiet about his mother's part in his father's and half-brothers' deaths, but still felt sick and angry about it.

'Why doesn't that surprise me,' drawled Northumberland. 'What of your wife's kinsman?'

Cicely decided to say her piece and leaned forward the better to see his Grace. 'I killed him with the hackbut which Husthwaite sought to kill Mackillin with.'

His Grace looked startled. 'You killed a man? God's blood, Rory, it seems you have chosen the right woman to stand alongside you in your Border domain. But tell me, who is this Husthwaite person?'

'He was a wily, sly cur who would have robbed my lady and her brothers of their inheritance but he, too, is no longer with us.'

The earl grinned. 'Then not a man to worry about. I wonder that you need my help at all when the pair of you are so able.'

Mackillin felt a swell of pride that his sweet Cissie should have won such praise from his kinsman. Since their first meeting, her courage had never been in doubt, but he was amazed that her nerve had not failed when confronted by her kinsman and the black-hearted Jamie Armstrong. It proved to him just how level-headed and resourceful she was and—as Harry had stated—a fitting bride for him.

'Tell me, Harry, have you captured Malcolm Armstrong yet?'

Instantly the earl's visage showed chagrin in the light of the coming dawn. 'I'm sorry to tell you, Rory, but in the confusion he seems to have escaped. Possibly some of his men might have, too.'

Mackillin frowned. 'That's bad news, but it can't be helped.'

'No doubt he'll head north.'

'Which means I cannot waste any time, but must return to Killin,' said Mackillin, his expression grim.

The earl agreed. 'He won't have got far. I'll have some of my men make a search for him, but they might not find him. He's a cunning devil. I don't intend waiting for them to find him, but will continue north without delay. Will you ride with us?'

'Aye. As soon as I can find a horse.'

'You should have no trouble doing so as some have lost their masters.'

Mackillin climbed down from the wagon before helping Cicely to the ground. The earl excused himself and left Mackillin and his lady alone. Lacking a cloak or surcoat, Cicely shivered in the icy breeze. Mackillin drew her against him. 'Are you cold, lass?'

'Aye,' she murmured, snuggling against him. 'I confess I am a little weary, too.'

'Not surprising considering what you've been through in the last few days. I suggest we share a horse—at least for the first stage of the journey. We can keep each other warm and you can rest against me.'

She greeted his suggestion with relief. 'Thank you, my lord. I confess to fearing that I might have shamed you by trailing behind and even dropping asleep in the saddle and falling from my horse.'

He smiled and ran a gentle finger down her cheek. 'I don't believe it. You are an excellent horsewoman. Besides, do you really think I would allow you out of my sight after all we have been through, my lady?'

Cicely felt a happy glow flood her being. 'It sounds so strange you addressing me so.'

'Aye, but it is true that you are my lady. I would have preferred our wedding night to be different, but, alas, even now our coupling will have to wait,' he said ruefully, 'but I promise you when the time comes…' He did not finish, but pressed his lips against hers in a long, sweet kiss. Then he took her hand. 'Let's go and find a mount suitable for our needs.'

It did not take them long to find such a horse: a grey stallion, broad in the chest and built for endurance. Mackillin lifted Cicely up on to the saddle and then climbed up behind her. She revelled in his closeness, watching his strong fingers take hold of the reins. Aware of the familiar scent of him, underlying the smell of dried blood, she remembered that it was not so long ago that he had been lying unconscious after being hit over the head by her kinsman. Suddenly she was overwhelmed by the thought that he could have been killed and tears slid silently down her cheeks.

One of his arms tightened about her. 'Why do you weep?' he murmured against her ear.

'No reason,' she said hastily, dabbing at her eyes with her sleeve.

'Of course there is a reason. Tell me the truth. We must have no secrets between us. Have you changed your mind about being my wife because you fear living in the Borders? Or have you remembered that you once wanted to marry Diccon?'

She thought he sounded anxious, so was swift to reassure him. 'Neither. I cry because I am relieved we have passed through extreme danger together and survived.'

Mackillin kissed the top of her head. 'Thank God the Armstrongs made the mistake of putting us together.'

'He underestimated your strength,' she said.

'And your cleverness.' He felt proud of possessing a wife who was not only comely, but courageous and clever, too. 'I know you will miss your brothers and your home, but pray God we will be able to visit them in the future. I'm of the mind that Jack should come and stay at my house in Kirkcudbright in the near future. I will introduce him to my master mariner and he can travel to Europe in my ship.'

Cicely was touched by his thoughtfulness. She considered it an excellent idea and said so, adding, 'I'm sure Owain will agree to it once he receives your courier, although he will not know that we are wed.'

'He was firmly of the opinion we should marry.'

'You broached the subject.'

'Aye. And as soon as possible I will send a messenger to inform Owain of our latest news.'

They both fell silent, wondering what he would do when he heard of their wedding.

Cicely's head began to nod and weariness overcame her. Aware that she had gone limp in his arms, Mackillin's hold on his bride tightened. It did occur to him that if Armstrong was lying in wait anywhere he was ill prepared to defend either Cicely or himself. So he steered his mount closer to his kinsman and spoke to him of his lack of a weapon.

'I will have a sword found for you,' said Harry. 'Although I doubt Armstrong will attempt an attack in daylight. I intend seeking shelter at the house of Sir Thomas Stanley's kin in Staffordshire before nightfall.'

The news satisfied Mackillin; although he felt a need for haste to reach Killin Keep, he did not expect them to arrive there without breaking the journey several times. His heart lurched uncomfortably when he thought of his mother and her duplicity. He was still undecided what to do with her when he arrived home, yet now was not the time to give it thought for his head ached and he was weary.

'No doubt they will be laying in supplies in case the king and queen should decide to stop by at their manor,' said Harry, rousing Mackillin from his reverie.

For a moment Mackillin did not know what his kinsman was talking about, then he realised and said, 'The royal couple are heading north?'

Harry nodded. 'No doubt they wish to have words with young King James and the dowager queen once again. This conflict is not over yet.'

Mackillin decided that it was over for him and Cissie. He had risked his life once for the Lancastrian cause, but he would not do so again; he had his bride to consider. He did not voice his feelings to his kinsman, knowing Northumberland's involvement in the Lancastrian cause was far greater than his. The Percys were sworn enemies of the powerful Neville family of whom the most famous was the Earl of Warwick, kin to Edward of York and his close advisor. Harry had no choice but to continue the struggle to be on the winning side in the fight for the throne of England.

By the time they arrived at the manor in Staffordshire where they were to spend the night, Cicely was awake and Mackillin had informed her of his kinsman's plan. Her face brightened. 'Kate is related to the Stanleys. One of Sir Thomas's uncles was her father.'

Mackillin said, 'I remember her mentioning Sir Thomas.'

Cicely lowered her voice. 'Kate's mother went through a form of marriage with him but they were young and his parents declared the marriage null and void, so they were both married off again to someone else.'

Mackillin was thoughtful. 'You realise, Cissie, this means that we are both related to the Stanleys now by marriage?'

Her lovely eyes widened. 'Indeed, I hadn't. Do you regard this as important?'

He smiled. 'It's always useful to have powerful allies, even if in this case they are English and unlikely to be of help to us once we cross the border into Scotland.' He dismounted and then lifted her down. She slid through his hands and their bodies touched in a way that roused him despite his weariness. 'I pray that our host provides us with a comfortable bed,' he murmured against her cheek.

Her heart seemed to flip over at his mention of bed, but she told herself that she had naught to fear from him. Had she not thrilled to his kisses? And those moments in the tub with him had been pleasurable and exciting.

A groom approached and led their horse away. Mackillin took her hand and, despite her outer calmness, it trembled in his grasp as they walked across a paved courtyard into a stone-built house with black-and-white plasterwork and wood beneath its eaves.

Northumberland had gone ahead of them, so that by the time they entered the hall, the lady of the house had already sent for refreshments and ordered bedchambers to be prepared for her guests. Harry made Mackillin and Cicely known to her. She led them over to the fire, bidding them to be seated and warm themselves. No sooner were they seated on cushioned chairs than a servant hovered into view, bearing a tray of steaming goblets and a plate of simnels and wafers.

Cicely could scarcely contain herself from scoffing the sweet cakes, but good manners prevented her from doing so. She had not eaten since the meal after her wedding and was famished. The mulled wine was fragrant and tasted delicious, but she had the good sense to refuse a refill. She was feeling light-headed and did not wish to nod off before the evening meal was served. The lady of the house made polite conversation, enquiring after her home in the north. Cicely told her that she was but newly married and had yet to be acquainted with her husband's manor.

Instead she described her previous home in Yorkshire and experienced a stab of homesickness. She was aware of her husband's eyes upon her from time to time—he was conversing with the lady's uncle—and hoped Mackillin considered she was acquitting herself well. Hopefully she would do so when she came face to face with Mackillin's mother.

It was a relief when a servant announced that the meal was ready. Cicely remembered her mother saying that hunger was the best appetiser and this proved true as she ate everything set before her: a bowl of pottage, baked lampreys in a syrupy sauce and a dish of junket sweetened with honey. She sipped sparingly of the excellent raisin wine, but the small glass of hippocras, flavoured with what tasted like cinnamon, ginger and cardamom pods, was delicious and the amount enough to cause her eyelids to droop.

'I deem my lady is ready for her bed,' murmured Mackillin.

Immediately Cicely forced her eyelids open and begged pardon. 'It has been a long day,' she said.

'Of course. We have been hearing of your abduction,' said the lady of the house, rising from her chair. 'Such a frightening experience, Lady Mackillin. I will call a servant to take you to your bedchamber. I pray that you sleep well.' Cicely thanked her prettily and accepted Mackillin's arm.

* * *

A fire was burning on the hearth in their bedchamber and candles had been lit and placed on a table. There was a stand with a pitcher of water and a porcelain bowl, as well as two drying cloths; a chest and a screen as well as a bed, which appeared narrower than the one in their lodgings at St Albans, occupied the rest of the space. Cicely considered the bedchambers at Milburn far superior. It did occur to her that maybe not all members of the Stanley family were as wealthy as Sir Thomas, but she was grateful for their hospitality, none the less.

The bed drew her eye. She found herself imagining lying alongside Mackillin, thinking she might have to cling to him, so as not to fall off it. She regretted not having her best silken night rail with her, knowing she would have to make do with the kirtle she wore. A sigh escaped her. It would have been good to bathe, but that was out of the question which was a pity. She would have liked to have come to him sweet smelling and wearing her prettiest nightwear. She stifled a yawn.

'Do sit on the bed, Cissie,' ordered Mackillin.

Her stomach quivered as she obeyed him. To her surprise, he knelt in front of her and proceeded to remove her boots. 'You should not be doing this, my lord,' she remonstrated. 'I should be helping you off with your boots.'

He grinned. 'No, lass, I would not punish you in such a way. They are heavy and you might topple over.'

His words amused her and she reached out and caressed his unshaven jaw. 'You jest, but you are kind. How is your head? Does it ache?'

'Not as much as it did.'

'You must rest,' she said with concern.

'It is naught for you to fret about.'

'I cannot help but be worried. That Jamie Armstrong was of a mind that you might not have recovered.'

'Sir Malcolm thought the same.'

She smiled. 'You proved him wrong, but even so you must rest.'

He raised his eyebrows. 'That is my intent—amongst others.' There was a gleam in his eyes that brought a flush to her cheeks. 'I will leave you and return shortly,' he said, getting to his feet.

She wondered why he was leaving her alone and then it occurred to her what he might be about. Her heart beat unevenly as she undressed and washed as much of her person as she could in the tepid water. After drying herself, she undid her braids. Unfortunately she had no comb to tidy her hair and so made do with her fingers to bring some semblance of order to her long tresses. When she heard his footsteps outside the door, she sat on the bed in her kirtle and attempted to calm herself.

Mackillin entered the bedchamber, pausing in the doorway when he saw her. Then he closed the door behind him and shot the bolt. Without a word he walked over and sat beside her, reaching out a hand to lift a strand of her hair. He curled it round his finger. 'I did not think this moment would come so soon when we left Rowan Manor,' he murmured. 'You know there is no need for you to be frightened? I will be gentle with you.'

Despite her apprehension, Cicely nodded and said, 'Now all the excitement of the day is over I feel strange and not sleepy at all.'

He was far from feeling that all the excitement was over, but refrained from saying so. Instead he proceeded to remove his boots and outer clothing before drawing her against him. He kissed the side of her neck before turning her round so that she faced him.

Cicely's mood had altered as soon as he had begun to undress and she felt a tide of desire sweep over her. She reached out to him, placing her arms about his neck, causing her breasts to brush the hard wall of his chest. One of his knees pressed her inner thigh. Then his mouth covered hers in a kiss that began with such gentleness that her lips were easily persuaded to part beneath the lazily wandering tip of his tongue. Instantly there came a change in him and now he kissed her with a passion that spoke of a hunger within. She responded with like hunger, instinctively arching her back and thrusting her lower body against him. She felt the low growl in his throat long before he gave it utterance.

'Do you know what you're doing to me?' he whispered.

'Tell me, show me,' she murmured dreamily.

He barely hesitated before tumbling her backwards on to the bed. He kissed her mouth again, plumbing its depths and tasting the sweetness of the mulled wine on her tongue. His fingers caressed the curve of her shoulder, but his attempt to ease down her kirtle proved difficult without lifting himself off her to undo the front fastenings. To do so without breaking off the kiss tested his ingenuity, yet somehow he managed it, but would not have done so without her compliance. Eventually he had to tear his mouth from hers so he could pursue other pleasures. She sighed as his lips blazed a trail of heat down her throat and between her breasts.

He gazed upon them and breathed, 'Perfection.'

'What's perfection?' she whispered.

'Your breasts.'

Her eyelids fluttered open and she stared up at him in the firelight. Her hand wandered down her throat to her bare breasts and the tip of her tongue darted over her swollen lips and she said unsteadily. 'I am glad they please you.'

'All of you delights me.'

He touched the rosy tip of a breast with a finger and then replaced his finger with his mouth. She had never felt such pleasure and then all thought faded and she was in a world that contained him and her alone, caught up in a storm of rising passion that threatened to overwhelm her in its intensity. Its strength took her unawares and was vaguely frightening, whilst at the same time it was exciting being swept away into unexplored physical realms.

His mouth held her captive and it swallowed the gasp of the momentary pain of his possession. Then he was moving slowly inside her and she felt as if that precious centre of her was unfurling like a rosebud opening its petals to reveal its heart to the sun. She was filled with a delightful warmth and wanted to draw him deeper and deeper inside her. She found herself moving in response to his rhythm, which was so tantalisingly slow that it aroused in her such a yearning that she was desperate for a fulfilment of which she had no conception.

Yet she gasped, 'Please.'

'What is it, sweeting? Am I still hurting you?' he murmured against her mouth.

'No. The pain was of no consequence. I have already forgotten it. I—I just don't want you to…'

'Stop?' he asked, a hint of laughter in his voice.

She buried her head against the warm skin of his shoulder. 'You will think me a wanton.'

'No, lass. Never that.' He drew back before plunging deeper inside her, thrusting again and again.

She responded by pushing towards him, until such a well of pleasure surged up inside her that she needed to cling on to him, feeling she might float away on a tide of bliss. 'I...I...'

'I know,' he declared unsteadily, and, with a final thrust, filled her with his seed.

Afterwards, he drew her close and buried his head against her breast. 'Next time there will be no pain and it will be even better for you,' he reassured her in a drowsy voice. Cicely wondered how it could be better. It had been wonderful! She lay a moment, listening to his steady breathing before drifting into slumber.

There was no time for lovemaking the following morning as they were still asleep when a servant came to rouse them at dawn. The earl wanted to make an early start, desirous of reaching his own castle at Alnwick as soon as possible. Mackillin was of the opinion that it would take longer than a day to do so.

By evening they had reached Yorkshire, enabled by Cicely riding a mount of her own at speed. The wind whipped bright colour into her cheeks, but she was weary and aching by the time they dismounted outside the abbey, where they were to break their journey. Frustratingly, there was no opportunity for them to make love as they had to sleep in separate quarters in the abbey's lodging house. Cicely wondered if she would have to wait until they reached Scotland before her husband could show her that their next coupling would be even better than the first time. At least he was able to write a message and send a courier to Milburn Manor with their latest news.

By late afternoon of the following day they had reached the wild but hauntingly beautiful landscape of Northumberland with its extensive forests and moors and its brooding castles. Mackillin spoke to Cicely of the time he had spent there, flying hawks, fishing and being taught how to fight with sword and lance, as well as studying languages, mathematics and ancient history under the auspices of his Percy kin's tutor. She listened, having spoken earlier of the pilgrimage she had taken with her mother to the priory at Whitby, founded by St Hilda. It was there that the decision had been made that England follow the Roman way of worshipping God, rather than the Celtic. A decision still disputed by some, thought Cicely.

It was dusk when Alnwick Castle came into view.

Cicely felt a shiver ripple down her spine as they rode towards the edifice, which stood apart from the town, overlooking the river. The huge fortification looked eerie against the darkening sky. As they approached the gatehouse a guard challenged them, but he soon realised it was his master leading the company. They passed through a stone gateway into an enormous courtyard that was soon crowded with people welcoming the earl and his men home. Cicely gazed at the huge many-towered keep at its centre and shivered again.

'Are you cold?' asked Mackillin with concern.

'No. The castle is just so…' She grimaced.

'There is naught to fear despite it is rumoured that the castle was haunted by one of its former masters,' said Mackillin, his eyes twinkling.

Cicely shot him a glance. 'But not now?'

He dismounted. 'Not once have I seen a ghost here despite having wandered its passages at midnight.'

'So tell me of this ghost.' She placed her hands on his shoulders and he swung her to the ground.

Mackillin whispered in her ear, 'His crimes were so evil that it was said the devil enabled him to rise from his tomb and his ghost wandered the castle and town, spreading pestilence in its wake.'

She slipped her hand through his arm. 'What happened to stop it?'

'They dug up his body and burnt it to ashes.

Afterwards the plague departed and the ghost was never seen again.' He kissed her cheek. 'So naught to worry about spending the night here.' Cicely thought that was a relief, but kept her arm firmly in her husband's as they entered the keep.

Despite the logs blazing in the enormous fireplace in the great hall, the air struck chill. The earl, who was standing by the fire with his lady, turned and said, 'Tidings for you, Rory. A messenger has been here from Killin Keep. Apparently none of the fighting men who answered the summons of Scotland's king have yet returned. Your mother was anxious about your safety and wondered if I and my men were back and whether I had seen you.'

Mackillin was filled with a sense of foreboding. 'Where is this messenger?'

'He left here this morning.' Harry hesitated. 'I did not mention to you that I dispatched a courier whilst in Stafford with news of our victory and your wedding. Naturally my lady—'

'Has informed my mother of the news,' said Mackillin in colourless tones.

'Aye.' Harry shifted uncomfortably. 'She thought only to relieve your mother of worry.'

'Of course,' said Mackillin, forcing a smile. He turned and thanked Lady Northumberland, adding, 'Lady Mackillin and I will ride for the border at first light.'

Harry looked relieved. 'I will provide you with an escort. With Armstrong still at large, who is to say that he has not gleaned men from those who deserted before the battle took place and might make an attack.'

With Cicely's safety uppermost in his thoughts, Mackillin accepted his offer.

Cicely found her husband distracted as they undressed. She had spoken to him twice and he had made no response. The third time she asked tentatively, 'Are you worrying about your mother and what she will think of your marrying me and the manner of our wedding?'

He did not answer immediately, but after a few moments he drew her down on to the bed beside him and said, 'I am certainly concerned about my mother and what she is thinking, but not in the way you suggested. I must tell you for your own safety that my mother is not to be trusted.'

Cicely was dismayed. 'In what way can't I trust her?'

'Neither of us can trust her,' said Mackillin, his hazel eyes sombre. 'Whilst the Armstrongs thought me still unconscious, I heard them talking. It appears that my mother schemed with Armstrong to destroy my father and half-brothers and...if I heard aright, my demise was also planned.'

Cicely gasped and turned in his arm and clung to

his undertunic. 'No! Surely a mother would not plan her son's death?'

Mackillin's expression was bleak. 'You would certainly believe that, sweeting, but…' His voice trailed off.

'But you don't,' said Cicely, feeling such pity for him that she drew him to her and held him in her arms. 'What are we to do?' she whispered. 'Do we pretend we have no notion of this plot against you?'

'I have thought of doing so in order to put her off her guard and see if she will make the attempt on my life herself,' he said, caressing Cicely's back.

'That is, of course, if we arrive safely at Killin Keep,' said Cicely. 'I presume you have thought of that?'

He nodded. 'I wish I wasn't taking you into danger. My plan was to make all secure for you first. I should really leave you here and go on alone.'

'No!' Her voice was firm. 'We married for better, for worst. We are in this together and I refuse to be left behind. Besides, do you wish us to part after what…happened when we…?' She hesitated to say the words.

He felt such love for her that she should broach the matter that he decided it would be a waste of time arguing with her. 'Of course not. How could I when you welcomed me so sweetly into your body?'

'I would do so again,' she dared to say.

He did not need a second invitation and when they made love this time it was with the knowledge that they both knew that the pleasures of the marriage bed could indeed be so delightfully unifying that both would want to die rather than be parted.

Afterwards she was filled with a sweet contentment, cuddling up against him, wondering if what he felt for her and she for him was that love which the minstrels sang about and Owain and Kate shared? It was in her mind that it could be possible that she had found what she had been looking for which she had once mistakenly thought she had found with Diccon. A tiny furrow appeared between her brows as she thought about her first love and she prayed for his safety and that he would find someone else who could love him as he deserved. No doubt he would be angry when he learnt of her wedding, but hopefully he would not wish to challenge Mackillin to combat. She would pray that he would accept that his life and hers now lay in different directions. At least her brothers would be pleased that she and Mackillin had done what their father wished and were now wed.

Suddenly it occurred to Cicely to ponder on the matter of Mary Armstrong. How would she feel when she discovered that Mackillin had married an

English woman? Was she involved in her father's schemes at all? What kind of welcome could she and Mackillin expect if—no—when they reached Killin Keep? She doubted it would be a warm one from either woman.

Chapter Fourteen

Cicely gazed up at the grey stone keep amidst landscape that at that moment looked dreary and unappealing beneath a louring sky. Her spirits plummeted even further than they had earlier when they had passed crows picking out the eyes of a dead sheep near a stone circle.

'When spring comes it will not look so desolate,' said Rory, rousing her from her reverie.

Cicely darted him a sidelong glance. 'I have made no complaint, my lord.'

A smile creased the corners of his eyes. 'No, lass, you're too well mannered for that.' He stared up at the keep yet again, conscious of the lack of a guard on watch. His concern had been that Armstrong might have already entered the building, but surely if he was here then Sir Malcolm would have posted a man to watch out for their coming. He caught a glimpse of a woman's face at a window on the first floor, but then it vanished.

Suddenly a door opened at the top of a flight of stone steps. They gazed up and saw a tall, black-clad figure standing in the doorway.

'It's Mother,' said Mackillin in an undertone.

'Is that you, my son?' she called down in a quavering tone.

Cicely sensed rather than saw him tense, but his voice was calm when he answered, 'Aye, Mother, it is I, Rory.'

'Come up to me.' She lifted her hand and beckoned him.

It seemed to Cicely that it was an effort for Lady Joan to make that gesture and would have felt pity for her mother-in-law if Mackillin had not already spoken of his mother's deviousness.

Mackillin murmured an order to the man at his side before dismounting and helping Cicely from her horse. 'Don't you want to go ahead and greet your mother on your own?' she whispered.

His craggy features were grim. 'No. There is naught I will say to her that you cannot hear. Besides, I want you to witness at close quarters her behaviour—so smile, my lady, and lift your head high.'

Cicely did so, but her pulse was rapid as she climbed the steps towards the woman whom she was about to supplant as lady of Killin Keep.

Lady Joan offered her cheek to her son. 'I thought you would never come. You knew my need and should have hastened home,' she scolded.

'You know my reasons, Mother.' Rory's lips barely touched his mother's cheek. 'May I introduce my wife, Lady Cicely Mackillin.' He drew her forward.

Cicely noticed the signs of former beauty in the middle-aged patrician features, but only for an instant did she consider aping her husband in kissing his mother's cheek. The gloved hand offered to her and the cold glint in the depths of the elder woman's grey eyes caused Cicely to scarcely touch that hand. 'I am delighted to meet you, Lady Joan.'

'So I should imagine,' said her mother-in-law, drawing her skirts close about her as if she did not wish to make further contact with Cicely. 'No doubt you will find this lowly keep not the least like your own home. If the messenger had not warned me of your coming, then you would find us in a worse state than we are. I have done my best to have a bedchamber prepared to your liking with the few servants I have here. You will find them sullen and unwilling and no doubt you'll soon be wishing yourself back in England.'

'Is that what you did?' asked Cicely, finding something to pity in the woman's situation despite what she knew of her.

Lady Joan's tall figure stiffened. 'What do you mean by that remark?'

'I thought it was obvious,' said Cicely, smiling warmly. 'You're English. I just wondered if you've ever wished yourself back home.'

Lady Joan darted a look at her son and then threw up her hands. 'It has started already,' she wailed. 'This wife of yours would be rid of me.'

Cicely was stunned by the accusation and hastened to reassure her. 'That is not true. Believe me, it is not so.' She turned to Mackillin. 'Tell her—I would that your mother was as a mother to me.'

'You have just told her yourself.' There was a hard light in his eyes as he looked at Lady Joan. 'Did you hear Cissie, Mother? Does the thought of having a daughter not delight you?' There was a thread of irony in his voice.

'You do not mean it.' Lady Joan took a scrap of lace and linen from her sleeve and dabbed at her eyes. 'How can I see her as a daughter when I know naught of her but that her father was a merchant?' She took a deep breath before rushing into speech again. 'And that you allowed yourself to be forced into a marriage with her because you took her into your bed beforehand as you would a common whore.'

The colour drained from Cicely's cheeks. 'That is not true!'

Lady Joan laughed. 'Naturally you would deny it, but why else would he marry you?'

'Hold your tongue, Mother.' Mackillin's voice was harsh. 'My wife was a virgin when she came to me as a bride. I married her because I care for her.'

His mother turned on him and her features were twisted with fury. 'You expect me to believe that? You're like your father. He stole me away from all I held dear and brought me to this Godforsaken place. She'll regret joining her life with yours. Mark my words, she'll rue the day.'

'Enough! Make up your mind between one or the other, but be warned—I am not a child that can be bullied and lied to any more,' he said sharply.

Lady Joan gasped and put her hand to her heart. 'You dare to speak so to your ailing mother. I have only ever cared for your well being.'

Mackillin threw back his chestnut head and laughed; it was not a pleasant sound. 'You resented me because I was my father's son. Perhaps you thought if I had not been born then he might have given you your freedom.'

Lady Joan fumbled for a chair and sat down. 'You should not speak of these matters in front of this—this merchant's daughter. I feel faint.' She put a hand to her head. 'Summon one of the servants. I need wine.'

'We all need wine,' said Mackillin, breathing deeply. 'And Northumberland's men need ale and food and a place to sleep before they return to Alnwick. Where are the servants? Where are Killin's men-at-arms? Where is Mary? You said in your message that she was staying with you.'

His mother glared at him. 'You think I would keep her with me, knowing you were coming home with another bride? The poor child was so disappointed, I had to send her away.'

'Where to? Have you had word that her father has returned?' he asked sardonically.

Lady Joan's eyelids flickered rapidly. 'I don't like your tone.'

'Did you provide her with an escort?'

His mother leaned back in her chair and closed her eyes.

Cicely looked at her husband and saw his lips tighten. 'Should I go in search of the kitchen and see what food and wine there is available?' she murmured.

His expression lightened. 'Aye, that would be useful.'

Lady Joan smirked. 'There is little wine and food in this place. It is almost March, so provisions are low. See what a mistake you have made in marrying my son, merchant's daughter, you'll receive naught of value from him.'

'Silence!' thundered Mackillin.

Both women visibly jumped. Cicely wondered at his interest in Mary, but did not speak of it. Instead, she said, 'It is not your son's responsibility to lay in stores for the winter or to purchase what is available from the nearest town if none is available on one's manor. It is the lady of the household's job to perform that task. As it is still Lent, then hunting for fresh meat must wait, but surely you have the means to make bread? There is the river to fish, and do you not have peas and onions and barley to make pottage?'

She did not linger to see the effect of her words on Lady Joan, but left the hall by an inner door. Still disturbed by the strength of the emotions between mother and son and what had been said about Mary, she tried to put it out of her mind. She was in a small space containing a chest, a small table and a bench; a stone staircase twisted upwards and downwards. She took the lower stairs and was almost at their foot when she heard voices.

She took several breaths before opening the door a few feet away. A glance around the room assured her that she had found the kitchen. Those present turned and stared at her. One of the men was grizzled-haired and had a snub nose. Immediately she recognised him. 'Robbie!' she cried, so delighted to see him that she ran over and flung her arms around him.

'There, there, Mistress Cicely, don't fash yerself, lass.' He patted her back awkwardly.

Immediately she drew away from him, sensing his embarrassment. 'I beg your pardon. I am just so relieved to see you.'

'I, you, too. Mackillin is with you?' he asked eagerly.

'Of course he is. We are wed now.'

'So I've just heard. I'm newly arrived, meself, with these men.' He indicated those in the company with a wave of his hand. 'Your father would be delighted.'

For a moment her face was sad. 'Aye. I only wish he could know that his last wish has come true. Still, perhaps he can see us from heaven.'

'Aye, my lady.'

There was a silence. Then Robbie said, 'Is it food and drink you're after, mistress?'

'It is indeed.' Cicely smiled and faced the eldest of the three women there. 'As you will have gathered from Robbie's greeting, I am your lord's wife. I would that you would not resent me because I am English, for when I married Mackillin I became part Scots, too.'

'Well said, mistress, them are words that Lady Joan has never said to any of us serving folk,' said Robbie gruffly. 'Now make your bow to her ladyship and prepare food and drink.'

Tears shone in Cicely's eyes. She thought it most likely that, if it had not been for Robbie, her presence here would have been resented. 'My thanks, Robbie. You must go and greet Mackillin.'

'Aye. I'll be glad to see him.' His eyes were bright. 'I have much to tell him.' He hurried out of the kitchen.

Cicely faced those remaining and asked some of their names. Then she requested that on the morrow one of the women should show her what provisions they had and where everything was kept. 'I know winter is almost over and so you will not have much in store—but thankfully spring is not far off.'

'That is true, my lady,' said the eldest maid. 'Will you be staying here for Eastertide?'

'I deem that is Mackillin's intent,' replied Cicely, suddenly remembering that she had planned to marry Diccon at that most holy time of the year.

She lingered a little longer, watching the mulled wine being prepared. When it was ready, she accepted one of the men's offer to carry it upstairs for her. But when they reached the hall, there was no one there. She bid him place it on the table and then told him to leave her. She presumed that Mackillin had gone with Robbie to the stables where no doubt Northumberland's men were tending their horses. She was so glad to have found

Robbie here because he was someone they could both trust.

'But where is the Lady Joan?' she asked aloud.

Her words echoed about the hall, which was now filling with the shadows of evening. Her ears caught the sound of a stealthy movement and she almost jumped out of her skin. 'Is there anyone there?' she called.

There was no answer, but again Cicely thought she heard a noise as if someone had drawn in a breath. With a heavily beating heart, she took one of the candles from the stand on the table and lit it from the fire. Then she searched the room, looking behind the wooden settle and under the table and also behind the enormous chest that stood in a corner. Then her eyes alighted on a screen and she tiptoed over to the fire and picked up a poker before approaching the gaily painted screen.

'Come out, whoever you are!' she ordered. 'And beware, for I am armed.'

There was a gasp and then a girl emerged from behind the screen. 'Who are you?' demanded Cicely, noting the shabby brown gown and was relieved that she was not Armstrong. 'Are you one of the servants?'

'You don't want to know who I am,' came the shaky reply.

'But I do,' said Cicely, guessing the girl was

scared of her. She held the candle closer to her face, to enable her to get a better look at it. She saw dimpled cheeks in a pleasant face, framed by wings of dark hair. 'Were you placed there to spy on us?'

'Aye. She told me I had to stay out of sight because she didn't want me sent away. I'd be happy to leave here. Perhaps Rory can have someone escort me to a convent in Galloway, far away from here. I'd rather that than return to my father's hall.'

'Your father?'

'Sir Malcolm Armstrong.'

Cicely gasped, 'You're Mary Armstrong?'

She nodded, linking hands together that trembled. 'Don't tell her I told you. She means you and Rory harm…' Cicely flinched. Mary hastened to add, 'But I don't—as Christ and His Holy Mother are my witnesses.'

'I believe you.' Cicely was astounded by this turn of events. How could Rory's mother believe that she could get away with concealing Mary Armstrong from them? 'Were you planning on remaining behind that screen all evening?' she asked curiously, convinced now that she had met her that Mary was no threat to her relationship with Mackillin.

The girl sighed. 'I was just about to come out of hiding when you came through the door.'

'And where would you have gone?'

'I sleep in an antechamber adjoining Lady Joan's bedchamber because she likes me close by. Sometimes she wants me to fetch and carry for her when she cannot sleep during the night. She's going to be furious with me once she knows we've met.'

'We'd have met sooner or later, so what does it matter? Whether you tell her now is up to you, but you certainly couldn't continue to conceal your presence from us.'

'You're right,' said Mary, looking relieved.

'But perhaps you'd best go or she might be wondering what's taking you so long.'

Mary hesitated before agreeing and left the hall.

Cicely lit the rest of the candles, which smoked quite dreadfully. She thought certainly they were not beeswax, most likely made from mutton fat. Once that was done, she poured herself a glass of mulled wine and thought she should have asked Mary not only where Lady Joan's bedchamber was situated, but where Mackillin's and her bedchamber was. She hoped that he would return soon as she wanted to tell him about Mary.

Cicely did not have to wait long because he reappeared a few moments later. 'You are alone,' he murmured.

Her lips curved in a delightful smile. 'Aye. And so are you. Did you speak to Robbie?'

Mackillin nodded, placing his arms about her

waist and bringing her against him. He kissed her. 'You taste delicious,' he murmured.

She pressed herself closer to him and watched some of the strain vanish from his face. 'Mulled wine. I will pour you some once you let me go.'

'In a moment. I need to beg your pardon for showing my anger earlier. I should have had more control.'

'You're forgiven.'

'Thank you.' His hands caressed her back before coming to rest on her buttocks.

'I have no notion of where our bedchamber is,' she said.

The lights in his eyes seemed to dance in the candlelight. 'I see the path which your mind takes. I, too, wish to go to bed, but we cannot yet.' He released her. 'I have matters of importance to tell you.'

'I, too, have news to impart. Mary Armstrong is still here. She was hiding behind the screen.'

He nodded. 'The servants told Robbie. How my mother thought she could keep her presence a secret from us amazes me.'

'I thought that, too.'

'But that is not the only secret she thought to keep from me.' He paused. 'Where is Mary now?'

'Most probably with your mother. I felt sorry for Mary. I would be her friend.'

'If that is your wish, then she must stay,' said

Mackillin, his expression lightening a little. 'For I hold her blameless in all this.'

'What is it?' demanded Cicely.

He hesitated only to take a sip of wine. 'Robbie came by ship to Kirkcudbright from Yorkshire. By chance he met up with those of Killin who fought at St Albans. They were travelling here when they came across others from Killin, but they were all dead. A sack was found in some bushes with a solitary batted brass lamp nearby.'

Cicely felt a stab of fear. 'Armstrong?'

'I fear so, but I have no proof. It could have been the Douglases or one of the other clans. I have ordered Robbie to have a guard mounted and to warn Northumberland's men to have care on their return journey.' His expression was strained and he took another gulp of wine before saying, 'One of the men had an interesting tale to tell Robbie, which had been told to him by his elder brother, who has since died.'

She felt a sinking at her heart, knowing from the tone of his voice that he was deeply disturbed. 'What is it?' She placed her hand on his arm.

'He said that my mother and Armstrong have been lovers for years. If that is so, then most likely she was definitely party to his scheming to destroy us Mackillins.'

'I am so sorry,' she said, distressed for him.

'Sorry, too, about Killin's men who were murdered.'

He sighed. 'It is a sad day.'

For a moment there was silence but for the crackling of the fire. Then Cicely said, 'What of Mary? Do you think she could be of help to us? She has no love for her father and I think she fears your mother.'

He nodded. 'I will need to speak to her myself and, until we discover Armstrong's whereabouts, you must stay close to the keep and not wander beyond the outer walls surrounding the herb and vegetable gardens and the outhouses.'

She saw the sense in what he said and agreed. 'What of you? Will you go in search of him?'

He did not reply.

His silence was answer enough for her and she squared her shoulders. 'What weapons do we have in store? I had to part with my bow and quiver of arrows and I need replacements and to practise, just in case Armstrong should come beating at our door while you are away.'

A smile tugged at his mouth. 'You would fight him?'

She returned his smile. 'I would shoot at him from the walls.'

'A much safer option, but let us pray that it will not come to that. I will have Robbie find a bow suitable for your size…but you must not go looking for trouble, Cissie,' he ordered, his smile fading.

'No,' she said softly. 'Where Armstrong is concerned, I am not such a fool as that.'

'Good.' He went over to the fireplace and took a log from the basket and rammed it amongst the glowing embers.

She watched his agile movements and her heart swelled with love for him. He had yet to say that he loved her, but his actions said so much about his affection for her.

The door opened and a couple of serving men entered carrying plates of food. A boy hurried forward with a bowl and a drying cloth.

'Just what we were ready for,' said Mackillin, smiling cheerfully at them. 'When you have finished setting everything down, one of you run upstairs and tell my mother and Mistress Armstrong to come and eat. Then fetch the men from outside.'

It was a good half hour later when Mary came hurrying into the hall. 'Rory, it is so good to see you.' She held out both hands to him. 'Forgive me for keeping you waiting, but your mother changed her mind about coming down and said just now that she will dine alone in her chamber.'

'So be it.' He stood up and grasped her hands. 'I

am glad you are safe. Cissie tells me that you were hiding from us. There is no need for you to fear us, Mary.'

'Aye.' She flashed a tentative smile in Cicely's direction. 'Your wife spoke kindly to me. I appreciated that very much, considering she might have resented me.'

'Why should she do that? It is some years since we last saw each other and no agreement was ever reached between our parents.'

She sighed. 'I know. Besides, I have not changed and you have. You carry yourself differently. You walk proudly now. You've seen so many exciting places and have learnt to fend for yourself and grow brave and true.' There was a wistful note in her voice.

Rory looked amused. 'I was a poor kind of creature, then. I am surprised you had a fancy for me at all. I had to go away before I could become my true self.'

'I wished I could have done so, but it is different for us females.' She turned to Cicely. 'Is that not so, Lady Mackillin?'

'In part it is, but a woman can still fight, only she has different weapons she can use.' Cicely patted the seat next to her. 'Come sit beside me, Mary, so we can become better acquainted, and do call me Cissie.'

Mary complied instantly. 'I am so hungry. I have

not eaten since breaking my fast this morning. Lady Joan was in a fury when she received the news that you were on your way here. She even considered leaving, but then she dictated a message to her cleric instead.'

His lordship shot a glance at her. 'Do you know whom this message was for?'

'My father.' She picked up her spoon as a serving man placed a bowl of pottage in front of her.

Cicely and Mackillin stared at her. 'My mother told you this?' he asked.

Mary gave a hollow laugh. 'You jest. I was hiding behind the screen.'

Cicely was curious. 'Do you make a habit of doing that?'

'Only when I tire of being treated like a lackey.'

'Did you hear where the message was to be delivered?' asked Mackillin.

She shook her head. 'Unfortunately, I did not.'

Cicely grimaced. 'What a shame.'

Her husband agreed, but then said, 'I would deem it a favour, Mary, if you would—'

'Keep a watch on her and let you know if aught untoward happens?' Her violet eyes twinkled at him.

He laughed. 'Exactly. My thanks.'

Cicely felt the teeniest bit jealous of their easy manner with each other and wished she had known

Mackillin in his youth. At that moment, Northumberland's men entered the hall and the matter was dropped. They continued their meal in silence.

After the table was cleared and the three of them went and sat close to the fire, Mary asked Cicely about her family. She was happy to talk about them and did so. Then Mary asked how she had met Rory, and Cicely told her of her father's murder and how he had saved her brother's life.

'It's just like one of the tales of derring-do that my mother used to tell me!' exclaimed Mary, her face rapt.

Cicely glanced sidelong at her husband. 'There you are, Mackillin,' she said. 'A story could be written about your ventures. Perhaps one day I will do so during the long, freezing winter nights up here at Killin. You can dictate to me those exciting happenings I played no part in.'

A smile lit his weatherbeaten face and there was a message in that smile that told her he was thinking of other ways they could spend those evenings and she felt quite breathless.

An hour or so later Rory and Cicely were in the marital bed. It had no curtains and it was pitch black and icy cold in the chamber. He had forced shut the swollen-with-damp wooden shutters as best he could. Beneath them a sheet covered a blanket that concealed a hair mattress. At least there were plentiful woollen blankets, thought Cicely as she waited for her husband to approach her.

For a moment neither of them spoke or moved. Then suddenly he shuffled closer and his arm went round her shoulders. 'Not the most luxurious bedchamber we have slept in,' he muttered. 'Forgive me, Cissie, for bringing you to this. I had intended to spend time making improvements to the place.'

'It is of no matter. I will enjoy sharing what needs to be done to turn this keep into our home,' she assured him.

With that said, she daringly toyed with one of his nipples. He quivered and her hand stilled, for she was suddenly unsure of whether she should have been so bold as to caress him there. Then he took her hand and placed it on his hip and now, encouraged, she caressed the line downwards, including the curve of his buttocks. How strong were the muscles there, she thought. In the darkness she pictured his naked body, aware not only of her own heartbeat but the thud of his beneath her ear. She jumped when his fingers touched her jaw and his lips found hers unerringly in the dark. When they made love, she could not resist moving in tandem with him and soared into a higher realm of pleasure.

* * *

They woke just before dawn and he took her with a hunger and swiftness that left her gasping for more. Afterwards they talked about their situation and what needed to be done. Then Cicely mentioned her need for a change of clothing.

'Perhaps Mary has a gown and undergarments you can borrow for now,' he suggested.

'I doubt it. The gown she was wearing was a poor thing. I must purchase cloth and make some new gowns,' said Cicely firmly. 'Either that or we send another messenger to Milburn, so that those I already have can be dispatched to me.'

'Until I discover where Armstrong is, I cannot put a man's life at risk for clothes, Cissie,' he said just as firmly.

She understood and said no more.

He pushed back the blankets and climbed out of bed. 'You rest a little longer. I will go and see if anyone is up and about.' His hazel eyes gleamed down at her. 'I hope that you have enjoyed your first night in your new home.'

She blushed. 'I cannot deny that I did.'

'Good.' He moved away from the bed, knowing Cicely was so essential to his happiness that if she was torn from his side then it would break him. He must find Armstrong and get rid of him.

Mackillin went downstairs to the hall and found

one of the men placing logs on the fire. After a few words with him, he went to check with the guards that they had seen naught suspicious. Then he visited the outhouses, including the armoury; the latter was almost empty, containing only a few rusty swords, a battered shield, a number of arrows and a couple of unstrung bows.

It was as he returned to the hall that he heard hurrying footsteps descending the stairs. He looked up and saw Mary. Her face was flushed and she looked frightened. 'What is wrong? Is it my mother?'

'I cannot find her and her best cloak and a couple of her gowns are missing, too.'

Mackillin said grimly, 'That doesn't sound promising.'

'You think she has left the keep?' Her voice trembled. 'Forgive me if she has done so. I did mean to keep my eye on her, but I was so tired, I fell asleep.'

'If she rose during the night, it is not your fault if you did not hear her.' His voice was calm, concealing his irritation. 'The guards did not notice anything amiss, although she could have slipped away when they were changing watch. The stable lad made no mention of any of the horses being missing, though.'

'What will you do?' asked Mary, clutching his sleeve.

'What is wrong?' called a voice.

Rory looked up and saw Cicely descending the stairs. 'Mother is missing. Mary informs me that her best cloak has gone and a couple of her gowns.'

Cicely drew in her breath. 'You think she has joined Armstrong?'

'It's possible. I must speak to the stable lad again.'

Whilst his wife ordered breakfast, Mackillin returned to the stables. This time he was told that his lady mother had placed her mare in the smaller stable, saying it had injured its leg and she wanted it kept away from the other horses. She had forbidden him to tend it, adding that she would do so herself. Immediately Mackillin went in search of it and found the stable empty. It was enough for him to rouse Robbie and the rest of the men before returning to the hall. There he ate a hearty breakfast and asked Cicely to see to it that food be made ready for him to take along on the journey.

'You are going in search of your mother and Armstrong?' He nodded. 'You know where to look?' asked Cicely.

'I have an idea. I could be away for several days, though.'

Cicely did her best to hide her fear. 'You will take Robbie and some of the men? And you will not take any risks?' she demanded, her hand resting on his leather body armour as she looked into his face.

Mackillin covered her hand with his own. 'Aye. But I will leave some of the men here for your protection. Northumberland's men will have to return home.' He sighed. 'I hate leaving you alone so soon.'

'It cannot be helped,' she said, holding back her tears.

He kissed her. 'Promise me that you will not wander from the keep?'

Cicely gave him her word. Then, with a cold chill about her heart, she watched him ride out until he and the men were out of sight.

Chapter Fifteen

Cicely stood up on the roof, looking out over the rolling windswept countryside of Mackillin's border domain. A few cattle grazed close to the keep, watched over by a herdsman. She had been informed that barley and oats had been planted and now the shoots had begun to break through the soil. Spring was on its way, but still her husband had not come. It was more than two weeks since he had left and sometimes she feared that he was dead. Yet something inside her would not allow her to give up hope, telling herself that she would have heard if he was dead.

Her bow and a quiver of arrows lay close to hand, just in case she should have need of them. During the long days and nights of his absence, she had done her best to fill them with useful toil, but it was not easy when she longed to ride out in search of him. In the evenings there were no books to read and she had not the means to make herself new clothes. Of course, she did spend time chatting to Mary and she had found quills, ink and a few sheets of paper, so had made a start writing down some of hers and Mackillin's ventures.

A sigh escaped her as once more her worried eyes scanned the now familiar scene. Then she froze as she saw several riders in the distance. Her heart began to thud, but she remained where she was as they approached. She was almost ready to fly downstairs, but as they drew closer, she realised with a painful disappointment that her husband was not amongst their number. Who were these men? At least she could not see Armstrong with them.

She decided to go down and speak to them. She climbed through the trapdoor, careful not to jam her bow in the opening, and hurried down the stairway to the hall.

Mary turned as Cicely entered and said excitedly, 'I was coming to fetch you. King James's envoys are here.'

Cicely could not conceal her astonishment. 'So that's who they are?'

'They have been here before. Come, you must talk to them.'

Cicely hurried outside to discover two of the guards conversing with the visitors. At the sound of her footsteps, one turned and said, 'Here's her ladyship now. She'll be telling ye that Mackillin's away and we don't know when he'll return.'

Cicely brushed past him and gazed down at the horsemen gathered at the foot of the steps. 'For what reason do you seek my husband?' she asked.

'The king orders him and his men to go to the aid of King Henry of England,' called up one of the men. 'There is going to be a great battle in the north of that country near York. Men are already gathering there.'

Cicely felt heartsick, remembering the cries of the wounded and dying at St Albans. She thought of more blood being spilt, more lives lost, more families grieving for their loved ones and was almost glad that Mackillin was not here to answer his king's command. 'I will inform my lord when he returns. God grant you a safe journey.'

She watched them depart and returned to the hall.

'So they wish for Scotland's fighting men to spill their blood for your king again,' said Mary, who had listened at the window.

Her words annoyed Cicely. She thought of the likes of Armstrong, pillaging and looting English lands. Then she thought of her brothers and Diccon and felt dizzy with anxiety. She sat down quickly.

'What is the matter?' asked Mary, worriedly, placing a hand on Cicely's arm.

'I am concerned for my brothers and my stepbrother.' She took several deep breaths and then rose again and wandered over to the fire. She kicked the log so that sparks flew up.

Mary followed her over. 'They will fight?'

'My stepbrother certainly will. The twins—? No. But even so, after a battle the bloodlust can still be on a warrior. Who knows what harm might be done to innocent folk then?'

'What are you going to do?'

'Wait,' she said shortly.

Mary sighed. 'That is all us women can ever do. If only Rory would come home, he would know what could be done to keep your brothers safe.'

'Where can he be?' cried Cicely, kicking the log again.

'Perhaps he has gone to Kirkcudbright,' suggested Mary. 'Lady Joan spoke of the port, saying that she had stayed in Rory's house before leaving for France a while ago.'

Cicely gazed into the fire and thought about Mary's words. 'I will give it another day,' she murmured. 'And if he has not returned, then I will take a couple of the men and go in search of him there.' She picked up the sheet she had been darning and abandoned two hours ago.

The following day Cicely was in the yard, issuing orders to one of the men when she heard a clamour outside. The man's head turned away from her and she fell silent, listening. Then her heart leapt as she recognised her husband's voice. Without more ado, she picked up her skirts and ran in the direction of the noise. And there he was at the head of his men. She saw his eyes brighten at the sight of her. A smile started within her like a shaft of sunshine that grew until it shone in her face.

'You've returned,' she said.

'Aye. I'm sorry I've been away so long.' He dismounted and covered the ground between them and swung her up into his arms and kissed her. For several moments after their lips parted, they remained close together, his gauntleted hands resting on her waist and hers against his chest, their breathing hurried as they searched the other's face. He badly needed a shave and a wash, but it was so good to look upon his dear face again, she thought.

'Something is bothering you,' he said.

She laughed. 'Of course I've been bothered. I feared you were dead.'

'I mean something else is bothering you.' He wondered if he should tell her that, having watched the changing expression of her face so often, he could almost read her thoughts.

'I am fine now that you are here.'

A stable lad had come running, so Mackillin left his horse in his capable hands. His grip on her waist slackened and he took one of her hands and began to walk towards the keep. 'I have much to tell you.'

'I should think you have after being away so long. Your king's envoys were here yesterday. King Henry requires your service again.'

Mackillin paused in mid-stride before continuing towards the house. 'There is naught for you to fear. I will not go. I have no intention of becoming involved in the affairs of York and Lancaster again.'

Cicely breathed the easier. 'That makes me happy,' she said softly. 'Although I fear for my brothers. The envoy seemed to think that the battle will take place near York.'

He wondered if her concern was also for Diccon, but did not say so, only squeezing her hand. 'I understand why you are anxious, but York is some leagues from Milburn, but as soon as possible I will send a messenger there.'

'What of Armstrong? What news of your mother?'

His lips tightened and several seconds went by before he said, 'My mother is dead.'

Cicely had not expected that news and her fingers gripped his tightly. 'How did it happen?'

'I found her in my house at Kirkcudbright. She had been strangled.' His voice was harsh. 'The place had been ransacked and the caretakers were missing. Later they returned after the news reached them I had arrived. They spoke of a man answering to Armstrong's description being there and ordering them out. I can only think that he and my mother quarrelled and he attacked her in anger.'

'Where is he now? Do you know?'

'Not exactly.' He fell silent.

She asked no more questions, deciding that it could wait until he felt ready to tell her the rest.

Mary greeted him as he entered the hall. 'I'm so glad to see you back, Rory.' Her face was anxious. 'Did you find her?'

He nodded. 'Later, Mary. I must wash and change my garments.' He went upstairs.

Mary turned to Cicely. 'What happened?'

She told her the little she knew. Afterwards they both sat, staring into space, remembering in their different ways the last time they had seen Lady Joan.

Mackillin returned to the hall within the hour and, over a meal, he told them what he had further discovered. 'I made enquiries about your father, Mary, and discovered he had taken a ship to France.'

Both the women were astounded. 'For what reason?' asked Cicely.

Mackillin took a deep draught of ale. 'He murdered my mother, so that was reason enough. He knew I'd be intent on bringing him to justice.

Anyway, my ship was anchored in the harbour, so I decided to follow him. Unfortunately the trail went cold when I arrived at Angers, so I hired a couple of men in the hope they could pick up his trail and returned home.'

He fell silent. Cicely reached out and covered his hand with hers.

'Father has kin in France, but he never mentioned the exact place to me,' said Mary, her eyes bright. 'I can only pray that he never returns.'

Cicely echoed her sentiments, but noticed that her husband did not.

Mary left them alone after the meal and for a short time they sat in front of the fire whilst Cicely told him of what she had done in his absence and showed him the pages she had filled with her writing. 'I will need more to continue the tale,' she said.

He nodded absently. She wondered if he had been listening to her at all. Soon after they went up to bed. He seemed content to just hold her in his arms and kiss her and she accepted that, despite his anger towards his mother, he grieved for her none the less.

The next day Mackillin sent a messenger to the king in Edinburgh, citing not only his having fought at St Albans and his subsequent abduction by Armstrong as a reason for not answering the summons this time, but also the loss of a number of his men and the need to protect his wife and his lands from his enemies. He offered to serve the king in any other way that he wished in the future. At the same time he asked Robbie to take a message to Milburn Manor. He did not send him alone, but arranged for a couple of the men to accompany him. The Borders were emptying of the clans, eager to fight on English soil again. A rumour had swept the area that King Henry had promised to return Berwick-on-Tweed to the crown of Scotland for its aid.

The snows of March had melted away and the sights and sounds of spring could be heard in the song of the thrush and the sight of newborn chicks and the wild flowers in the meadow. The last few weeks had drifted by and Easter had come and gone; still there was no news from Robbie or the king's envoy. Cicely and Rory had occupied their time in a variety of activities. Sometimes they shared pastimes, such as exploring the extent of his lands. On another occasion they had ridden into Kelso, where they had worshipped at the abbey. As it was market day, she had also been able to buy woollen cloth, linen, paper, ink and quills. This delighted her. Not once did he mention their visiting his house in Kirkcudbright and, although she thought she understood why, it saddened her because he had spoken of it being his favourite home.

On the days when he was occupied elsewhere, hunting or speaking to his newly appointed steward, she organised the cleaning of the hall, or set to fashioning new clothes and making sheets for their bed. For an hour in the evening, she gave time to her writing, although she had yet to get Mackillin to talk further of his travels.

It was the second week in April when she realised that she might be with child, but she kept silent, wanting to be certain. As it was, a couple of days later they received news of the battle of Towton in Yorkshire, brought by one of Mackillin's mariners, whose eyes were bright with a mixture of excitement and horror as he told his tale over a tankard of ale.

'The Lancastrians and Yorkists have fought a great battle. They say never have so many men been killed on English soil before in such a conflict.'

The blood drained from Cicely's face and she had to sit down. 'When was this?'

'Palm Sunday.'

Mackillin placed a hand on his wife's arm, concerned that her feelings for Diccon could be deeper than he had feared. 'So who was the victor?' His hazel eyes were intent on the mariner's face.

'Edward. It's rumoured that when the news reached York of his victory it spread like wildfire. King Henry and Queen Margaret took their son and fled for the border. They're saying more than twenty thousand men died.' The man swallowed. 'Don't bear thinking about, does it?'

'No,' rasped Mackillin. 'Names! Do you have any names of the fallen?'

The mariner cleared his throat. 'Your kinsman Northumberland was amongst the slain and they say many reivers were slaughtered.'

It was Cicely's turn to show concern for him, knowing how upset he would be at that news. If it had not been for Northumberland, she and Mackillin might never have escaped Armstrong's clutches. 'I'm so sorry, Rory,' she murmured.

'Me, too,' he said on a sigh.

Afterwards, Mackillin spoke at length to the mariner but he did not tell Cicely the content of their conversation.

It was late afternoon the following day that Mackillin was informed several riders were approaching the building. Cicely was practising archery in a meadow at the back of the keep, so immediately he sent someone to fetch her. 'Perhaps it's Robbie and the men,' he said.

'I will go and see.' Mary did not want to miss out on the excitement. She stood at the top of the steps and tried to focus on their faces. She recognised Robbie amongst the eight riders, one of whom was a woman. 'You have returned, Robbie,' she called down. 'Rory and Cissie will be so glad. But who are these folk with you?' she added.

The riders reined in their horses and a man in breast armour shouted, 'Who is it that asks?'

'I am Mary Armstrong. State your name and I will inform Mackillin that you are below.'

'Tell him that Sir Richard Fletcher is here with Master Owain ap Rowan, Jack Milburn and the servant Martha.'

Mary felt a thrill of excitement as she gazed down at the knight's face. 'I will tell him.' She stepped back and collided with Mackillin.

'I heard all,' he said before she could speak. His expression was grim—he was wondering why Diccon was here.

Mary faced the visitors again. 'Welcome! Come inside and rest after your long journey.'

Diccon gazed at the comely lass who stood just above him. 'I thank you for your welcome, Mistress Armstrong,' he said, dismounting.

Mary took two steps down so she could see his

face the clearer, considering him handsome, despite the fresh scar on the left side of his face. Suddenly there came a whistling on the air and she staggered back. Martha let out a cry of dismay. An arrow jutted out from beneath the girl's collarbone.

Diccon hurried forward and caught her as she fell. She moaned as he carried her into the shadowy lee of the stairway and set her down on the ground. Mackillin's gaze flew towards the bushes a short distance away and he caught sight of a man concealed there. Taking his dagger from his belt, he went for him, knowing now that the mariner's information had been correct.

Several things happened at once. Cicely came round the side of the keep, carrying her bow. Martha dismounted and went to Mary's aid. Seeing the visitors there, Cicely was filled with gladness, although her mood was tempered by her concern for Mary. Then she realised that Mackillin was not present and looked about her. As she saw him running away from the keep, she saw his quarry. He was placing an arrow in what appeared to her to be a hackbut. In that moment she recognised Armstrong. Hastily she reached for an arrow and fixed it in position and let fly.

Mackillin was but yards away when he felt the movement in the air that signalled Cicely's arrow sailing past him. It took Armstrong's hat off and was diversion enough to cause him to drop his bow. Mackillin launched himself at him and plunged his knife into his enemy's chest. Armstrong stared up at him with hatred in his eyes and then his head fell back.

Mackillin said a prayer and then stood up and turned to see Cicely coming towards him.

She threw herself at him. 'Oh, my love…'

He caught her against his chest. 'Your arrow…'

'I know! It missed its target.' Her expression showed chagrin.

'But you still saved me, sweeting.'

Robbie came hurrying over to them. 'Well done, Mackillin. And you, your ladyship,' he added hastily.

'I missed him, Robbie,' she said forlornly.

Mackillin grinned. 'You need more practice. Now let's get back to the keep.'

'Mary is hurt,' said Cicely, worriedly.

Mackillin nodded. They hurried back to the keep.

Owain and Jack greeted them with cries of relief and informed them that Diccon had carried Mary into the hall and Martha had gone with them.

'You must come inside,' said Mackillin. 'You have ridden far and must be in need of rest, food and drink.'

'We wouldn't argue with you there, Mackillin,' said Jack, smiling at his lordship and his sister.

'I can scarcely believe you're here,' said Cicely, hugging him.

He returned her hug briefly and then released her.

'We've brought you gifts. Martha thought you might need some clothes and I have fetched the Flemish glass that Father had made for you.'

Cicely clapped her hands in delight. 'Hopefully it will fit the opening in our bedchamber, if not we will find somewhere else for it.' She looked a question at her brother.

He winked. 'Aye. We've brought that.'

Cicely did not linger, but hurried on ahead into the hall to give orders to the servants. Mackillin told her to tell them to serve the best wine that he had sent from France months ago. 'I want a feast worthy of our guests,' he said.

While the food was being prepared, Owain and Jack brought in a small chest and placed it on the table. 'Here is your dowry, Cissie,' said Owain, shaking his head at her in mock reproof. 'I never expected to have to chase the pair of you all the way up here to deliver it. It's in coin, for I was certain that you and Mackillin might be in need of silver and gold.'

Mackillin could not speak for a moment and then he glanced at Cicely and squeezed her hand before saying, 'I took her without the dowry, Owain. I have money of my own.'

'Don't be a fool, man. She's going to lead you a merry dance and has expensive tastes,' said Owain with a laugh. 'Besides, it was Nat's wish.'

'Accept it,' said Cicely, smiling at her husband. 'I have plans to add a few luxurious touches to this keep. A tub for a start. Now you will excuse me. I am neglecting my duty. I have left Diccon and Martha tending Mary and I should be at her side.'

She went over to where Mary was stretched out on the settle and greeted her stepbrother and maid with equal warmth, before adding, 'I see you've already removed the arrow.'

'Sir Richard took it out,' said Martha, beaming at him. 'He really seems to know what he was about.'

Diccon glanced unsmiling up at Cicely. 'I need more cloths to stem the blood,' he said gruffly.

'Then I will fetch some.' Cicely wondered why he had come when it was obvious he was vexed with her. She sighed, wanting all those she cared for to be happy on this day. As she made to turn away, she heard Mary say, 'You've gentle hands, Sir Richard.'

'My mother was a healer, a wise woman,' he muttered, 'so is my sister. She would have been here if she was not with child, so I have come in her place to give our good wishes to our stepsister and her husband.'

'I am glad you came,' whispered Mary. 'She was concerned for the safety of all her brothers.'

'Her brother—so that's how she sees me now,' he said, glancing over his shoulder.

Cicely caught that glance and smiled. 'I, too, am pleased you came.' She blew him a kiss and then hurried from the hall, hoping that perhaps he and Mary might prove to be of comfort to each other.

Three weeks later Mackillin and Cicely said their goodbyes to Owain, Diccon and Mary. The latter's recovery had been swift and the suggestion that she travel south and visit not only York but London, where she could watch King Edward IV being crowned, was too good an invitation to turn down. One of the maids was to accompany her. It seemed to Cicely and Mackillin that romance was in the air for those they once believed they were intended to wed. They, themselves, were to leave Killin for a short while to visit Kirkcudbright. She wondered if they would have been going if they were not seeing Jack board Mackillin's ship. Owain had also wrung a promise from his host to visit him and Kate during the summer.

The journey to Kirkcudbright was accomplished without any difficulty. The Borders and the south-west of Scotland were looking their best. She was not looking forward at all to saying her goodbye to her brother, remembering the last time had been her final farewell to her father.

She had voiced her fears to her husband and he had said sensibly, 'You can't prevent him going, Cissie.

The sea and foreign climes call to him and it would be wrong to harp on about the danger when there is so much pleasure and excitement ahead for him.'

She had agreed and said no more.

The harbour at Kirkcudbright was just as exciting and colourful as Mackillin had painted it in words and when the parting from Jack came, she said her farewell as cheerfully as she could. 'I would like to visit Europe one day,' she said wistfully, gazing across the shining surface of the water. 'You are fortunate, Jack.'

'I know I am.' He gave her a bear hug and a kiss on the cheek before turning to Mackillin and holding out a hand. 'Thank you for letting me travel on your ship and for everything else you have done for me and mine.' There was a glint of tears in his blue eyes.

Mackillin shook his hand vigorously. 'Take care of yourself, laddie. I've said all I'm going to say to you about that. Keep in touch by courier and then we'll know where to find you if we decide to join you—or, if that isn't possible, when to expect your return so we can make ready for you to stay with us.'

Jack thanked him again before going up the gangplank; he did not look back. Cicely rubbed away her tears and hand in hand with her husband left the harbour.

* * *

She woke early the next morning to the sound of sparrows under the eaves and seagulls in the harbour. She realised that Mackillin must have left her to sleep, rather than disturb her. She sighed with pleasure and then lifted her head and could just about make out his strong features in the faint light. To all appearances he was still asleep. His breathing had not altered when she moved, so she felt free to continue gazing at him and found pleasure in doing so. He looked younger in slumber; the faint lines at the corner of his eyes were barely discernible. Obviously any problem that he might have had about returning here where his mother had been murdered had evaporated. Impulsively she kissed him lightly on his eyelids, nose and mouth.

He wrinkled his nose and she drew back, but he reached out a hand and took hold of her chin. 'Where d'you think you're going?' he murmured.

Without waiting for a reply, he brought her face close to his and kissed her with a depth of hunger that caused her to respond in like manner. She felt a stirring against the fabric covering her abdomen and a tiny pulse throbbed between her legs. The colour rushed to her cheeks as she felt him pleat the fabric of her best silk night rail, shortening it little by little until he lifted it over her head. He dropped the garment on the floor and drew her close to him and whispered against her mouth. 'There's naught to fear, lass. Trust me.'

She laughed. As if by now she did not know he was to be trusted. He kissed her gently and then rolled her over so that she was flat on her back. Then lowering his head, he began to caress her skin with his lips—face, throat, shoulders—before burrowing his face between her breasts whilst his fingertips caressed her nipples with a gentle stroking movement. Such sweet seduction was sweeping her on to a plain of feeling that she was familiar with by now. His mouth replaced his fingers, stepping up the pleasure so that tiny sighs escaped her. She would have had him keep his lips to her breast by holding him captive by his chestnut hair for longer, only he broke free and turned her over. She gasped as he ran his tongue down her spine, caressing her buttocks before darting between her thighs, at which point she protested.

He caught her wavering hand and then came a flicker and a fluttering like that of a butterfly diving into the heart of a flower in search of nectar and she gasped again. Her embarrassment at his kissing her in such a spot was drowned by her need for him to continue and he did so with a gentleness that made her sigh. Moments later such pleasure exploded inside her that she could not contain its reaction. She arched her back, uttering his name in a throaty whisper. 'To think that once I never knew such bodily bliss existed.' Her voice was deep and husky. 'Now you take your reward as my father wished.'

And he did. Within moments he was inside her and it only took seconds for her to catch his rhythm. Waves of pleasure rippled through her again and again; she felt fulfilled as he came inside her. 'I love you,' he said, 'body and soul and with all my heart.'

'Oh, Mackillin,' she breathed.

'Do you not think it is time you dropped the Mackillin and called me Rory, my love?'

'Rory.' Her tongue and lips felt as if tasting the word. 'What does it mean?' she asked.

'It means Red King and most likely was brought to Scotland by the Norsemen who invaded our country in the dark times.'

'So you are named for a red-haired barbarian,' she teased.

'Without doubt, and you are named for a saint. In the past many a saintly woman tamed a barbarian king. Alliances were forged that brought peace in place of war.' His hazel eyes twinkled down into her blue ones.

'So you believe that a wife's task is to influence her husband and bring out the more gentle side to his nature?' she asked.

'Aye.'

She smiled and, reaching up for him, said, 'It is also her role to provide him with children.'

He stilled and gazed at her with a wondering expression in his eyes. 'Are you saying…?'

'Aye. I am with child. God willing it will be an heir for Killin. If not, then we must try again,' she said with a mischievous expression on her lovely face.

Rory gave a whoop of delight and brought her so close to him that not a feather could slip between them. 'Oh, my heart, you are all that I want in a mate. You provide me with all that I need in life.'

'I am pleased to hear it. You are all I want, too.' She kissed him on the mouth and murmured in a teasing voice, 'So, take me again, my barbarian, and let me tame you with my love.'

HISTORICAL ROMANCE

LARGE PRINT

MASQUERADING MISTRESS

Sophia James

War-scarred Thornton Lindsay, Duke of Penborne, can hardly believe the news when a beautiful stranger comes to London proclaiming to be his lover. Caroline Anstretton is on the run and desperate. Courtesan or charlatan, Thorn is intrigued by both sides of this mysterious, sensual woman. Could she be the one to mend a life he'd thought damaged beyond repair?

MARRIED BY CHRISTMAS

Anne Herries

Josephine Horne ignores convention. She never intends to marry, so why should she be hedged about with rules? When loyalty to a friend demands Jo risk her own reputation, she doesn't hesitate. Then she meets handsome Harry Beverley…and her ideas about marriage begin to change…

TAKEN BY THE VIKING

Michelle Styles

They claimed they came in peace, but soon Lindisfarne was aflame. Annis of Birdoswald fled in fear, but she could not escape the Norse warriors. One man protected her – Haakon Haroldson. The dark, arrogant Viking swept Annis back to his homeland, taking her away from all she held dear. Now Annis must choose between the lowly work that befits a captive, or a life of sinful pleasure in the Viking's arms!

MILLS & BOON®

HIST0208 LP

HISTORICAL

LARGE PRINT

SCANDALOUS LORD, REBELLIOUS MISS

Deb Marlowe

Charles Alden, Viscount Dayle, is intent on reform, having misspent his youth. Forced by circumstance to hold a title he never wanted, he's determined to live up to his noble name. Sophie Westby is the last woman who should attract his interest – and yet she captivates his wary mind, and tempts him with her exotic beauty…

THE DUKE'S GAMBLE

Miranda Jarrett

Eliot Fitzharding, Duke of Guilford, finds the thought of matching wits with Miss Amariah Penny very exciting. But there is no avoiding the fact that she runs a gaming house! When a gambler accuses Penny House of harbouring a cheat, Guilford comes immediately to Amariah's rescue. But soon the pair risk becoming an item of choice gossip themselves…

THE DAMSEL'S DEFIANCE

Meriel Fuller

Emmeline de Lonnieres swore she would never belong to a man again, so she is plunged into confusion by her feelings for Lord Talvas of Boulogne. His powerful charisma is irresistible, but she cannot give what she knows he will eventually demand – marriage. A demand she knows he will make when he discovers their passion has created the tiny new life growing inside her…

HISTORICAL

LARGE PRINT

HOUSEMAID HEIRESS

Elizabeth Beacon

An heiress, thinks spoiled Miss Alethea Hardy, should rise late, dress elegantly and marry well. A far cry from her new responsibilities – up at dawn to fetch and carry for her betters! In running away from a repulsive proposal, Thea has ruined herself. Until she meets Marcus Ashfield, Viscount Strensham, who seems to see the beautiful woman behind her dowdy uniform…

MARRYING CAPTAIN JACK

Anne Herries

Despite being the belle of every ball, Lucy Horne can't seem to quell her feelings for a man she has met only once before – the enigmatic and dashing Captain Jack. Jack Harcourt is determined to put the bloody battlefields of France behind him and find a suitable wife. But secrets from Jack's past threaten to confound his plans – and he cannot offer a beautiful girl a tainted name…

MY LORD FOOTMAN

Claire Thornton

When his family is threatened by a greedy blackmailer, Pierce Cardew, Viscount Blackspur, becomes convinced that the recently widowed Comtesse de Gilocourt knows more than she is telling, and takes a job that will keep her *very* close. But soon, playing the detached footman becomes almost impossible when all he wants to do is take his mistress to bed!

HISTORICAL

LARGE PRINT

THE VANISHING VISCOUNTESS

Diane Gaston

The prisoner stood with an expression of defiance, leather shackles on her wrists. Adam Vickery, Marquess of Tannerton, was drawn to this woman, so dignified in her plight. He didn't recognise her as the once innocent débutante he had danced with long ago. Marlena Parronley, the notorious Vanishing Viscountess, was a fugitive, and seeing the dashing man of her dreams just reminded her she couldn't risk letting anyone get caught up in her escape…

A WICKED LIAISON

Christine Merrill

Anthony de Portnay Smythe is a mysterious figure. Gentleman by day, he steals secrets for the government by night. When Constance Townley, Duchess of Wellford, finds a man in her bedroom late one night, her first instinct is to call for help. But the thief apologises and gracefully takes his leave…with a kiss for good measure. And Constance knows it won't be the last she sees of this intriguing rogue…

VIRGIN SLAVE, BARBARIAN KING

Louise Allen

Julia Livia Rufa is horrified when barbarians invade Rome and steal everything in sight. But she doesn't expect to be among the taken! As Wulfric's woman, she's ordered to keep house for the uncivilised marauders. It would be all too easy to succumb to Wulfric's quiet strength, and Julia wants him more than she's ever wanted anything. But what future can there be for two people from such different worlds?